EVERYBODY'S HUSBAND

The Victoria Topping Story

JEANNE REJAUNIER

Copyright © 2016 Jeanne Rejaunier

All rights reserved.

ISBN-13:
978-1539084112

ISBN-10:
1539084116

DEDICATION

For Victoria
May she find peace and understanding.

CONTENTS

Dedication

Acknowledgments

EVERYBODY'S HUSBAND

About the Author

Books by Jeanne Rejaunier

Critics' Comments

ACKNOWLEDGMENTS

This book is a true story. It is based on handwritten letters from and frequent phone conversations with Victoria Topping over a period of more than two years.

CHAPTER ONE

"I've seen you somewhere before."

The woman standing next to me at the Saks Fifth Avenue perfume counter was trying to recall where.

"I know -- the Phil Donahue Show -- the one on bigamy!"

I did my best to smile, trying to strike a balance between graciousness and aloofness in hopes that this encounter wouldn't become an invasion of privacy, as many often did.

The woman continued, "I was in the audience that day and I felt so sorry for you. Everyone did."

"I know. About two dozen people came up afterward offering to pray for me."

"And Phil kept patting your shoulder asking if you were all right. What a horror story you lived through with that man you married! I do hope things are better now."

"They are." I felt kindly disposed toward the lady, as she was sympathetic and seemed genuinely concerned for me.

She said, "This husband of yours actually had twenty or more other wives you never knew about? Amazing. Well, I do hope you've done what you said you would on the Donahue Show. I hope you've written a book."

I told her I intended to begin doing that soon.

"You should. This story has all the ingredients -- alcoholism, wife abuse, co-dependency with a twist. Your husband wasn't only a bigamist, he was also a gigolo, a sociopath, and a con man. You had your hands full, all right. Tell me, are you still in love with this skunk, or have you gotten him out of your system?"

I laughed. "It would probably take an entire book to answer that question," I said.

"Well, do it, do it," she said, preparing to move on. "I'll be looking for it!"

Shortly after this conversation, I decided to phone a psychic in California I'd heard a lot about. I'd always meant to call Joan Brooks but never had. Now seemed like as good a time as any. I dialed her number in Rio Oso, near Sacramento.

"Hello, Joan," I said. "My name is Victoria Topping and you've been highly recommended to me. I'd like to set up a phone reading."

I was pleased Joan said we could do the reading on the spot. After touching on a number of other areas of my life, Joan came to the subject of my bizarre marriage to Allen Topping and my intention of writing about it.

Uncannily, Joan alluded to many of the incidents that appear in this book. She also told me that contrary to official record which lists Allen Topping as having died March 1, 1989, he is still very much alive. This confirmed both my own and others' convictions.

"There's no question," Joan said, "Allen Topping is alive. He hasn't been in this country for about three years. He's living in Canada, somewhere in the northwest, Vancouver or Saskatchewan. One of his various wives helped him stage a phony death and pull an insurance scam. Another body, not Allen's, was quickly cremated; there was no autopsy; in fact, the body was cremated without a death certificate. They've changed all the identities. There's a lawyer involved as well, a man who sets these deals up and gets paid for it.

"Various palms were greased. The mortician, for one. These people have covered their tracks well. You wouldn't be able to trace their whereabouts yourself, but the book will smoke them out. Allen and his accomplice will surface, don't worry. Either someone will recognize them or the insurance company will come forward raising hell. The truth will come out."

Then Joan said, "Allen nearly ruined your life, but he also gave you something unique, something that will make for an unusual book. But you must do it soon. Don't lose any time."

Why the urgency, I wondered?

Joan said, "Allen and his accomplice are already planning another scam, this time with the woman as the phony death victim and Allen as the beneficiary. Allen Topping is not a well man. He won't be around that much longer, maybe only about another year, two at the most. If you want to smoke him out, you'll have to hurry because he's not long for this world."

"That really puts the pressure on. I've been doing a lot of thinking, Joan. How to tell the story? There's so much to say. Where do I begin?"

"Just start at the beginning. Tell it the way it happened."

Joan made it sound so easy. That night, I took her advice and started at the beginning. I began writing

EVERYBODY'S HUSBAND

CHAPTER TWO

Jamaica, BWI

The kitchen offered one of the prettiest views of our plantation -- mango and banana trees, tall pines, king palms, and tropical flowers that grew in profusion: purple bougainvillea, white jasmine, yellow calandra. From the window, one could see a serene group of twenty pink flamingos gliding in their natural rock pool habitat. I always liked to spend time here with Cook. Nana had gone to see the barristers and now Cook and I were making pablum for the litter of puppies. Cook wanted to give them cornmeal husks and leftover rice.

"In my day, no dawg eat pablum!" Cook insisted good naturedly.

"Star's puppies love it, Cook," I answered, reaching for the milk. "Look how much they've grown lately."

"Watch it, no upset me board, Ma'am," Cook chided, wiping a place on the counter where a spot of white mixture had fallen. "Ever since them little dawgs com' inya, me kitchen's no the same at all. Me no mind you big dawg, but them twelve little puppies -- mmmm!"

"Don't worry, Cook, I'll help you clean," I offered.

"No, my darling, don't your hands in hot water. Your hands too delicate."

I finished spooning the mixture into small bowls and laughed. "Do you suppose my Prince Charming won't love me if my hands are red, Cook?"

"Prince Charming, Prince Charming! Him is all you think about, my sweet child."

"Yes, indeed, Cook. In another six years, when I'm eighteen, Nana will send me to London to finishing school to prepare me for a proper marriage. Prince Charming will propose, I shall accept, we will love each other forever and live happily ever after!"

After I fed the litter, Cook let me help her mix Silly Bobs, the recipe for which had been in my Nana's family since Elizabethan England. Nana would be hosting a small gathering for Boxer Day, the day after Christmas, at which she would serve the Silly Bobs. As I poured in the ingredients -- milk, cider, brown sugar, vanilla, and lemon zest, I thought not without trepidation about the upcoming occasion. I didn't like it when Nana had visitors. People made me blush, then they'd laugh and

I'd want to run away and hide.

I just couldn't wait till I was grown up so that life would become pure bliss and happiness with Prince Charming, the man I'd been fantasizing since I was seven years old. Everything would be beautiful when we got together. I'd never again think about being an orphan, having no mother or father, brothers or sisters. I loved my Nana dearly, she was all I had in the world, but I was so frightened of losing her.

I knew she was ill and I was always afraid to be bad lest she go to heaven and I be sent to an orphanage. I'd overheard conversations with her doctor about her heart. One day Nana asked me if I would like to learn to knit. Always wanting to please her, I accepted, but for some reason I couldn't follow the directions. Immediately after this aborted lesson, Nana had a heart attack, for which I blamed myself afterward. I was six years old.

I must always be good, always behave like a lady, never complain or speak harshly, and do as I was told so that Nana would be happy with me and we could stay together until Prince Charming whisked me away.

"Cook, how do you suppose Prince Charming and I will meet?" I asked. My daydreams had created endless scenarios, but I wanted Cook's opinion.

"You're a big whoman now, my darling. We can look into the sea shells and see what kinda man dem have fie you," Cook suggested.

"The sea shells?" I didn't know what Cook was talking about, but I felt an undercurrent of excitement as she glanced around furtively, then lowered her voice. "My sweet darling, we don't tell nobody our secret, nobody."

With great anticipation, I followed Cook to the servants' quarters and waited while she searched through a bureau drawer. Was Cook going to divine the future for me? I knew she had been born with a caul, the sign of a seeress, and I'd always been eager to have her tell my fortune, but Nana had never permitted it. Oh, if Nana should ever find out!

Cook extracted a white silk handkerchief, then beckoned me to sit down on the bed. Wrapped in the handkerchief were a number of small, shiny enameled white shells with brown markings, all about one half inch in diameter. Each shell was different, yet all of them looked like sweet little faces with large mouths. I wondered if these shells came from our native Jamaican beaches or from elsewhere, as I had never seen anything like them before.

Cook lowered her girth onto a cane chair, bent over, then raised her arms upward with the shells cupped in her hands. She closed her eyes and intoned something in a strange language that I had never heard her speak before. Then she threw the shells to the floor. After a moment she nodded, a slight smile on her face, and murmured something inaudible.

"What? Oh, Cook, do tell me!" I begged, unable to keep silent.

After a long pause, Cook opened her eyes and looked at me directly. "Child," she said, "yah sweetheart soon come fie you."

"He will? How soon, Cook? Tell me! Where will we meet?"

Cook tossed the shells once more, then touched a few of them with her index finger. She seemed to be studying their pattern. She said, "You'll in upa States."

"America? How wonderful! And will he be handsome, Cook? How will I find him? What will Prince Charming look like?"

Once again, Cook threw the little shells and studied them carefully before answering my questions. She said, "Him have yellow hair, him have blue eye, but sweetheart, one eye is no good. Him father have much money, own eerplane and big boat, nuff things."

I asked Cook several more questions, including Prince Charming's name. She told me he had the same name as his father, and that his initials were A.T.

"Him bring you good times, bad times," Cook predicted. "Him wang go fah. And a high whole heap o' wedding ring." Cook shook her head, unable to explain the symbology of the many wedding rings. "Bat you give him you heart and it work out fie you, you mark my word. It's in your stars. He's definite fie you. Wid him, you have a debt to pay."

"A debt? I'll gladly pay. Tell me, will we have many children, Cook?"

There was another long silence. Finally, Cook said, "Wid you piknie, you have pain. But keep strong, keep good, be careful." Her voice lowered and her face became solemn. "I see blood wid piknie. Watch you self. Avoid blood!"

"I promise to be careful. But you're certain I will find my Prince Charming in America soon, Cook?"

"From God in heaven created world, this one fie you. The Lord give him, mark my word, as God is up in heaven, this one fie you!"

Something in Cook's manner gave me goose bumps. She was looking at me with a strange, penetrating glance as I listened in rapt silence. "Massa God, him make Adam and Eve, man an whoman. Always one, always look foh de otha. No matter how fah, always cam bak togethea. Caant live one widout de otha. You and him be one, two peas, one pod, batty and bench, one spirit."

"Yes, yes," I murmured softly, engulfed in an awesome power that I had never ever felt before.

"Go through thick and thin, live it out. You remember, child, when times are tuff, look black, stick wid him. It gwang get betta!"

I wanted to know more, but just then, we heard Nana's chauffeur-driven Deusenberg touring car approaching on the gravel outside the window. Hastily, Cook put the shells away and we both left the servants' quarters.

Although I begged her many times after that, Cook would never read the shells for me again. She said they had already told me all I needed to know.

CHAPTER THREE

The flight from Kingston, Jamaica to New York City was only half full. For most of the trip I peered out the aircraft porthole hoping to avoid curious stares, so that no one would notice my red my eyes and swollen face. It was obvious I'd been crying for days. Would my sorrow never cease? What I had dreaded all my life had finally came to pass: Nana had died and I was alone in the world, with the exception of a dowager godmother I hesitated to contact. I was sixteen and a half.

It was frightening yet exciting to know a new part of my life was beginning. The piano, violin and fencing lessons I'd never cared for, the dancing which I loved and thrived on, all were in a past era. Strangely, although Nana had always told me I'd be a rich woman after she died, her estate had left me with practically nothing, according to the barristers. So it seemed I would have to get a job of some sort. Perhaps I could join a riding club or find a position in a stable? I was crazy about horses. I relaxed in my seat and closed my eyes.

I'd have to find an apartment where dogs were allowed. My mind wandered to poor beautiful Star, confined to a crate in the baggage compartment in the belly of the plane. She must be feeling neglected and confused. But in another few hours we'd be reunited.

I wondered what kind of work I should look for. I couldn't spend my days behind a desk, since I was unable to type. They liked pretty girls for modeling, and I was tall enough to model.

My thoughts turned to the prophesy Cook had made with the sea shells when I was twelve. I would meet my Prince Charming in America, and soon, Cook said. I prayed this would happen immediately, as I urgently needed Prince Charming now. Marriage would be the ideal solution for my predicament, to meet the man of my dreams, have him sweep me off my feet, love and cherish me forever, provide a home, take care of me, and live happily ever after together. I was reminded of my dear Nana's warnings about my being "too thin to be a good wife." Models were always thin. So maybe until Prince Charming was a reality, modeling would be my best option?

When the Statue of Liberty loomed below, I knew we were arriving. The wheels of the aircraft were grinding as I gathered my hand luggage and prepared to land. What new adventures lay ahead of me in this strange city of my birth which I certainly didn't remember? I closed my eyes and fantasized.

New York City --- Fifth Avenue and all the fabulous shops and stores! I could envision all the chic frocks and beautiful accessories I'd buy. But then it hit me. Using what for money? A worrisome thought raced through my mind: at my age, would I be able to get a job? Perhaps if I piled my auburn hair on top of my head I'd look more sophisticated. Nana always said things worked out for the best. Since I had nothing to go back to, from here on in I'd definitely have to make that statement come true.

I hailed a taxi and asked to be conducted to a safe, inexpensive hotel where dogs were permitted. The driver dropped me at one near Gramercy Park. Good, I could walk Star across the street in the park.

I struck out with high hopes, but reality soon set in when I had no luck at all finding a job. After that, I spent another week seeking other solutions, grasping at straws, meeting nothing but blind alleys and cold despair. What was to become of me? Finally realizing that my options were exhausted, I had no choice but to turn to my godmother for help.

Dorothea del Drago, a boarding school chum of my Nana, known in society columns as the Baroness dell'Aqua zu Längele Boncompagni, Marquise de Rochemont, and Contessa Marsigli, was a filthy rich American born heiress to three fortunes who had married any number of times to impeccably mannered, titled European gentlemen short on money. Dorothea moved in sophisticated circles and was socially connected all over the world.

Dorothea and her friends were two generations my senior and we were worlds apart. I knew Dorothea wouldn't want an orphaned teenager around cramping her style; nevertheless, with my back to the wall, I swallowed my pride, got out my address book and dialed her number. My godmother told me to pack up my belongings immediately, take my collie and come in a taxi to her maisonette on East 82nd Street. The houseman, Amos Blackman, would pay the cab and take charge of caring for Star.

In the foyer of her sumptuous five story town house, Dorothea greeted me with a mechanical smile, her diamond clad arms outstretched.

"Victoria, darling," she intoned, planting two perfunctory kisses on either of my cheeks, European style, "how I miss your dear Nana. But it's so lovely to see you, child."

Dorothea had changed little since the last time she dropped in on Nana and me at the plantation, except that I could tell she'd had a recent face lift, coming on the heels of several previous ones. She had dark auburn hennaed hair that gave a pasty look to her extremely fair skin. Dorothea was tiny, not more than 4'11' tall, and weighed less than 90 pounds. She wore nothing but high cork platform Carmen Miranda shoes which she had made to order, trying to appear taller. Even with these, she looked like a shrimp.

Dorothea assigned me to a guest room and bath on the third floor. I took a long bubble bath and went to sleep.

That night I dreamed the recurring dream I'd had since I was a small child. I was on an ocean liner dancing with a tall handsome man. I wore a long black sequined gown, and my hair, combed on top of my head, shone like a copper crown. Was this the Prince Charming my Nana had promised and Cook had prophesied? In my dream Prince Charming had no face. I had the feeling that something wonderful was going to happen to me.

There was a knock at the door. Amos, the houseman, stood with my breakfast tray with a pink camellia in a crystal vase on it. Star, excited at seeing me after a night of being banished to the kitchen, waited patiently by his side, her wagging tail thumping on the thick carpet. Amos was a quiet black man who spoke with a deep southern drawl. One could never hear him walk.

He set up the tray and left. Star knocked me to the floor, kissing my face and neck. I ate my breakfast with her lying at my feet. When Amos returned to collect the tray and Star, he told me Madame had requested that I dress and appear at her rooms in one hour, and that I should be ready to go out with her.

"Come in," Dorothea called out in response to my knock on her sitting room door. She put down the large glass of herbal tea she'd been sipping and motioned to me. "Sit down, child," she invited.

The chairs were all Louis Quinze antiques that looked uncomfortable, but I took one.

"What a lovely lady your Nana was," Dorothea began. "It was all so sudden   such a shock. And how terrible for you, alone in the world. Tell me, if it's not too painful,   did she suffer?"

"I don't think so," I replied, knowing Dorothea would ask me about Nana's death. "Nobody told me very much. One day she had a heart attack. She gave orders I was not to see her. Then I was told she passed away in her sleep. It didn't take very long." I didn't tell Dorothea how angry I felt with Nana for leaving me flat, how rotten I thought it was of her to die that way. Such thoughts wouldn't sound polite and I didn't suppose Dorothea would understand.

"I am very puzzled about this estate business," Dorothea mused, shaking her head. "I believe there must have been a mistake in the probate. I intend to have my attorneys investigate. Of course, our being Americans dealing with these people makes the task more difficult, but rest assured I will look into the matter."

Dorothea took another swill of her tall glass of tea, and said, "One other thing, child."

"Yes, Dorothea."

"We prepare a modest European style breakfast at home -- toast, juice, coffee. But we do not serve an evening meal except at dinner parties. New York, as you may know, has a terrible roach problem, to say nothing of rats."

"I heard all cities have roaches and rats."

"Not like here. I've lived all over the world, dear, and believe me, New York is the worst, which means we must be very careful. It's quite unfortunate, and the problem is becoming increasingly aggravated. Of course, I'm sure the reason for this is the vast number of Puerto Ricans who keep coming here. These people throw their garbage out the window, you know."

"They do?"

"Unfortunately, yes. At any rate, I wanted you to know the rules of the house. There are several excellent restaurants as well as lovely coffee shops within a six block radius of here, so this should pose no problem for you." She waved her diamond encrusted arm. Then, peering more closely at me as if seeing me for the first time, she frowned. "We'll have to get you a complete new wardrobe," she concluded. "Are you ready to leave?"

Off we went to Saks Fifth Avenue, Blooomingdale's, Bonwit Teller, Bergdorf's and Henri Bendel. The two of us looked like Mutt and Jeff, Dorothea taking tiny bird like steps in her six inch platforms, I five foot nine, trailing, towering over her in my spike heeled pumps.

I was wide eyed with anticipation, hoping to see all sorts of glamorous socialites and movie stars. Although none were on tap that day, the new purchases my godmother treated me to were excitement enough. As in a trance, I followed Dorothea into the cab with all the attractive flowered boxes containing my new clothes and cosmetics. Next on the agenda was Elizabeth Arden, where they did my hair and makeup. I was walking on cloud nine.

Attired in one of my expensive new dresses, I stood in the drawing room by Dorothea's side at the white marble fireplace. It was the following evening and Dorothea had invited fourteen Manhattan socialites to cocktails and a sit down dinner. The arriving guests walked down three steps to the old polished cobblestone floor, and one by one I was introduced to everyone.

I didn't know any of these people, but well mannered girl that I was, was polite to all. It was going to be a boring evening, I decided. Little did I realize in just a matter of minutes my lifetime dream would come into focus: I would meet Prince Charming in the flesh.

Allen Topping arrived escorting his sister Barbara. Talk about love at first sight! Absolutely, without the slightest doubt, I knew the instant I set eyes on this divine being that we belonged together. As Cook had said, "It's in your stars. Mark my word, as God is up in heaven, this one is fie you." His initials -- A.T.! My soul mate and spirit companion, my twin flame! Deep within my heart and soul, a responsive chord was struck; there was no question that Allen was the partner I would spend the rest of my life with, the man of my destiny.

He was exactly as I wanted my Prince Charming to be: tall, blond, handsome, charming, debonair, well mannered. When we were introduced, I noticed how remarkably blue his eyes were and that he had a beautiful large smile. He held my hand, pressed it to his lips, then turned to the cocktail tray Amos was passing around.

I started shaking from emotion as I felt a thrill approximating dying and going to heaven. Did he feel it too? Silly, he was old enough to be my father. Could a man of his worldliness possibly take an interest in a girl as young and unsophisticated as I? Why was it I wanted his attention so desperately? Did he know I was his female counterpart, ordained from time immemorial? My heart was beating so wildly, my stomach churning, my head spinning out of control. I'd never felt this way before.

Barbara Anne Topping, two years her brother's junior, was tall, slim, milky white skinned with nearly coal black hair and dark brown, snapdragon eyes. She wore the palest white rice powder and dark, blood red lipstick. Later, when I would meet their mother, Anne Topping, I would realize Barbara was her double.

Barbara and Allen kept Amos busy supplying them with drinks. It seemed the two Toppings drank more than the other guests, but since they didn't appear drunk I dismissed the thought from my mind. I knew very little about the Topping family at this time, only slivers of gossip that Allen's cousins Dan and Bob Topping were notorious. Owners of the New York Yankees and the Brooklyn Dodgers, they had married numerous film stars, including Lana Turner, Arline Judge, Kay Sutton and international ice skating champion Sonia Henie, among others.

Dorothea's Chinese style dining room was filled with priceless antiques from the Ming dynasty. She had seated me between Allen and a titled gentleman named Michael something, who turned out to be the fashion editor of Harper's Bazaar. I'd mentioned my modeling aspirations to Dorothea, so perhaps it was no accident Michael was here tonight. He asked me a number of questions about my life, past and present.

Although I was excited and intrigued, it was Allen Topping who had my fullest attention. He captivated me so, I kept fantasizing him in the role of the knight I'd known would ride up on his white charger and love me forever. All during dinner Allen turned on the charm. He was playing footsie with my sandaled feet. Ingenuously, I asked him if I should move my legs out of his way. He smiled broadly and said of course not. That was when I noticed his right eye was blind and crossed, the result, I was to learn later, from a World War II accident. Oh, my God, I thought, as Cook's words came to mind. "Him have blond hair, him have blue eye, but sweetheart, one eye is no good." It was utterly uncanny. I couldn't stop trembling.

Allen had stopped drinking to eat, but Barbara was swacked to an embarrassing degree, so he asked to be excused to see his sister home. I was disappointed he made no reference to our getting together again. I thought, there must be a way. Nana had promised me Sir Galahad, and Cook's prophesy had been too eerily accurate. I knew Allen and I would reunite.

The next two weeks were hectic. Michael of Harper's Bazaar arranged a makeup and photo session with his magazine, which turned out to be grueling. After seeing my tests, Michael and his assistants recommended I go on a diet to shed ten pounds, no matter that I already was nearly rail thin.

After heeding their advice, several weeks later, on Michael's recommendation, I had an appointment with Amanda Gill, the high fashion modeling agency maven, who offered me a contract with the agency. I was overjoyed. I was soon going to be rich and famous! And then somewhere in this big city I'd find Allen Topping again and my happiness would be complete.

The taxi radio was playing Harry Belafonte's "Jamaica Farewell." Very a propos, but I wasn't going to be sad or homesick. I had a new career to look forward to. I couldn't wait to tell my collie, who understood every word I said, all about it.

I was lonely for Star's company and wanted to care for her myself. Poor baby, always locked in the kitchen with Amos. He was kind to her, but she often whined forlornly, which upset me, and the only time I saw her was in the morning when Amos brought her in with the juice and coffee.

I felt constricted at Dorothea's. Besides, I was beginning to discover things about my godmother my Nana had neglected to tell me, or perhaps hadn't known. Dorothea was in many respects a somewhat strange lady.

One of her husbands had been a top echelon Nazi who'd escaped to Argentina with Dorothea and a Rolls Royce in tow. The Rolls' entire front end was pure gold smuggled out of Portugal just shortly after Dorothea's last private audience in Germany with Adolph Hitler, a man she admired greatly.

Dorothea showed me a prized autographed photo of the Führer and told me stories about the trips she made between New York and Buenos Aires during World War II. The FBI came to see her off on the boat every time. Once they even cornered her at the town house as well, and tore her platform shoes apart. Dorothea, with only a sheet covering her naked body, lay in bed snarling at the G's: "Ruin one more shoe and you're getting a bill. They're made to order and they cost $400 apiece."

The townhouse had eight bathrooms, one Dorothea's in which no one else was ever permitted; another one used exclusively for laundering Dorothea's lingerie; a third for servants; a fourth for lovers; and the remaining fourth for guests such as I.

My dog and I would stay here only until I'd earned enough money to get our own place. It wouldn't be that much longer, I promised Star.

My first booking was the following Tuesday. In short order I found out how tiring modeling could be, but nevertheless I did enjoy the work. As my assignments increased, so did my hourly rate. I was starting to feel independent and successful. I was making excellent money.

As far as getting my own place was concerned, I'd gotten into a big ruckus with Dorothea, who insisted I was too young to live alone. I broke down in tears and cried for hours. Hearing me sobbing in my room, Dorothea eventually capitulated and promised that for my seventeenth birthday, she would find and furnish an apartment for me with a little yard for Star.

Dorothea kept her word. By the end of July, she had found me a first floor flat on 71st and Fifth with a tiny yard with grass and flowers for Star. I could walk Star in Central Park.

The first time I saw the apartment I fell in love with it. The bath and dressing rooms were adorable; the tub looked out into the walled garden. The linen closet was filled with thick pure cotton oversized aqua colored towels, loads of Arpège bubble bath and perfume. The floors were covered with aqua wool carpeting.

The bedroom contained a king size bed with aqua sheets and quilt to match the bath and carpeting. The living room had a white marble fireplace that was almost a duplicate of Dorothea's. Directly under it was a polished old cobblestone floor covered with a blue Persian rug. A sliding glass door opened to the garden. Dorothea decorated the place with French cherry wood furniture. This was her birthday present to me, and I moved in the very next day, August 1st.

I ran to Gristede's around the corner to buy necessities, including a bag of Purina Dog Chow for Star. I put everything away and unpacked my clothes. Star watched, wagging her tail, as if sensing a new chapter of our lives was beginning.

I climbed into the bubble bath. It was then I realized that there was but one thing missing in my happiness. Allen Topping. What an indelible impression he'd made on me and how terribly, achingly much I wanted to see him again. His name was engraved on my soul, for he was my male counterpart, my animus. Forever and always my pledge and devotion to "A.T." would be absolute. Once we were united, nothing in the world could ever keep us apart, for "whom God hath joined together let no man put asunder." My heart hammered. I was passionately in love with Allen. But how would I find him again? To my chagrin, Dorothea had removed the Toppings from her Rolodex with the explanation that she hadn't known they drank so heavily. She'd only met them briefly before, thought they were an amusing pair, but after that dinner party, they were doomed to be erased from her life forever. What was I to do? I had to find him.

I fell asleep dreaming the dream of my childhood, with Star behind my knees in the huge bed.

It was late November. I'd been in the apartment nearly four months when I ran smack into Allen, colliding as we emerged from the subway stairs into a premature snowstorm.

He seemed delighted to see me and offered to escort me to my apartment. Walking in the cold, holding his hand, the certainty was ever more definite. Yes, yes, yes, this was the man I'd longed for and dreamed about my entire life. By now, I hoped he sensed it too. I invited him in to have coffee and meet Star. They hit it off at once; he suggested that he could walk her during the day when I was out.

I said I'd have keys made and he could pick them up.

My sexual feelings were aroused every time I thought about my Prince. I imagined our melding, the tenderness and sweetness, the waves of sublime joy that would envelop us as we consummated a sexual embrace. Relaxing with Allen, I got to know him better. There was no sense of rush or urgency. We'd sit talking for hours, and for over two weeks he made no move to touch me. I found myself longing to be near him, thinking of him every waking hour. When we were together, I ached for his touch. When would he come physically close to me? I wanted him as I could never in my dreams imagine wanting anyone. When Allen was ready for me, I was ready for him.

One Friday evening when he returned from taking Star out, I took his snow covered cashmere coat and hung it up in the hall closet.

The three of us sat on the rug in front of a roaring fire. Allen reached for my hand and I started to shake. I wanted him, God I wanted him, this man who was the love of my life. I knew it was going to happen, and oh, how I wanted it. I trusted Allen completely. My surrender would be absolute, no fears, no holding back. At last, everything was right.

As his arm encircled my waist he slowly drew me close and held me until my trembling stopped. He put his hand under my chin, touched his lips to my eyes, my cheeks and ears, and then very carefully, he brushed my lips. At first my heart beat so fast I felt like it would pound itself to death. Then I reached up to him and we melted together.

He kissed me again and again. When he opened my blouse to kiss my nipples, I felt like a fire was burning inside me, making me feel like liquid gold. He carried me into the bedroom and put me on the bed gently, still kissing me.

Undressing a woman was not new to him. He showed a practiced yet tender skill as he removed my clothing quickly and gently, then undressed himself as well. In the bathroom he picked up a bottle of Nivea Skin Oil. He came to me and began massaging me all over. Then he started to kiss my entire body very slowly and deftly until I pulled him to me and he melted into me. I felt like we were molten gold and both one.

We made love all night long until neither one of us could do anything but sleep. The following day was Saturday. Star pushed open the door with her paw and stuck her cold snoot in Allen's face. He laughed, opened his eyes and said, "I love you both."

He dressed to take her out before she had a flood. After I bathed I drenched myself in the Arpège perfume Dorothea had selected for me. I brushed my teeth, combed my hair, and donned a pink terrycloth shortie robe. A warm feeling of elation and happiness came over me when I heard the key in the lock and realized Allen was back.

He undressed again and took a shower, I gave him a new toothbrush and he started a fire in the fireplace. I brought our hot chocolate into the living room and we snuggled together before the fire.

He kissed me and said, "I just want you to know something, my darling. I'm madly, deeply in love with you."

How I had dreamed of hearing those words. "I feel the same about you, Allen," I said softly, with awe and gratitude. How warming it was to be united with my love and to experience a feeling like no other.

We talked for hours until we finally fell asleep in each other's arms before the fire. I awakened hours later to find him gone, but he'd left a note and one red rose. He said he loved me and would see me tomorrow early morning, that he had some business to attend to. He had a chicken baked for me and some milk and eggs in the fridge. I wasn't hungry so I left the chicken, put on my jeans and a sweater, took Star for a walk, fed her and went back to sleep.

Once again, I dreamed my recurring dream, only now Allen's face was the man I was dancing with on the ocean liner.

I slept until I heard his key in the lock. He came in full of snow and I jumped into his arms, snow and all. He stopped long enough to take his coat off and remove my robe. He smelled funny when he kissed me but I couldn't figure out what it was. Not to worry, he loved me and I loved him with all my being and always would.

Eventually I would learn that funny smell was vodka.

He took a shower, brushed his teeth and asked if I'd eaten. I said no. He went to the kitchen and returned with a tray. He'd cooked poached eggs for two, toast and milk. We had a picnic in bed.

He gave me another sensuous Nivea massage first and then we

made love for unknown hours. When we woke he told me we must talk.

I said, "All right. What?"

He said, "I'm married and I can't get a divorce. But I haven't seen her for three years."

My heart dropped down to my feet and I started to cry. He took me in his arms and tried to comfort me. Oh, my God, my God, I thought, Cook's prophesy with the "whole high heep o' wedding ring." This was what it meant. I had never known such utter heartbreak.

Allen quickly reassured me. He wanted to marry me, he'd get a divorce somehow. Then he said, "I could live here with you." He'd get me a ring and we'd tell everyone we'd eloped to Maryland, he suggested.

I agreed, and he settled into the apartment a week later. Then he moved in several bottles of Anjo Rum, Plymouth Gin, Canadian Club and J & B Scotch, some rye whisky, vodka and vermouth, practically enough to open a barroom. I told him to store his booty in the kitchen cabinet, I didn't drink and wasn't planning a cocktail party to celebrate our "marriage" as yet.

All I knew was I was blindly in love, that Allen Topping and I were destined to be together, because "as God in his heaven created man and whoman," this one was for me! Somehow everything had to work out for us.

It was written in the stars.

CHAPTER FOUR

Domestic bliss was going to be a pleasure to embrace; everything seemed perfection. Allen said he'd never felt this way about any woman in his life. Then he told me there was but one thing the matter with our relationship. He didn't like my name.

"What's wrong with my name?"

"Victoria? It's ugly as hell. I love you, darling, but I hate Victoria. Likewise, 'Vicky' sucks. We'll have to get you a new name. Hmmm, what shall we call you?"

"Well, my middle names are Alberta and Frances."

He grimaced. "Victoria, Alberta and Frances! You have to be kidding. Did they think you were in line for the British throne? Christ Almighty. I know -- I'm going to call you Troy."

Where he got that name I'll never know, but to please Allen Topping, I became Troy. And Troy it was, from that moment on.

Modeling was going great guns. I was booked all day most of the time, often working until I could drop. I was making good money and it was I who paid all household expenses. That seemed fair, since I was working and Allen wasn't. Allen received a small check from the Veteran's Administration once a month for the loss of sight in one eye, which as far as I could tell was the extent of his resources. His father was a multimillionaire, but I gathered there was an estrangement of sorts. I didn't know at the time Mr. Topping was giving his son money. I wondered why Allen was unemployed and why he seemed to drink more than most people. I told him he ought to cut down on the cocktails and get a job.

I had several thousand dollars in the bank when Allen suggested a joint account. Since I loved him the idea seemed appropriate and I readily agreed.

Allen spent a good deal of his time indulging his hobby of photography with me as his favorite subject. He was a crackerjack photographer and the agency flipped for the 11 by 14 tests he did of me, saying they helped get me a lot of work. There was another type of photo layout Allen shot of me, however, which no eyes would ever see if I had anything to say about it.

One day he handed me a package. The wrapping said Frederick's of

Hollywood. He said. "Put this on for me."

First I pulled up the black silk hose, then hooked the black lace garter belt and black satin and lace shell bra, then stepped into a pair of black five inch high heel pumps. There were no panties.

I asked, "Allen, where are the panties?"

He said, "You don't need any, sweetheart."

I walked out of the dressing room. He looked me over and said, "Now, parade for me. You know, dance a little, wiggle a bit."

I turned red all over and he roared. "You're blushing, silly. Yeah, walk over there   that's it. Bend over. Okay, now put your leg up on the chair. I want to look at your rose."

I did as requested, wishing he wouldn't ask me to do these things, but they pleased him so I did them. It just embarrassed me and seemed very peculiar. To make him happy, I posed for a set of photos. After one roll, he laid the camera aside, put out his cigarette, yanked the garter belt off me and threw me onto the bed. He was very aroused and was kissing and biting me all over, until I cried, "Allen, please, you're hurting me."

"Sorry," he said hoarsely, and went about making love to me like a madman. He had me in every position he could think of, some of them highly uncomfortable, like wrapping my legs around his neck. He muttered, "Oh, those fantastic long legs. They drive me wild."

Then he said, "Here, sit up on me. This is what you call spinning, honey."

He tried to make a spinner out of me but at my nearly six feet, I was too tall. He told me that short girls make great spinners. One minute he was violent and then he'd get gentle and soft and loving. I couldn't figure him out.

But there were a lot of other things about Allen I didn't understand, either. I wondered why he wasn't closer to his family, why he hadn't introduced us yet. Often he would come home complaining about his parents and his stepmother. When I questioned him further he'd rant and rave, then start drinking more. Apparently Allen felt betrayed by his father for the divorce from his mother and remarriage to the stepmother he detested, Gladys ("Glad Ass") Topping.

According to what Allen told me, his father had financed movie star Joan Crawford's career. Mr. Topping Senior used to like to cover Crawford's body with honey and lick it off. Allen also related how his father made Glad Ass drink tea by the gallon, after which they'd get in the tub naked and he'd have her squat down and pee on his face. This, he said, was known as a "golden shower."

The Toppings Sr. resided at One Beekman Place in the city, and also maintained homes in Greenwich, CT, Palm Beach and Old Quogue, Long Island. They had a 150 foot yacht moored at their beachfront homes and kept a private plane in Teterboro, NJ. It was all exactly as Cook had predicted, "Him father have much money, own eerplane and big boat, 'nuff things." Mr. Topping ran Topping Bros., a wholesale hardware concern. Of course, he had the same name as his son! Everything fit.

I'd not met Allen's father. Then one day a few months after Allen and I were together, the phone rang and when I said hello, a male voice said, "Victoria, this is Allen's father. How are you?"

I told him I was just fine. I couldn't help but picture him having a golden shower, or perhaps a taste of honey.

He said, "I'm not saying congratulations, because I think you have made a mistake. I would like you to sign some papers that would put my son Allen Jr. where he will get professional help. I would give you a sum of money to take care of you, but my great concern here is I would like to help my son."

Mr. Topping had 37 years to help his son. Where had he been? Out of politeness, I kept my thoughts to myself.

"Look," Mr. Topping said, sensing my disinclination to do what he was asking, "I'll give you one million dollars if you'll sign these papers. It will help both of you. Please."

"I'll think about it, Mr. Topping, but I don't really want to do it."

He said, "All right, you think about it and I'll phone you again."

"Goodbye, sir."

We discussed it a few more times; eventually, Mr. Topping had to accept my love for Allen was not for sale -- at any price.

Although I was doing well financially as a model, most of my bookings were bread and butter catalog work. That wasn't where the prestige was, and Amanda thought I was capable of much more. One day she invited me into her office to talk. She said, "Victoria, you can be one of the top girls in the business, but you need European experience to get there. A year's training in Paris would make all the difference in the world to your career."

Paris? I was intrigued.

Amanda continued, "New York photographers and fashion editors want to see more than just good test shots, they want to see a portfolio with a pile of tear sheets   actual color prints from top fashion magazines."

"Well, I have plenty of tear sheets from my catalog work."

"That's not what I'm talking about," Amanda replied, and showed me what she meant from a messy pile of papers on the corner of her desk.

I saw the immediately that the European photography was more artful and interesting, the pictures full of drama and passion. By contrast, my New York work looked corny, pedestrian, and dull, the poses phony and contrived. Sears, Montgomery Ward and J. C. Penney were just another world altogether. I understood what Amanda was saying about Europe bringing out a model's full potential.

"You've got the raw material, Victoria," Amanda said, "height, bone structure, grace and distinction in front of the camera ...you're a natural. The question to ask yourself is: do you want to earn at your present level or double, even triple or more your current earnings, start doing more important work, and become one of the five top models of your era?"

"I want to go as far as I can," I assured her. "I want to be the best model I can."

"Good. There's only one way to do it," Amanda said. "I'd like to send you to Paris next month. How would you like to live there for a year?"

"Live in Paris for a year? Work there as a model? Oh, my God! Oh, wow!" I was overwhelmed at the thought.

"We can arrange to fly you there on the first. The agency maintains three apartments in Paris where we send our girls for grooming in the European tradition. We keep quarters in other European capitals as well, but I have a feeling Paris is the place for you.

"We have one upcoming vacancy in our Paris flat on the Avenue Foch in the 16th arrondissement. Very posh location. You'll love it. You'll be living with four of our models: Ilse, a delightful German girl; Gunilla, a lovely Swede; Cindy, another American -- she's from California, the same age as yourself; and Donatella, who's Italian. You're all completely different types, and I know you'll get on famously together. Everyone speaks English, so you won't have a problem communicating with your roommates."

"Oh, my gosh, Amanda ... I don't know what to say! Do you think I'll get by in France with my schoolgirl French?"

"Don't worry. I've been sending my girls for several years and they all do just fine with French, no matter how lousy it is to begin with."

"I can't believe it, Amanda! Paris! And you picked me to go!"

"I have a lot of faith in you, Victoria. Spend that year working for the French photographers and doing runway work and I guarantee you'll have this town by the tail when you come back to New York. You'll get the choicest bookings and your income will jump sky high. So how does this strike you? Do you think you want to go?"

"Absolutely, yes! Oh, wow, am I excited!"

"I know you'll need a little time to think it over and to get your affairs in order. But I'd like to have your answer in a few days so we can start making arrangements next week."

I was so elated I could scarcely contain myself. In fact, in my excitement I even temporarily forgot about Allen.

But out on the street, I remembered him. If I left for Paris, what would happen to us? How could I bear being separated from him an entire year? Suppose he met somebody else? Then it occurred to me that Allen could come to Paris with me. After all, he had no reason to stick around New York, since he had no job.

That night when I told him about my offer, Allen looked at me as if I must be insane. "Paris?" he repeated. "Who the hell wants to go to Paris? It's a lousy, expensive, overrated city."

"Oh, Allen, I've never been there, but I've always dreamed of going. I'm sure it's so romantic and beautiful! It would be so wonderful to be there together."

"What the hell would I do there? Jack off in some fucking café? I don't even speak the goddamn language. I hated French in prep school. It was my worst subject."

"You might feel different today. You might do some photography there."

"Listen, I've been through the American tourist in Paris scene and I'm not the least interested in a repeat performance. In the first place, I detest France as a nation and can't stand the French people. Those frogs are the most arrogant and disgruntled people in the world, they all have lousy dispositions. Not on a bet am I going to go and live among the French."

"But couldn't you bend a bit for me, Allen, for the sake of my career? Amanda says it would put me way out front of the competition."

"I don't give a shit what Amanda says. You're doing pretty goddamn well right now without Paris. These modeling agency cunts are all the same. They just want to control, that's their problem. They can't let well enough alone."

"But it's such a break for me, and it's only for a year and it's an honor to be selected, and if I say no I'm afraid I'll never have another chance, and I want to go so much!"

Allen went to the bar and mixed himself a drink. He said, "Troy, you have to make up your mind what's important. As far as I'm concerned, you and I are important."

"Allen, you're the most important thing in my life. But I don't see what one has to do with the other. As long as we're together, that's what counts."

"Together, yes, but not in Paris."

"It isn't as if you had a position here, Allen. If you were offered a job in China or Japan, I'd go there to advance your career."

"It's not the same thing."

"Why not? I'm the earner, I'm the one who's making money. I can't do this modeling stuff forever, I can only do it while I'm young. It will help us both to have more money for our future together."

He shrugged. "So go there for a year, if that's what you really want. I'll miss you, Troy, but if we're apart for a year, there's no guarantee about our future together. You've always talked about having a home. You want animals, you want to raise horses and dogs on an estate in the country. That's your dream. Honey, how can we do that if you're off in Paris?"

"Couldn't we do it after the year in Paris?"

He swirled the liquid in his glass and gazed at it before he took another swallow and said, "No. If we went to Paris that would take me away from some things I'm working on here, things that could bring your dreams to reality."

"But what about marriage, Allen? Are we just going to go on living together? I love you, I want to be your wife, really married to you."

"Baby, you know we'd be married by now if I could get the divorce from Trudy. Well, look, I didn't want to mention this because I wanted to surprise you at the proper time, but the picture has changed some, and it is entirely possible that I'll have my divorce in the near future. I'm working on it for us, and then we'll definitely get married."

"Oh, Allen, do you really mean it?"

"Yes. I didn't want to talk about it before it came through, but I have to bring it up now because of all this Paris bullshit. It just wouldn't work for me, Troy."

I felt let down, like he'd popped my inflated balloon, the dream I'd had of modeling abroad, but at the same time, he was holding out hope of my dearest wish, to be married to him.

"Honey, if you and I were man and wife right now, do you know what I'd say? I'd say no wife of mine goes to Paris on a whim, Amanda Gill's big plans notwithstanding. I'd say your place, Troy, is by your husband's side. Right now I consider us as good as married. The only difference is a slip of paper. But you're still my girl, my baby, and you belong to me. And I still say no to Paris, unless you want to spoil a beautiful relationship. You're a free agent and you're the one who has to decide. I just pray you're wise and mature enough to make the right choice."

Allen put some extra ice in his drink and twirled the cubes around with his finger. After that, as far as he was concerned, Paris was a closed issue and he refused to discuss it further.

The way he'd put it to me, I became very frightened. I felt not only would I lose Allen if I went to Paris, but that marriage was imminent and I'd be throwing over a chance for everything that was really important in life. Besides, Allen had undermined my judgment and I had no faith in my ability to make a decision.

This juncture marked the end of the "honeymoon." After that, our relationship gradually started becoming less and less euphoric.

One time a couple of months later, Allen had lost his apartment key and borrowed mine because he said he'd be needing it that afternoon, whereas I was booked on an all day modeling assignment and wouldn't be home till late. He said he'd have my key copied and would definitely be there to let me in when I was through for the day. I waited outside the apartment for two hours.

Allen finally showed up drunk, had not copied the key and had totally fouled up my schedule for the following day when I had an early call. When I tried to explain to him that I not only needed a good night's sleep but had to get up at the crack of dawn to wash and set my hair, he tried to make it seem like I was being a prima donna.

Already, my modeling career was starting to suffer.

CHAPTER FIVE

During the two years Allen and I lived together in my apartment, our love was tested many times over. There were the blissful times of happiness that I lived for, but then, our difficulties could be sheer hell.

Eastertime, when we'd been together less than a year, Allen disappeared into thin air for a whole month. My heart ached. I felt betrayed, but I was impotent to do anything, since I had no idea where on earth he was.

Always, I recalled Cook's prophesy that there would be good times and bad times with Prince Charming, but that I should stick with him through thick and thin because it was meant to be and it would get better. In the meantime, stress was killing me. My stomach and intestines were playing havoc, everything I ate came out on both ends and it felt like my heart had sunk into my gut, where it kept pounding relentlessly. Acute, painful cramps persisted for weeks until I looked like a skeleton. I couldn't believe Allen thought so little of our relationship to run away. Why? Why? Was he afraid of being happy, afraid of commitment? Cook had certainly been right when she'd spoken about black times. Stick it out? I didn't even have that option now. Would Allen and I even see each other again?

Finally I regained enough strength to go out romping in the park with Star. It was a beautiful spring morning. Coming toward me, I spotted a modeling friend, Margery Scott, strolling arm in arm with her naval Lt. Commander boyfriend. We stopped to chat.

Margie said, "Bob and I are married now, as of six months ago."

"Congratulations," I said, smiling. "I'm so happy for you."

At that very moment, Allen Topping appeared out of the blue, ambling over, joining our group casually as if he were a long lost friend. The feeling of having been wronged was so total my heart fell to my stomach. Purposely, I neglected to introduce Allen to the others. What could I say? "I'm married too, and this is my husband?" Margie really was married and I wasn't. Besides, Allen was no husband, he was a skunk who'd loused up my life, Prince Charming or not. After what he'd pulled, I would have been ashamed to introduce him as my spouse.

Margie and Bob left me their calling card, which I quickly dropped into my purse. I turned to leave, ignoring Allen.

He was furious. "Why didn't you introduce me?" he demanded, hot on my heels. "Are you ashamed to have your friends know I'm your husband? Ashamed of me? Answer me, Troy."

When trying to put me on the defensive didn't work, he changed tactics with a running dialog designed to get back into my good graces. He was sorry, he was a jerk, he loved me, you are my one and only love, I can't live without you, I need you, and so on and so forth, ad infinitum, ad nauseum.

We reached the apartment. I unlocked the door, let Star in, gave Allen a piece of my mind, stepped into the vestibule, slammed the door in his face and bolted it shut. He hammered and shouted outside for half an hour until I threatened to call the police.

It was a few weeks before I saw him in the flesh again, not that he didn't phone every hour of the night and day.

One day Allen's mother, Anne Topping, rang up. "Troy dear? Are you all right?" Allen was a fine one to talk about my not introducing him to a casual acquaintance -- he'd yet to show me the courtesy of an introduction to his mother, something I did not understand.

Before I could answer her mother, Barbara Topping got on the line. She said, "Troy, Allen is beside himself. My brother is making himself ill because he loves you so."

"What's he doing about it? Drinking rum to ease the pain?"

Anne, on the other extension, said, "Darling, won't you please reconsider? Allen's not drinking, and he does love you."

"So he tells you. But what he does is another matter."

Anne said, "May Barbara and I come to see you tomorrow? We won't bring my son. Allen is so sorry, Troy. But we'll come alone. Perhaps we can take tea together?"

"All right, but only if Allen definitely won't be there."

Anne said, "Darling, I'll see to it."

So I was finally going to meet Allen's mother. I hoped I wouldn't get a nervous stomach again. Star seemed to sense something was up; she kept coming to me and giving me her paw and wagging her tail. With that uncanny sixth sense that animals have, she knew something important was going down.

I dressed carefully but casually. At two pm the bell rang, and there stood mother and daughter. Anne Kelly Topping was a strikingly beautiful, tall, slim, dark haired woman who looked exactly like her daughter. I had heard from Allen his mother had been a Ziegfeld Follies showgirl, and given Anne's glitzy background, I was expecting someone far less refined than the aristocratic, gentle mannered woman who now stood smiling at me.

"Mrs. Topping?"

"Yes, dear. But you must call me something more familiar than `Mrs. Topping.' After all, I'm your mother-in-law. I'm so happy to finally meet you, Troy. Would you like to call me Anne?"

"Thank you, yes, Anne. Come in, please "

"I'm Barbara Topping," Barbara said in a loud voice, extending her hand. "We met one evening at the Baronessa's "

"I remember. How do you do, Barbara?"

Anne and Barbara sat on my satin divan while I took a seat facing them. Star lay down at Anne's feet, wagging her tail. We all laughed. It took Star to break the ice.

Anne said, "Troy, you must try to understand Allen. I love my son dearly, but sometimes he can be impossible. He doesn't mean this behavior the way it could seem. I see my son from a different perspective entirely than you do, and you love him in a different way than I do."

Barbara piped up, "He's a devil, Mother, and you know it."

"I'm sure he hasn't told you all the nasty things he's done," I said.

Anne said, "He has told me how very much he adores you, that you eloped, that he doesn't want to live without you. He also admitted to me how cruel he's been to you. You poor child -- and that's what you are. Allen should be a lot more protective of you." Barbara, antsy from being without a drink in her hand, had risen and was looking around the apartment. Anne, taking notice, frowned. "Barbara, please," she said, "sit down and have your tea."

"For heaven's sake," Barbara said, "don't you have any liquor around here?"

"I threw it all down the loo when Allen left. I don't drink it and he's not here anymore. Reminders like rum, vodka and the like I don't need."

"Where did you get all this?" Barbara asked, waving her hands around.

"It was a birthday gift from Dorothea."

"And you're the long legged godchild Allen fell in love at first sight with at her dinner party that night. He sure works fast, that brother of mine. I guess the Toppings owe that baroness, or whatever she is."

Anne, watching me glare at Barbara, said, "Barbara, please be a lady. I would like to see Allen and this girl be happy together. It appears they're very much in love and I know well how love can hurt a young girl."

Barbara shut up and drank her tea.

Anne said, "Troy, dear, I have an apartment at the Carlyle, and I'm inviting you to tea tomorrow. Allen will be there, Barbara will not, and I would like you, Allen and me to talk this problem out. If he gets out of hand I will dismiss him, I promise you. Will you do me this favor ... and honor?"

Anne looked so sweet and so sad I couldn't refuse her. "Yes, I'll be there," I said. "But I can't promise anything beyond that."

Anne smiled and rose. "Barbara, let us be off," she said. "I'm sure Troy has some thinking to do."

Barbara said, "All right, Mother. But let's stop on the way for a cocktail."

"You may do as you wish, Barbara ... after you see me home."

As they prepared to leave, Anne stretched out her arms to me. "Come here, Troy," she said, smiling, then gave me a warm hug. "I'll see you tomorrow then?"

"Of course."

When Anne embraced me, I felt such an outreach and bonding. If only I'd had a real mother, I thought wistfully, longing to linger in Anne's arms. Allen and Barbara were lucky to have such a lovely mother. I wished I'd been as fortunate. What was that enchanting fragrance she exuded?

I asked about her perfume.

"That damned Emeraude," Barbara answered, wrinkling her nose in distaste. "She never uses anything else. Coty launched that fragrance in 1921, and Mother will never switch to anything else."

As Anne walked out with a gentle smile, Barbara tried to take my hand, but for some reason I pulled it away.

I was left alone with Star and that captivating aroma of Emeraude that lingered for the rest of the night.

I wasn't anxious for tea. Allen would try to con me again with his mother to help him. I wished I could take Star for moral support. Who else did I have? My stomach was starting to hurt again, so I phoned the doctor for more medication and had the pharmacy send it over. One pill and the pain and pounding stopped. I went to sleep with Star and my dreams to comfort me.

I was in for a rough afternoon. Damnit, I wouldn't take Allen back, no matter what. No, I didn't want to go to tea at all, but I'd promised Allen's mother. I was very fond of her already, this woman who was to become the only mother other than my Nana that I ever had.

I arrived at the Carlyle dressed in a suit, and was announced by the concierge. Anne greeted me at the door, wearing a floral chiffon tea frock that looked like vintage Mainbocher from the 30's that would never go out of style. We embraced. I sat on a green chair, which "enhanced my auburn hair," Anne said.

Allen arrived twenty minutes later. He smiled at me, winked at his mother and kissed her on the cheek. I was nervous being with the two of them. Allen took a seat on the couch next to Anne, facing me.

Allen was sweet, he was sober, and apparently had been on the wagon for a while. We went through all the niceties until Allen said, "Darling, this meeting was Mother and Barbara's notion."

"No, it wasn't," I said. "It was your devious idea to get back in my good graces. You're a demon, Allen Topping."

Anne interrupted, "No, no, now, no fighting. You two are in love and should be able to live together and be happy. Allen, I know you've been cruel to Troy. You've brought me many daughters-in-law, but never before a motherless child. You have to take care of her. She needs you. You've been unfair and you have behaved improperly."

Many daughters-in-law? What a peculiar turn of phrase! I wondered what Anne meant by that, but as the gist of the conversation was going in another direction, I let it escape my mind for the time being.

Allen was starting to get angry, very likely because of Anne's comment about the many daughters-in-law. He growled something at his mother, to which she replied, "Allen, I promised her this would not happen. She didn't really want to come."

Allen sat down, smiled and behaved himself again. He said, "I'm sorry. I guess I want you back so very much I get angry at the drop of a hat." He stood up, put his hands behind his back, looked at me with utmost sincerity and said, "Darling, in front of my mother and upon my mother's soul, I swear I will behave properly, I will work, I will care for you. I promise there are no other women in the world for me but you, Troy, it's you and only you, and I will love and treasure you forever."

"Sure. I've heard that song before. Allen, why can't you keep a promise just once?"

"I will, I swear. No more scenes, no more trouble. Sweetheart, please?"

"I'm not going to let you make me ill and unhappy anymore. You'll have to prove it to me, and frankly, I don't know how you ever can."

Both Anne and Allen, each in their own way, kept up the pleas, the pressure, the reassurances, the built in guarantees. Finally, as much for Anne's sake as Allen's, I negotiated a peace treaty. "You'll have to show me you've turned over a new leaf, Allen," I said. "There's no way it could happen overnight. The way it will have to be, if anything is possible, is that we'll start dating. It will be like a trial courtship. We'll go to the beach, to a movie, we'll have dinner maybe a couple of times a week. I can't do it any other way."

"That sounds reasonable enough," Anne said. "Is it fair as far as you're concerned, Allen?"

He said, "Ok. Not my idea of what I want, but Troy's the boss now."

Anne said, "Yes, Allen, do it her way if you really love her. You can stay here in the guest room. She's got to learn to trust you again."

"Why don't the three of us go to the beach tomorrow?" I suggested.

"I avoid the sun," Anne said, "but the two of you should go. A splendid idea! Yes, go, have fun, swim, how nice. And remember, Allen, you stay here with me."

It was time for me to leave. When Allen tried to kiss me, I looked at Anne and said, "See? He just won't keep his word."

Anne said, "Allen, don't touch her. From now on, you'll have to phone her for dates. Don't be so impatient."

"Allen will be phoning day and night," I said.

"No, he won't," Anne reassured. "He'll be staying here with me. He'll keep his word, he'll be a gentleman, and the two of you can work out the rest. Troy, you just have to learn to trust him, dear."

"Yes, if he justifies it."

"You go on home now and relax, dear," Anne said. "Everything's going to work out just fine. I'll have another talk with this son of mine."

"Thank you, Anne. Thank you for tea."

"I'll see you again, dear, no matter what happens."

We said goodbye just as Barbara walked in loaded.

"Oh, God," Allen groaned, "this is all we need now."

It only took three weeks of dating. One Saturday we returned from the beach, I with a bad sunburn. When I emerged from the shower, Allen was standing in front of me with Nivea in hand. He said, "You need a light massage on that burn."

I wrapped up in a towel. Allen loosened it and began caressing my back with that magic touch of his. He undressed, turned me over and stroked on Nivea all over me. He kissed me again and again all over my body, and as usual I melted. He felt it. He knew he had won me back.

We made love all night. At one point the phone rang. Allen picked it up and said, "Yes, Mother. All right, Mother. It's wonderful. No, I'll behave, I promise." His favorite word, I promise. Of course I believed it, now more than ever.

When we awakened we had a talk. I said, "Allen, if we're to create a life together, we've got to start with a firm foundation -- trust, love and friendship. Can we do that? Because I sure can't do it alone."

He said, "You're so right, darling. I love you so, and I'm so ashamed of myself."

When I told Allen about my recurring dream of Prince Charming, the man with no face, he said, "We'll just have to put my face on him. We'll build a marriage, put my face on Prince Charming, and be madly in love forever. Would that please you, my love?"

I cuddled in his arms, and again inhaled the aroma of sun and sea that I would smell all the days of my life. We held each other like that until we fell asleep and I dreamed my dream again. But the prince still had no face.

When we woke he said, "I love you."

"Why?"

"Well, you've got skin like silk, you're a wonderful lover, and you take me somewhere into outer space, a place where no woman ever has ever made me feel like that, Troy. You're the cleanest woman I've ever known, the most pure. You're just vastly different from all others. Besides, you're beautiful. Good enough reasons?"

I thought for a moment. "I guess that's a start. But I hope you'll think of a few more reasons someday."

He said, "I will, I'm sure. Girl, you are too much! You're perfect, and I adore you."

I turned my head to notice Star had opened the door and entered the room. Now she was putting her cold black snoot on Allen's chest, inviting him to take her for her morning constitutional.

Allen and I both laughed. "Nature calls," Allen said, reaching for his trousers and Star's lead. "Don't go away, honey. I'll be right back."

CHAPTER SIX

To my enormous relief, Allen definitely did seem to have turned over a new leaf, and our happiness continued unabated for several months. If here or there a lapse occurred, I tried to understand since the overall picture was more positive than negative. I'd invested a lot in this relationship and I wanted it to succeed. Prince Charming had proven he could be my all in all. Doing everything possible to make our relationship work was worth it, even if, as Cook had predicted, it should take a long time to achieve my ultimate dream.

Time and again patterns repeated; as the road got bumpier, there were more separations and reconciliations. Each time I thought we were through, Allen would woo me back and we'd agree to try one more time.

Never knowing how long the happiness would last kept me on a tightrope, feeling anxious. I was often resentful. Perhaps this was the reason I had become tense sexually. Allen was having difficulty penetrating me; I was closing myself off to him. I was suffering from a condition known medically as dysparunia -- painful intercourse. We talked about it, and Allen thought he had a solution.

"I'm going to the store. I'll be right back," he said and was out the door in a flash.

I let out a sigh, afraid to be happy with this man who was the love of my life. I had taken a bath and was filing a fingernail when he returned. A man followed him in with three cases of Dom Perignon champagne.

"You promised to stop drinking, Allen," I reminded him.

He took me by the shoulders and sat me down, saying, "Hush, I'm not going to drink it." He paid the delivery man off and closed the door. "Come on, sweet baby, it's not going to hurt a bit. We're going to have some fun. Just wait here. I'll be right back."

He carried one case after another into the bathroom. What was he going to do, toast us in the loo?

First I heard a cork pop, then the trickle of fluid going into the tub. Then another pop and more fluid being poured into the tub. This went on for about half an hour, until Allen emerged, took me by the hand and guided me into the loo. The tub was full of champagne and red rose petals.

"Come on," he said, removing my robe and sitting me in a tub of champagne. Was this a new trick? Allen sat on the side of the tub sucking the wine off my fingers, my arms, my nipples. He turned me over and then licked champagne off my ears and back.

"This is for you, darling," he said, "I want to get you crazy so I can make love to you without hurting you and love you over and over forever."

"But it makes me feel all sticky."

"That's ok. You can bathe yourself later." He lifted me up and out of the tub to lead me by the hand to our bedroom. Incense was burning, there were rose petals all over the bed, and I was very excited. He rubbed me everywhere with perfume, then licked the wine and perfume off me, all the way down to my feet. When he started sucking it off my toes I screamed and jumped.

"What's wrong?"

"It tickles. You know I can't stand to be tickled."

He laughed, pulling me into his arms, where we stuck together. He moved round and around, up and down, on top of me. He said, "I want you to want me so bad you can't stand it. I'm going to spoil you for any other man for your entire life."

As he was kissing my face, my hair, sticky with wine, got in his mouth. I said, "Please let me shower this wine off me? I like Nivea better."

"Okay. But be quick about it, sweetie." He had an erection so huge I had never seen it quite so extended before.

When I'd showered and returned, he grabbed me and told me to get on my knees and elbows. I was afraid he might have sodomy in mind. Instead, he kissed my rose over and over, holding it apart with his hands.

The moment he entered my vagina from the rear, I felt like a wild animal. He was slowly going in and out, twisting his organ with artful skill, as well as using his little finger on its root. I went crazy. Then, varying the positions, he tried something we had never practiced before: Imsak, said to be a special Arabic method of male retention. In this technique, the male sexual partner spurs his female consort on toward repeated, ever more satisfying heights of sexual pleasure while he delays his ejaculation. This continues any number of rounds, each more intense than the previous one. Porfirio Rubirosa is said to have kept Barbara Hutton totally mad for him via Imsak. Allen told me that harem keepers were able to satisfy ten women a night with this method, and that since he had no harem, I alone was receiving all the benefits for my own exclusive pleasure. Mutual ecstasy is enhanced to an incredible degree with this technique, but few men have the skills to master the techniques.

In Imsak, one pursues heightening sexual pleasure up to the point of orgasm, which the woman may achieve at any time and in any number; she may enjoy as many orgasms as she wishes, but the male must wait until the end. The man may pull out up to ten times, allowing the erotic fire of mutual arousal to build with each successive penetration, so that when the mutual tidal wave arrives, it comes straight from paradise. Allen was a past master at Imsak.

But there was more. In one of the endless, intensely exciting rounds, Allen guided us both into a twilight zone of rest. As he lay quietly on top of me he instructed me to open my eyes.

Looking deep into my soul, he said, "Tell me you've never had a lover like me." I did as he wished. Then, never removing his gaze, he said, "No man in this lifetime will give you the pleasure I give you. No man will satisfy you as I do." His voice sounded strange and distant, as if coming from another part of the universe. He made sure to synchronize our breaths and never removed his eyes from mine as he asked me to repeat affirmations pertaining to how no man could ever be what he was to me.

Although I was exhausted, we kept on making love. He was wearing me out! He turned me on my back, continued the twisting and the finger until I must have come a dozen more times, until we both fell dead asleep.

Allen was right. I would never be tight or hurt again. My dyspareunia was cured for good. For the first time that night, I had deep vaginal orgasms. I screamed, I cried, I went crazy. When the last of my long, satisfying climaxes subsided, Allen said, "I'm going to get wine all the time." We both knew no one in my life would ever make me feel like he did. Even so, I felt Allen had hypnotized me while we'd been making love.

I awakened in a state of bliss. When Allen woke he smiled and said, "Rest assured I will have every blessed morsel of you, my darling."

I searched his handsome face for some sign of his mood. My answer came when for a split second he gazed at me and in that brief moment, I saw malice, anger and venom glimmering in his eyes. Then suddenly it seemed he pulled a shade down and the nasty look was gone.

I would live to see the day when I would remember that look. I wanted to ignore it, never to see that anger again. The exquisite sexual sensations we had shared were soft, delicate, wild, and I agonized how to reconcile them with that baleful glance that swept into his eyes. There was the magic, the losing myself and drowning in love for him. But I was beginning to recognize his dual nature.

How I wish I had seen that baneful look the night I met Allen. I didn't know how cruel, cunning, merciless and bitter he could be. These qualities were not necessarily directed at me, but I was to bear the brunt of it.

He had initiated me into a magic I had never known and would never forget. Now, thinking of that, I dismissed the swift coldness that had appeared in his eyes. Let me stop thinking and just be happy. Allen was my love and he could always transform my world into rapture when I was in his arms. I dozed off again. When I awakened he was looking at me with a smile.

"God, how I love you," he said. "And you, are you happy?"

"Allen," I said, "you know I'm always in heaven with you. I want it to be like this forever."

"It will be," he promised. "We love each other, so it will be."

Remembering that look in his eyes, I wanted assurances. I said, "Allen, I love you. I want to get married. I'm ashamed of living with you this way."

"We'll be married as soon as I can get free," he promised. "I love you and I want us to be married, so don't ever be ashamed of being in love. I feel you're my wife anyway. I've told everyone we're married."

No matter how much money I made, I never had any. One week I was shocked to find the funds in our joint account were insufficient to pay the rent. At home, I found Star sitting outside the apartment. The landlord had locked us out; my key wouldn't work; the lock had been changed. Luckily I had enough money to go to an inexpensive hotel with Star.

All my belongings were in that apartment -- personal papers, diary, family photos, everything I valued. The weather had turned freezing, it was snowing now and I was walking around without a coat, galoshes, or gloves. Allen had told me he'd paid the rent from our joint account but hadn't; now he'd disappeared, and along with him, my bank balance. I couldn't believe it. Had I really lost both the man I loved, my beautiful apartment, my life's belongings, and all my money? I was so hurt that through my tears I was gasping for breath. This time Allen had gone too far. I mourned the death of my illusions, my hopes and dreams.

At this point, my modeling bookings had dwindled to a fraction of what they'd once been. Allen had fouled me up with the agency on more than one occasion. In the first place, Amanda had been upset when I turned down Paris, so was not pushing me into the major markets. In addition, my reputation had taken punches from other directions. Sometimes Allen interfered with my bookings by expecting me to cancel at the last minute or for the remainder of the week to accommodate his schedule. Furthermore, there were times where I'd cried my eyes out the night before, thereby ruining the next day's shooting. Models have to watch those late, sleepless nights, and stress was taking its toll. I was no longer as fresh and enthusiastic as before.

A model has two approaches for being in demand: either she creates excitement by being a new face, in which case photographers and fashion editors will make initial allowances because she's green and hopefully will develop; or she becomes established, having proven herself to be thoroughly professional and reliable. At this point I was neither of these.

I thanked God, though, that I was still earning enough money to make ends meet. I worked all I could to get enough money to pay off the landlord so I'd be able to get my clothes out of the apartment. Apparently Allen had gotten his out in the nick of time.

A couple of weeks after the lock out, Allen located me and phoned saying he wanted to get together. All the time we were apart, I was in so much pain even my bones hurt, although I was unaware that this is a common symptom of repressed anger directed at the self.

I let him have it over the phone. He said, "Go on. I deserve this."

"When are you going to get my stuff back? When are you going to get me another apartment like that one? There's nothing you can do to make this up to me, Allen."

He said, "Let's meet. Let me come over and we'll try to make things right. I only borrowed the money. I'll pay it back."

"No, Allen, since apparently you've failed to get the message, let me spell it out once and for all. It's over. Don't call me again, just leave me the hell alone!"

Shaking with rage, I banged down the receiver.

Allen initiated another of his campaigns. There were more calls and attempts at negotiated settlements from his family, flowers and gifts, love notes and funny cards; I was besieged with phone messages. Every manner of persuasiveness was brought to bear. How could I be so cruel? Allen had learned his lesson. He needed me, he was lost without me.

I shut him out for three weeks. Then Anne had a birthday party and I was invited. How could I not go? I was so fond of Anne. Allen was there too, of course, and it was impossible to snub him. In the convivial family atmosphere, we were soon communicating again. But I wasn't sure at this point that I could go back with Allen. I felt I needed space, time to myself to think things over. Even bearing Cook's amazing prophesy in mind, and given the promising outcome Cook had said our relationship would have, I still wasn't ready.

Then I got a call from Anne, asking me to come to the Carlyle, saying she had something important to tell me. Always happy to see Anne, I embraced her warmly and followed her into the living room.

"Troy, I wanted to talk to you because I know Allen has been mean to you lately, and I believe it's time you knew some reasons why he behaves this way," Anne began. "You know that Allen was wounded during World War II, but I don't believe you realize that it affects his behavior. You're his wife; you should know." She indicated a brief case at her side. "I have all Allen's Army medical records here. Let me explain and then you may read the reports yourself. All right?"

I nodded agreement. Anne continued, "Allen Jr. enlisted at the age of nineteen. He was a strong, healthy young man. He trained as a paratrooper and was assigned to the 501st Division of the 101st Airborne Paratroops, sometimes called the `Screaming Eagles' by the Germans, or the `devils in baggy pants'. It seems the Germans were afraid of these boys.

"As Allen told me, they were paratroop infantry and could take no prisoners; they moved too fast to feed them, so they had to kill them. He jumped into Holland a few times before D Day on mapping missions, to make contact with the underground, and to do reconnaissance on enemy installations. He also saw battle at Ardennes and in Normandy in northern France. In one of these places he suffered a wound which left him with a shell fragment in his skull, for which he was treated at the 192nd Hospital, England.

"On his second mission, September 24, 1944, he jumped in Veghel, and took an .8 mm shell on the right side of his face. He was taken to the University of Brussels Hospital, where the shell was removed. That was the accident that left him blind in his right eye and almost caused losing the sight of his left eye as well. His entire face and head were full of fractures. He sustained cranial nerve damage, among other things.

"They transferred him to a hospital in England, where a steel plate was placed on the top of his skull. As soon as he was on his feet again, but still an inpatient, he went A.W.O.L. Now, Troy, you won't like hearing this but you must know. At this time he met a woman rumored to be an English duchess whose husband was presumed dead, and he married her. Daphne was her name. I understand she was lovely with British schoolgirl skin, amber eyes, finely chiseled features, the hair a light shade of auburn bordering on titian, the figure tall and slim.

"A month later while they were still honeymooning, they were in the garden of her manor house together, when out of the blue, a handsome, aristocratic man in an RAF uniform appeared in their path. To make a long story short, the husband was very much alive. Allen Jr. became agitated and the two had a rather violent altercation. Allen, the loser, was taken back to the hospital from which he was A.W.O.L. He had no recollection, so he says, of his marriage to the duchess. This time he was wheeled into a stockade hospital, where they continued to treat him. It appears from the reports that a part of his brain was further damaged by this incident."

I was looking at my mother in law in horror. "Why didn't you tell me all this before, Anne?" I asked.

"I really didn't think his behavior would get worse, so there was no reason," Anne said. "I assumed everything was running smoothly, especially after he fell in love with you, darling. But now I don't know, I felt I must explain it all to you. He needs our love so desperately. We mustn't turn our backs on him, dear."

I said, "Anne, do you think Allen's injuries have caused some form of mental or emotional instability?"

"Yes, Troy, that's just it. There is impairment in his cognitive faculties. Allen can't always discern right from wrong or know what's expected of him. The condition makes him somewhat unstable, subject to emotional ups and downs. He has developed a nervous constitution. You've seen how he tends to drink to excess to deaden the pain."

"Oh, poor Allen. I had no idea."

"So we really must not fault him too greatly for his sudden mood shifts and his seeming confusion. Darling, he does not mean to be cruel, and I know it hurts him when he hurts you. If you could only be patient with him."

"Is he still married to the duchess?" I asked.

"No. Their marriage had no validity, as her legal spouse was alive."

When I read the reports, my heart fell down to my feet. Now I could understand Allen so much better. Adequate reason existed for his actions. War injuries caused the irrational, seemingly reprehensible behavior. Allen couldn't help it, he wasn't responsible. As Anne had said, more than ever, he needed my love now.

Had this been a skillfully orchestrated strategy? I never knew. But my response was heartfelt. Right after seeing Anne, her son walked in the door, put his arms around me, and all he pain I'd been feeling turned to tenderness and compassion. Of course I forgave him, we moved in together in temporary digs, he with ten suits and all his accessories, including his prized World War II uniforms and medals.

When I had enough money to wipe out the old debt and get my clothes, I asked Allen to take care of it while I was working. I was dying to change clothes and have a warm coat to wear.

Instead Allen disappeared again and was nowhere to be found. On the third morning my patience gave out. I was so furious I took a razor blade and slashed every one of his custom made Witty Brothers suits to ribbons, his Brooks Brothers button down shirts, all the shorts and even his shoe laces. I left the World War II uniforms in tact.

He arrived back that evening, ashamed. He'd spent the money and hadn't retrieved my belongings, which I never saw again. When I showed him what I'd done he was angry as hell, but that made two of us.

I picked up my purse and Star's lead. Allen walked over to me and slapped me in the face. He stood there, glaring. I saw him raise his arm and make a fist. The next thing I knew, that fist landed in the socket of my eye.

I left with Star, hailed a cab and went to another apartment hotel.

It was a dreadful place but no one would hit me there. I had enough money to pay four weeks' rent. Still in shock, I took to my bed and called for a doctor, who came every day for four days and gave me shots that made me sleep. Finally the doctor, an old German man, told me whatever was wrong with me, I must get up and face it. No more shots; they were addictive.

He said, "You look like a strong girl, but remember, please, you are not. You must be careful."

By now my modeling career was in shambles. Although I tried to make excuses for not being able to honor my bookings, it was no use. I was now poison as far as the agency was concerned, a victim of the "Bad Boyfriend Syndrome," death to a model.

I cried in Amanda's office when she told me she was dropping me from the agency roster.

"I hate to do this, Victoria, because I like you and I always believed in your potential," Amanda said. "But our reputation is on the line."

I begged and pleaded, promising there would be no further mishaps. "On my word of honor, from now on things will be different," I swore through desperate tears.

"Victoria, you could have been one of the biggest models of your era," Amanda said. "Unfortunately you let this man get the upper hand. Given the fact that he's so much older than you, I understand it. However, in a tough, competitive, professional world, we simply can't make concessions."

"But it's over now," I sobbed. "Allen's gone from my life forever."

"Want to bet?" Amanda said prophetically. "Men like him use young naive girls like you. We've invested a lot of time and effort in your career, and for a while everything was on the right track. But then -- "

Amanda was talking to me like a mother, but she was at the opposite end of the spectrum from Anne Topping. "What do you see in him?" she asked. "Why Allen Topping? What's the appeal?"

"I love him," I explained lamely, knowing I could never put my deepest feelings into words.

"Look, if you have a weakness for older men, God knows there are scores of rich, charming sugar daddies out there looking for models to be their mistresses. Honey, they'll lay the world at your feet, and unlike this jerk, won't ask you to put up with bullshit. Want a man to take care of you, Victoria? I'll give you a list of a dozen potential sugar daddies right now, men who call every day, begging me for introductions, men just dying for a girl like you. Is that what you want?"

"No, I'm not looking for a man to pay the bills, Amanda. It's love that matters to me, not money."

"Then find a nice, healthy young man to settle down with. This modeling game doesn't last forever, darling. There's nothing like it when you're young, but unfortunately it ends."

"But I am young now, Amanda. And I want to model. Honestly, I know I misjudged Allen's behavior, but I mean it when I say I've learned a lesson. Please give me another chance, Amanda, please!"

Amanda appeared to waver for a moment. I thought she almost gave in. Instead she said, "Ok, Victoria, let's leave it this way: for now, you're out. Come back to me in three months if you really mean what you say about being finished with this guy. He doesn't deserve you in any case, so for your own good I hope you mean it. If you do, we'll talk then about the possibility of getting you started again."

It was a small hope to cling to. I'd known my modeling days were numbered. I guessed this was Amanda's way of easing the pain. Still, I did hope for another chance. In the meantime, I decided to apply for a night job, which would enable me to keep days open in case the agency reconsidered and called me again. For now I had to do everything possible to get Star and me out of that dump.

At this point, I didn't see how it could work out with Allen, love notwithstanding. I felt guilty, after all Anne had told me, for not trying harder. I'd done my best to be patient and forgiving. If Allen couldn't be held responsible for his actions, I felt sorry both for him and for the mother who was so loyal to him. But I was not Allen's mother, and now I just wanted to think of myself, of my own health and sanity.

Luck, for a change, was on my side, or so it appeared. A friend who owned some cocktail lounges gave me a job checking coats and selling cigarettes. My friend also offered me a tiny furnished sublet that she assured me was safe, as it was in a gay area. As if that weren't enough, this friend introduced me to an extremely attractive, rich, very nice man named Don who owned an airline.

In short order Don became enamored of me and asked me to think about divorcing Allen and starting a new life with him. I didn't tell him Allen and I weren't really married, as I was ashamed of the deception, but did say I needed time to mend. As much as I liked Don, I didn't feel in a stable enough place emotionally to become involved in another serious relationship. The wounds Allen had created were far too recent.

One evening when I returned home from a date with Don, lo and behold, who was sitting in my place but Allen. There was a huge bouquet of pink camellias on the table with a card from Don. Allen started giving me the third degree about the person who sent the flowers.

"Who is this son of a bitch?" he shouted, obviously insane with jealousy. "What are you doing with this asshole? What gives him the idea he can send you flowers? Doesn't he know about us? Does he think you're available, for the Christ's sake? Doesn't he know you have a husband?"

Coldly, I said, "I won't dignify your questions with answers, Allen. And you better get out of my sight before I call the police and issue a complaint!"

Allen would have hit me, but Star knocked him to the ground and lay on top of him so he couldn't get up. That made him laugh, but he was still angry enough to throw a ring at me. The ring hit me above the eyebrow and I started to scream. Allen got up and left.

I was sobbing when Don phoned. Don said, "I've never sent a girl camellias, asked her to marry me and had her burst into tears." I couldn't bring myself to tell Don about what had happened with Allen.

He was leaving for Europe, Don said, and would phone again upon his return.

I wanted to escape the city with all its ugly memories and go far, far away where Allen Topping would never find me. No Prince Charming could be so oblivious to my feelings. My dream had collapsed. I simply could take no more. It was now clear I couldn't live with Allen Topping. The problem was, it was so very hard to live without him. Which was the lesser of two evils? Cook said we belonged together and things would get better, but I simply could not go on exposing myself to such emotional destructiveness. Again, I wanted space. I wanted my freedom -- at least for now.

I phoned a friend, Cynthia Holly, who arranged a job for me out of town, a dancing gig in a nightclub in Washington, D.C. I asked Cindy never to reveal my whereabouts to Allen or to anyone associated with him, and she promised to honor my request. Cindy even arranged for an apartment in D.C.

We rehearsed every day for two weeks, seven days a week. I loved to dance so it helped heal my broken heart. Maybe in time I'd be able to put all the past horrors behind me. I thought Allen was out of my life forever. He'd never find me in Washington.

But find me he did. Immediately prior to opening night, he phoned. Cindy, the friend I'd trusted not to reveal my whereabouts, betrayed me by giving into Allen's persuasiveness. Her story was he cried, begged, bullshitted and sweet talked her. "You just can't say no to the guy," Cindy explained. Cindy too? So I wasn't the only one unable to resist Allen's persistence.

Now I was the one he was begging, bullshitting and sweet talking.

"Allen, why do you keep after me? Surely, you have other women. Just leave me alone. Why do you always track me down? I don't need your abuse. I've had enough. I loved you, but I'll get over it. There are other men in this world."

"Are you through now? It's my turn. Let me speak, darling. I love you with every cell in my body, heart and soul, and I always will."

"This is tiresome, Allen."

"No! You must believe what I say. Somehow, I must prove it to you." The old con again. "Troy, I have to talk to you. There are some new developments, changes in the wind ..."

"A leopard doesn't change its spots, Allen. I thought I could deal with it. I can't. It hurts too much."

"Can we just talk, honey? Look, I realize I've made some serious mistakes, I've been a louse, and you've every right to feel the way you do. But for old time's sake ..."

"Forget old times. Old times were bad times."

"Can't we talk as two civilized, adult human beings? Please let's not be bitter. If this whole thing has to end, I accept that I'm the cause, but let's just see one another one final time to end on a positive note "

Hearing the sound of Allen's voice filled me with painful conflicting emotions -- anger, hurt, despair. Why couldn't he leave me alone? I wanted peace, not turmoil, but he kept hounding. His mother was calling as well, begging me for her sake just to see him, let him explain. She was afraid for her son, Anne said, afraid what he might do to himself. If only I'd do her this favor, talk to him in person. I was being pushed from all sides when all I wanted was privacy and space to do the dance gig I'd been hired for, and get my life together.

Ignoring my wishes, Allen arrived from New York in a green Cadillac Coupe de Ville convertible. I was beside myself, furious. I'd made it clear he was unwelcome, and now here he was, barging in.

"Honey, I drove a great distance because you're the most important thing in the world to me," he said. "Please, hear me out. I only want to talk."

He managed to make me feel guilty and cruel for turning my back, then sighed deeply and said, "If we must end it, let's not hate each other."

"I don't hate you, Allen. I just don't think you and I are good for each other."

"If you don't hate me, then talk to me. We'll be calm and intelligent, mature people."

I didn't want to open the door again, especially now. Arguing and explaining were too exhausting. I was already drained.

Allen didn't look well, I had to admit. He played that card too. "I'm on my ass," he sighed, his eyes beseeching. "I can't eat, my nerves are shot to hell, all I do is shake all over ... there's nothing left of me. If this is the price for my behavior, I wish to God I'd wised up sooner. Troy, oh Troy, honey, I'm sick in my heart. Please don't do this to me."

"I'm sorry, Allen. You should have thought all this out sooner. Actions have reactions, they have consequences."

"Oh, God," he moaned, with tears in his eyes, "don't tell me I've destroyed the thing that meant more to me than anything in the world. Troy, have you turned utterly away from me? Is there no hope?" He looked stricken.

The last thing I needed was a scene like this, especially given my priorities of rehearsals, obligations, responsibilities. The timing was wrong. I couldn't seem to make him understand that. He just kept it up.

"I should have realized... I learned too late ... if only I could undo all my mistakes ... I'd give anything to turn back the clock and make it all up to you. You're such a beautiful person. You deserve so much better ... what can I ask ..."

I kept saying no, Allen kept on pressuring. He was making me crazy, destroying my peace of mind, forcing me to address his questions and statements, issues and non issues, manipulating me verbally and strategically. I was distraught. He had intruded on my sense of independence, he was stirring things up. God, if only he'd let me be. But he wouldn't give up hounding and pounding, and he was confusing me endlessly, until I broke down in tears from sheer frustration. Then he became tender and sensitive. He stroked my hair, wiped my tears away, soothed me with soft words and endearments.

After several hours of listening to Allen's entreaties, his promises and apologies, of hearing him bare his soul and seeing him cry real tears, of being forced to explain my position over and over and being backed into a corner and having all my buttons pushed, it was just as I'd feared, no use. Once again, Allen had conned his way back into my life. He'd broken me to pieces, and now he'd gotten me to agree to come see his mother. It would be a healing experience for both of us. We wouldn't rush back into a reconciliation, we'd take it easy. We'd give it time and then we'd see.

He collected Star and took us back to New York.

I was never to dance in that nightclub in Washington.

CHAPTER SEVEN

We were going to relax -- no pressures, just a nice family visit. My shattered nerves would be relieved being in Allen's mother's reassuring presence. She was my oasis. Surely, her wisdom and influence with her son could make everything better.

The three of us, plus Star, rented a place in Woodstock, New York, in the country. The house was pleasant and comfortable, although I'd never seen a coal stove before, an anachronism to someone raised in the Caribbean. Allen shoveled the coal and cooked us egg sandwiches on it. We were almost happy.

I felt very close to Anne and enjoyed hearing the stories she told me about the Topping family.

"There were three Topping brothers who came to America from Wales," she said. "One went to Canada and became a highwayman and they hung him, one entered the railroad business, and my ex-husband's branch of the family went into manufacturing heavy hardware and marine equipment. Nobody else will tell you what I've just told you."

I certainly hadn't been expecting Barbara Topping, but then, unannounced, she arrived with one of her live in drinkers, the Group Theatre/New York Critics award winning actor Art Smith, and all hell broke loose. Art was rushing around back and forth to Western Union, picking up fifty dollar handouts from his pal, actor Karl Malden, known for his American Express commercials (Art had either "left home without it", or didn't have one) while Barbara was busy leaving chaos in her wake.

The more I got to know Barbara, the worse impression I got of her. No two ways about it, Barbara Topping was an arrogant, loudmouthed, drunken hellion. The first time I met her at my godmother's was more than enough anti-social behavior than I cared to be exposed to. Yet another time, in the middle of a Manhattan snowstorm, Barbara was in her customary inebriated state and unable to find a taxi. She peeled off her mink coat, lifted her skirts, flashed her naked genitalia at a millionaire's chauffeur driven limousine, flagged it down, hopped in dragging me behind, and ordered, "The Colony Club, please, driver." I was mortified.

At the age of 17, Barbara had been married in St. Patrick's Cathedral to an elderly gentleman some 50 years her senior named

Jacques Frey. Her drinking ruined that, so following the bust up, Barbara took on a string of lushes each of whom was many years her senior, all with white hair. All of them were as obnoxious as Barbara herself, and all seemed to resemble Mr. Topping Sr., whose hair had turned white as well.

Barbara and Art had descended on Woodstock while I was out shopping. Anne was upstairs in bed with a sprained ankle. Barbara tried to hit Anne for whiskey money and Anne turned her down. With that Barbara yanked the sheets, blankets and spread off her mother's bed and in a fit of temper threw them down the stairs. This is what I found upon my return.

I told Allen he should not have allowed this to happen, particularly since his mother not only had no servants on hand to pick up the mess, but also because of her sprained ankle. Obligingly, Allen gathered up the bedclothes and remade his mother's bed, then told Barbara and Art Smith to clear out of the house.

We played checkers that night. Allen was very sweet and promised there would be no more scenes. I tried to get him to speak about his past, although it was like pulling teeth.

He said, "Mother is an old Irish biddy and she was foolish as hell to divorce Father. What did she expect? He'd done this nonsense before, she knew all about it, but she didn't run off and divorce him."

"Why are you so adamant about their divorce?"

"Because he didn't want to marry Glad Ass but Mother played into her hands."

"People get over divorces, Allen. Why can't you accept it?"

"Because it interferes with my life, goddamnit, my inheritance, a whole lot of things. Glad Ass gets all the money, the old whore. It's not right on either of their parts, Father or Mother, to do this to Barbara and me."

"How did it happen? Do you think your father fell out of love with your mother? Did he just fall madly in love with Gladys?"

Allen was looking at me in a way that seemed a cross between pity and incredulity. He laughed the bitter, maniacal cackle I would come to know so well and said, "Not bloody likely on any score. God, if you could meet Glad Ass you'd never ask such ridiculous questions. The slut was a prostitute in Arkansas. You should hear the way she talks. As if that god awful accent isn't bad enough, she sounds like an Ozarks cat. Father met her at some dive on 3rd Avenue."

"I really don't understand you, Allen."

"Don't try," he said. "Honey, when Barbara and I were small they started driving us nuts. Mother and Father kept us waiting on meals all the time while they downed the martinis. They were always going out to dinner and leaving us alone. One time there was a terrible storm. Barbara and I were left with two ignorant Irish maids. The maids locked us in a dark closet, supposedly to protect us. I still remember being scared as hell and trying my damndest to comfort Barbara. I was so angry with Mother and the old man, I never forgave them."

"Allen, you can't keep being so hateful to your mother. She's suffered so much, and now you and Barbara torture her more."

He said, "Let's forget it. I do not wish to speak about all this ever again. Period!" He pushed back his chair, went to the bar, poured himself a stiff drink and stepped out into the back garden.

I tried to follow but he started shouting at me, "Go to bed, Troy, you're tired. Good Christ, you're skinny! You are so goddamn skinny I can't believe it. Gain some fucking weight." His mouth was snarling in a vituperative manner as he flashed me an ugly basilisk glare.

I went upstairs to bed. I thought about the things Anne had told me about Allen's war injuries. For a long while I lay in bed, shuddering. Then, slowly, the tears came, until I cried myself to sleep.

I had just decided I'd dance for a while, and was tying the ribbons on the toe shoes I'd brought along with me when Anne called from her room, "Troy, dear, please come here."

"Coming, Anne," I answered, smiling as I entered her room. Allen was out somewhere. "What is it, luv?"

Noting my leotard, toe shoes and hose, Anne asked, "Are you going to dance now?"

"I'd like to," I answered. "I haven't rehearsed for a month. I'll be getting stiff if I don't."

"Before you do," Anne said, "please have a seat. I have something I'd like to speak with you about."

I chose a big comfortable chair and pulled up my legs.

"Darling," Anne began, "I know you love Allen Jr. terribly, as I did his father, and I want you two to be happy. Recently I've been doing some deep thinking about both of you. As you know, I've been concerned about Allen Jr.'s drinking and his behavior toward you at times, and I thought well, maybe if they had a baby he would behave nicely and I know you would be happy. I would be delighted if you gave me a grandchild, and if it was a boy, maybe, just maybe Allen Jr. would make his peace with his father."

"Anne, nothing would please me more than to give you a grandchild, and have Allen's child. But I don't know that he'd feel the same way. I know it sounds funny, but I'm not sure Allen is quite ready for fatherhood."

"So often young people are not, but confronted with the reality of a bundle from heaven, they change."

"Still ... "

"A child does alter our focus, Troy. Parenthood forces one to rethink priorities, to put someone else first, to cease being preoccupied with our own concerns. Believe me, dear, being a parent brings out the best in all of us and reveals hidden resources we never knew we had. I'm sure Allen would rise to the call."

"You think so?"

"Oh, my, yes. After all, Allen is already well past the age when most young men become fathers for the first time. It would be one of the most enriching experiences he could have. As for you, Troy, I know you're young, but many young ladies have been mothers at your age. In fact, in Shakespeare's day it was the norm."

"They do say it's nice to be young with your children."

"Yes, dear," Anne agreed. "Oh, Troy, I do believe you could be even happier with Allen Jr. if there were a child! A child does solidify a loving union. I'm not trying to run your lives, but I know how happy I was when my son was born, and how proud his father was of both of us. Mr. Topping couldn't stop kissing me even in the hospital while he was holding Allen Jr., perhaps because I had given him a son, which he so wanted. Darling, you know I was very young at that time too, not as young as you are, but close to it."

I had an important question to ask my mother-in-law. "Anne, you know what you told me that day at the Carlyle about Allen's war injuries," I began. "You're sure there's nothing congenital ... nothing in Allen's genetic history ..."

"No, dear, absolutely not. Allen was a perfect specimen until he was wounded in the war. I'm his mother; I know."

I said, "I do often worry about Allen's erratic behavior."

"I know, dear. And this is why having a baby seems like such a good idea to force Allen to wake up. Darling, if you can just be patient with him. No one is perfect. All marriages have these rough spots."

"I'm just not sure Allen would agree to having a child if I asked him, though."

Anne smiled, holding her finger up to her mouth. Her voice

lowered. "Don't ask! He needn't know, dear!"

"Oh, Anne, you mean to just go ahead, get pregnant on purpose, take it upon myself, trick Allen and then stick him with it?"

Anne's smile was conspiratorial. "Women have been doing just that since time immemorial, darling. It seems the lord gave us females a certain weapon to use. God knows we have little else in our arsenal."

"But it would seem so dishonest to me."

"Ah, youth!" Anne said. "Troy, dear, some day you may realize that strange as it sounds, `dishonesty' is one of the best traits a woman can have in life!" She was smiling at me as her brown eyes twinkled.

I didn't understand what she meant and looked at her, puzzled. Anne merely said, "Anyway, I thought I'd plant a little seed with you rather than with my son."

I lifted my chin out of my hand, stood up and sat down on her bed. I embraced her and said, "Anne, I would adore having Allen's child and giving you a grandchild. I hope it will happen someday."

"You're such a good girl, Troy. We have such nice chats together, don't we, dear?"

"Yes, we do. It's wonderful for me. I never had a family. Being part of the Topping family is important to me."

"I know that, dear. Perhaps that's one reason I want to protect you and make sure you and Allen stay together. I believe you two need each other very desperately. I know sometimes Allen gets in dark moods. If you can just bear with him, stick with it, through thick and thin ..."

Where had I heard those words before? "Stick wid him, through thick and thin ..." Cook had said that. And now my mother-in-law was telling me the same thing.

"Don't think I'm trying to interfere with your life, darling. I just feel there are things I must say, given the benefit of my perspective, and the mistakes I've made myself and have seen others make. I would hate to have you make those same mistakes, dear. If I could save you from them ..." Anne patted my hand. "It's been such a pleasure for me, spending time with you, dear. In many ways I feel closer to you than I do to my own daughter. Now, give me a kiss, go downstairs, and be careful while you dance."

I really loved Anne as well as being madly in love with her son, loved the idea of us being a family. I imagined all of us, three generations of Toppings, all together, Allen and me holding our child, and Star kissing the baby's hand.

Since our coming to Woodstock, things had been going fairly

smoothly. Anne's presence helped a lot. Allen was trying harder, and his lapses had been few. I'd begun to think once again it might be possible for us to have a real chance, especially if Allen and I were married, really married.

True commitment could make all the difference in the world. I smiled to myself. Maybe I should take my mother-in-law's advice, pull a pregnancy on Allen. I'd have a part of him to hold and love forever. Then Allen would have to get a divorce and we'd be married. In my imagination I could see Allen, his mother and father, the baby and me all in church while the minister married Allen and me and christened our baby. In my mind's eye, Allen was standing by the fireplace, smiling, sober, the proud daddy, taking pictures of us all. Then he walked over to Anne, picked up the baby, put his other arm around me and said, "I love you all, but most of all, this sexy, baby wife of mine." I was so happy the tears ran down my face, as Allen leaned over the baby to kiss my tears away.

We went to a movie that night, "Camelot." Sir Lancelot was so handsome, I thought, but Allen, my Lancelot, was even more so. Impetuously, I reached for Allen's penis and whispered, "Let's go home." I couldn't wait to get back to our bedroom. Upstairs, I leaped into his arms and kissed him like crazy. I unbuttoned his shirt as he unzipped the back of my dress and unhooked my bra. As our clothes fell to the ground, I turned to see Allen standing in his bikini pants and shoes. He finished undressing, went to the bed and said, "You angel, come here." The perfumed Nivea was in a marble topped drum table next to the bed. He reached for it, removed my panties, and then massaged me until I thought I'd rise off the bed. I wondered if this were the right time of the month. Could it happen tonight?

Vague promptings drifted through the back of my mind as I heard Cook saying, "Wid you piknie you get pain. Avoid blood." But I decided not to think about it. There were too many good dreams to concentrate on now.

Rummaging through the Woodstock attic one day, I found some old pre Civil War copies of Harper's Magazine, one of which contained an article about the Topping family lineage. I learned that the House of Topping was said to be older than that of the houses of York or Lancaster and that the Toppings came to the British Isles with the Norman victors. In France, their name most likely was Toppin, Toppinge or Toppingue.

The article contained an interesting section headed "The Gypsy Prophesy of Lord Topping." It seems a famed Lord Topping had two sons, thus passing his title in a direct line was supposedly assured; however, a gypsy gave him the disturbing prediction that this would never be the case. There was great danger in store for his sons, the gypsy said; it looked doubtful that either of them would live long lives.

The most crucial period would be immediately prior to their twenty-first birthdays. Lord Topping must be on his guard at this time, for if the sons lived to see twenty-one all would be well.

In order to prevent disaster, the elder son was locked in a tower for months. One day preceding his momentous birthday, the weather turned freezing cold. Some fagots -- sticks tied together to burn for fuel -- were sent up via a window. Inside the basket was an asp, which bit the lad and he died.

The second son was never out of sight of his tutor. On the day before his twenty-first birthday, someone called to the tutor from just a few feet away. The tutor turned his head for only a matter of moments, and when he looked around again, the boy lay face down, drowned in two feet of water.

I wondered if Allen knew about Lord Topping. He was very proud of the Topping heritage and often boasted about his noble lineage and illustrious line of forebears. He'd mentioned that Toppings had been original, early 17th century settlers in towns like East Hampton, Long Island, Greenwich, Connecticut and nearby Tarrytown, that some of them had also been a part of Cotton Mather's colony in New England. Wherever we went, Allen always brought a framed copy of the family coat of arms along. He'd promised to take me to historic "Gracemere" in Tarrytown, the mansion in which he'd been raised, once the eponymous dwelling of his paternal grandmother, Grace Bell Topping.

I started down the stairs to show Allen what I'd discovered about his ancestors. Just then, I heard mother and son arguing and stopped in my tracks to listen as their voices became louder.

Anne said, "Allen, this is no way to talk to me. Lower your voice. I went to Clearwater to get a divorce because I couldn't stand any more abuse from him. By abuse I mean his womanizing, the gossip all over New York connected with it and the whole family hearing about his escapades. You and Barbara were grown and had left home anyway. The two of you have a fixation about your father, and you've both been ungrateful children."

Allen bellowed like a roaring lion, "Mother, don't you realize you ruined our lives by divorcing him? Now we shall inherit nothing!"

Anne said, "Hush, Allen. Don't presume to know things you don't really know at all."

"You didn't have to do it, Mother, there was no reason you couldn't have stayed with the old man. You thought he'd run after you, didn't you? Stop you, beg you to reconsider? When your ultimatums didn't work, you thought to spite him, but you only ended up spiting yourself and your children."

"Contrary to what you think, Allen, I didn't divorce your father to hurt you and Barbara. How was I to know he'd cut his children off? But that's your own and Barbara's doing, not mine. If I were the two of you, I'd get back in his good graces again. He's your father. You're his only children. There's no reason for antagonism if the two of you would swallow your pride."

"You know we've tried, but the stubborn old bastard won't give an inch. He says I'm a constant source of embarrassment, I should get out of his sight. As for Barbara, he doesn't approve of her choice of drinking companions. He's a fine one to talk. No, Mother, that's a lost cause and you know it. Face it, Mother, you screwed up. You're the one. You did this to all of us. We could have stayed together as a family. So what if Father had his outside life, his stewardesses, his whores and chorines, the Joan Crawfords and the rest of the sluts. How does that harm you? The family could have continued. Tell me what you accomplished, Mother, tell me."

"I will not have you talking to me this way, Allen."

"Just face the facts, Mother."

Anne said, "I am facing facts, and what I see is not a very pretty picture. I see that you're following in your father's footsteps ... and his father's before him. That poor child upstairs whom you had the gall to marry will live to see the day when you hurt her as your father hurt me and his father before him hurt Grace Bell Topping."

"I've told you I love Troy very much, Mother. You don't know what you're saying."

"How many daughters-in-law have you brought me? How long is this going to go on with all these women? Trudy gave you a child you deny is yours, your own flesh and blood, a beautiful daughter who's the spitting image of you. Allen, how can you keep denying this child? And let us not forget how you threw Marnie down the stairs so she lost her baby. Son, what are you going to do when Troy gets pregnant?"

"That's a long way's off, Mother. Troy's just a child herself."

"You know it would please your father if you had a son. Let me pass that tip along, Allen, a son could make a big difference with your father. I do worry about Troy, though. Troy's got some fire and spirit in her, but is she any match for you? I know you too well, and I'm afraid for her. Allen, I will always protect Troy."

"I'm your son. Why do you always take her side?"

"Because this time you married a child with no mother."

"I love Troy. She doesn't need you to protect her, she has me."

"I hope you mean that, Allen. You've brought me many daughters-in-law but never a motherless child before. I will do everything in my power to make sure Troy doesn't get hurt. She's different. The others could defend themselves. Trudy was well into her 30's, Mariana also a divorcée; that Pat had sure been around the block, Cheryl Ann was no blushing bride by a long shot, Emily was just an out and out opportunist; as for Millie -- "

"That's enough, Mother. I don't need your full accounting."

"The point is Troy is defenseless. She reminds me of myself as a young girl. Someday she may give me a grandson to carry on the Topping line, and let's hope her husband will be ready for the responsibility."

Allen said, "Are you quite through, Mother? I resent your interference as well as your contemptuous offer to protect her from me. As for a child, if Troy should have one, you know perfectly well Father would support her forever. Especially a son! That settled, may I please ask you to stay out of my affairs, and mind your own business, you old Irish biddy!"

When Allen went on calling his mother names, I shouted at him from the stairs to stop. Quickly entering the room, I said, "I thought you were a gentleman, Allen."

He said, "Sorry, sweetheart," and put his lips on mine. I broke away from him to embrace Anne. Tears were streaming down her cheeks. I said, "I'm so sorry, he oughtn't to speak to you like this."

A short while later, Allen took me to see Gracemere. The mausoleum like greystone turreted castle, dominating the Tarrytown landscape, was perched high on a hill. It was monstrous, somber, ugly, dark, cold and ominous. It had ceilings as high as Gothic cathedrals, a 150 foot living room with fireplaces at either end, a six car garage, friar and belcher gargoyles, and stained glass windows. The place gave me the shivers. It was as if the spirits of Allen's long dead ancestors hovered around, as if all the sorrows and ugly deeds of generations of Toppings were contained within. I couldn't imagine living here. I was sure it was haunted and couldn't wait to leave.

Recalling the conversation I'd overheard between Allen and his mother, I was disturbed by Anne's repetition of "many daughters-in-law" together with her list of their names. I'd overlooked her previous reference to this topic; now I wondered what she meant. I knew about the alleged duchess, but were there more? Once again I was reminded of Cook's words, "and a whole high heap o' wedding ring." She hadn't been able to explain. Could this have something to do with it? Did Allen have a secret life I knew nothing about? I asked him point blank.

He turned to me and took my hands. "Troy, darling," he said. "As you know, I'm married to a woman I haven't lived with in nearly a decade. I'm a normal man and yes, there have been other women in my life over the years. My mother is a traditional woman of the old school and doesn't approve of the idea of `free love' or `living in sin' or whatever you wish to call it. So I have brought women to her who, for the sake of convenience, I've introduced as her daughters-in-law. I stretched the truth out of respect for my mother. It was a harmless subterfuge that never meant anything. Only you have meant anything in my life, darling."

My eating disorder had worsened and I was mere skin and bones, down to eighty-five pounds now. Allen insisted I try drinking a milkshake, so I obliged and immediately puked it up all over him.

Barbara was back and her drunken antics continued driving everybody crazy. Once I looked at Allen's sister I thought how beautiful she might have been had she not been smashed all the time.

Barbara's one saving virtue was her ability in the kitchen. She loved to cook, and once told me the drunker she got the better she cooked. Ultimately, gourmet food or not, I could take no more of Barbara, and I insisted we leave and return to Manhattan.

CHAPTER EIGHT

Now Allen and I were starting a new life together, going traveling. Whence and whither? To what end and purpose? I wondered, but wasn't told. Allen packed up the green Cadillac, Star jumped onto the comfortable back seat and we all zoomed out of the city for parts unknown. I wasn't to see the Big Apple again for many years. It was sad to be leaving everything behind, but now maybe Allen could get a divorce and we really would get married.

With no seeming agenda, we passed through the southern states, cutting across Georgia, heading toward Texas. He wanted to show me the whole country, he said, to share a beautiful travel experience and broaden my perspectives. It seemed there were many forts in Texas and he was anxious to show all me all of them. Allen's intentions were good but the trip was torture. We drove twelve hours a day with poor Star bored and restless in the back.

We crossed the border at El Paso, entered a Mexican hellhole, and then it was back to Texas. It was pitch dark when we arrived in Midland in the dead of winter. We took the one dinky motel in sight, went to bed freezing and couldn't get warm. Star was wedged between us, but even her fur coat and body heat didn't help. My teeth were chattering and to my chagrin I discovered this fleabag had no heating system.

I was glad to leave Texas and the other southwestern states. They were all so brown and dead looking compared to the east.

I didn't know how to drive at that time and Allen steadfastly refused to teach me. In retrospect it makes sense that he wanted to keep me as helpless and dependent on him as possible.

With Allen at the wheel, at long last we hit Los Angeles. He steered the car onto the Sunset Strip and pulled up to the entrance at the Garden of Allah, former palatial home of Russian film and stage and screen great Alla Nazimova. I was delighted there were flowers and that it was warm here, that we had a spacious, sunny suite and could spend time outdoors swimming and napping in the sun. "Him wang go far," Cook had said. He would take me traveling to many places, she predicted, and Allen was doing just that. But what about marriage?

What would happen to me? What was I doing here? Why had we come? I was terrified not knowing what the future would hold. I kept thinking how I had no home or family, no place to go. Allen was my life and hope, but I felt like his prisoner. I loved him but hated the feeling of not having control of my destiny. All the days of my life I would never forget this time.

One evening we stopped at an impressive home with its shades drawn. I asked Allen whom we were going to see. He said this was the home of Dorothy Parker, a famous aging writer he knew from back east who had once held court at New York's Algonquin Hotel with a group of other famous writers of yore. He said he'd go inside and be right out.

I waited over an hour. He didn't say a word when he returned, nor during the entire time we were driving back to the Garden of Allah. The liquor on his breath, however, was unmistakable. It was only much later I learned that Dorothy Parker, like Allen, had an alcohol problem, that Allen had tapped her for money, and that while I waited in the car, he'd been rolling in the hay with her. In due time I'd find Dorothy Parker was only one of a series of elderly women for whom Allen Topping functioned as stud on demand.

There was a part of Allen's life I wasn't privy to, a mysterious dark side which had only been hinted at up until now: Allen Topping was a bigamist, polygamist and a gigolo. I knew about the so called duchess, I'd heard about the "many daughters-in-law;" there had been evidence I'd disregarded that he was accepting money from other women. Dorothea had warned me about his boozing and gallivanting in bars. She'd done some checking; times I believed Allen was meeting people on business, Dorothea said, he was actually in the company of two or three women who were picking up his bar tabs. I didn't believe this information. I also had no idea that Allen's father had been giving him money all along. I guess there was a lot I didn't know or didn't want to know about Allen. It would be some time yet before I would acknowledge such things.

One morning he had some business to take care of and planned to be back late. I had no idea where he'd disappeared to. He didn't return for another day, when he told me to get dressed up because he wanted to take me shopping. Where did he get the money, I wanted to know. On a business deal, he replied. When I asked about his staying out all night, the excuse was he'd had to go up north. In his pocket I found a match cover from the Santa Ynez Inn, which was not exactly "up north."

I pressed him for the name of the party he was involved with in this business deal. Allen identified her as a sanitarium patient on leave named Jean Ward Smith, said that she'd had an affair with John F. Kennedy in Palm Beach, and that her ex-husband had been the U.S.

Ambassador to Cuba. It turned out that Jean Ward Smith was yet another middle aged woman generous with her money who was more than grateful for Allen Topping's sexual favors. It also turned out that Allen had falsified her identity. It was not Jean Ward Smith whose ex-husband had been ambassador to Cuba and had an affair with JFK, but Florence Pritchett Smith, who was married to Ambassador Earl E.T. Smith. There was also a Jean Smith who was a Kennedy herself, JFK's sister, married to Steven Smith. And then, there was the Jean Ward Smith who had given Allen money.

Thanks to Dorothy Parker and this Jean, (although still unbeknownst to me) Allen and I went on a Rodeo Drive shopping spree in Beverly Hills. In one store he brought me a turquoise and white print dress, white high heel shoes and a purse to match. When I stood up in the heels I was as tall as he was. I'd grown two inches since we'd met. He put his arms around my shoulders and said, "My baby wife."

I said, "We're not married yet."

He said, "I'll see to it soon, I promise."

He then took me to a beauty salon and told the hairdresser to make my hair blond, a process that almost burned my head off. I missed my auburn hair and didn't like the ash blonde color at all. It took a lot of getting used to. Allen was trying to make me into somebody else. I wondered why.

Late that evening, we pulled off the Hollywood Freeway onto Alvarado Street, a rundown area in East L.A. not far from Skid Row. I wondered what we were doing in such a crummy place. Allen parked the car in front of a derelict hotel, got out and told me he'd be right back. From my vantage point in the front seat, I could see Allen talking to someone at the registration desk. His body blocked my view at first, but a few minutes later, I noticed he had shifted his stance enough for me to make out the desk clerk's features. I did a double take.

The man looked exactly like Allen, only a decade and a half older. Who was this person? He had to be a relative. The resemblance was uncanny -- same hairline, eyebrows, eyes, nose, square jaw, even the lips and teeth. Coloring, expression, mannerisms, height and build were identical.

When the clerk came from around the desk to accompany Allen to the door and the two of them stood there chatting for a brief minute, I was able to catch an even better look. Even the neck and the set of the wide shoulders were the same. It was as if I'd stepped into a time warp, previewing Allen fifteen years hence.

"Who is that man?" I asked when Allen returned.

"That's Hal," he replied nonchalantly.

"Hal who? Hal Topping? I didn't know you had relatives in L.A."

"Hal's not a Topping, no. However, there is a branch of the family in California, mostly ranchers and investment bankers. Dr. Norman Topping, the famous immunologist who discovered the rabies vaccine, now Chancellor of the University of Southern California, is a Topping relative."

"Who's Hal, then? He looks just like you, except older and more down and out. What's he doing working in a dump like that hotel?" Curious, I fired a series of questions at Allen, but he wouldn't answer.

It would be many years before I realized this man was Joan Crawford's brother, Hal Le Sueur, and that there was more of a connection between the Le Sueurs and the Toppings than I could possibly dream.

The next day we window shopped at Tiffany's, Van Cleef and Arpel's and Marvin Hime, ogling all the diamonds and emeralds. Allen kept telling me his mother had these things and he was so sorry he couldn't give me the jewelry, servants and other luxuries I deserved.

"It's you I love, Allen. I don't need jewelry and furs. What I need is a home and children, and I want to get married."

He looked at me and smiled. "You're so silly," he said. "But if that's what you want, it's within reach. I'm about to make a lot of money in Mexico."

"How?" I asked.

"This is the deal: I have access to Tyrone Power's estate in Cuernavaca through a pal of mine with a Mexican wife. The place is going to be sold and made into a resort. So play your cards right and all will be well."

He dropped me off at the Garden of Allah, saying he had to trade this car in for another model. Allen was always changing cars. This time he returned with a white four door '59 Mark 9 Jaguar with a C head, which he said had been customized in England. It had a smart red leather interior and was very comfortable. He always picked cars that would be comfortable for Star as well.

Back at the Garden of Allah, Allen told me he was mad about me, then made love to me, Nivea first, for hours. In the morning he announced we were going to Tijuana. It was a short spin to the Del Coronado Hotel in the San Diego area. We checked in, drove to the border, parked the car, and walked across into Baja California.

The Avenida Revolucion was seedy and ugly, I thought. One Mexican outside a bar shouted, "Señor, bring your sister in," which Allen gave evidence of intending to do until I protested. He then sat me on a donkey, placed a huge sombrero on my head and shot a roll of film, while flies buzzed overhead and fleas jumped off the donkey onto my skin. My dress smelled gamey now, but that didn't seem to faze Allen one bit when he took me to a whore house and tried to sell me into white slavery. Truthfully, despite the beaded curtains and dim lighting, I had no idea that this was a bordello until the madam told me in broken English that Allen should be ashamed of himself for trying to make a deal to employ me there. Allen had a knack for pulling pranks like this.

I forgave him when he spied an office with the sign "*Abogado*," which he said was Spanish for attorney. The sign said the *abogado* did divorces. I waited in the anteroom while Allen and the *abogado* conferred in back.

In a half hour, Allen came out smiling, took my hand and said, "Let's go." When we were alone, he gave me the glad tidings. In about a week his divorce from Trudy would be final.

I knew very little about this Trudy, just that she was somebody from Georgia or Oklahoma with whom he'd spent a weekend on a yacht. About a month later she came up pregnant and he married her to give the child a name, although he swore it wasn't his. In addition to overhearing Anne chastising Allen about the situation, I'd also learned from Barbara that Mr. Topping had made financial arrangements for the child. Nevertheless, Allen claimed his sole motive in the marriage was to be a good Samaritan.

As far as Allen had led me to believe, Trudy was his one and only about to be former wife. Despite Anne's references to the "many daughters-in-law" and Cook's "whole high heap o' wedding ring," I still would have been surprised to learn the extent of Allen's marital unions, that there were multiple wives in the background and that in the future there would be a string more, many running concurrent with our own impending marriage.

Back at the Del Coronado, Allen reached toward me and invited, "Dance with me?"

First we did the tango. Then he held me close as we rocked together, and he whispered in my ear, "Marry me, Troy. Make me the happiest man alive. Say you will,   please?"

Tears of joy welling in my eyes, I looked up at him. "Yes, yes, yes!" I exclaimed. "Oh, Allen, I'm ecstatic!"

He kissed me thoroughly, then said, "Tomorrow, my love, we leave for Mexico City. An apartment will be waiting for us there upon our arrival. We'll be married along the way."

Allen kept his word, and we were wed in the state of Morales two weeks later, on August 31, 1959. I didn't feel like a bride at all, but I did feel more respectable now that everything was legal, or so I thought. I also expected that now Allen would be making some money, we could go back to New York and be happy.

He drove east in Mexico toward Hermasillo. It was hot and the Jag lacked air conditioning. I closed my eyes, feeling the desert sun like fire on my skin. Relaxed and sleepy, I curled up on the seat and lay my head on my new husband's lap. It was sundown when I awakened, ill. Allen took me to a clinic. The doctor who examined me said, "Señor, she is exhausted. She needs a rest."

Our next motel was freezing cold. I was anxious to get this trip over and done with to return to civilization. Why were we traveling, where were we going, and for what reason? How long were we staying? I never knew precise answers to these questions. Allen was vague about specifics, other than the fact that this trip was supposed to put us on the map financially. And he always took control of everything -- money, time, plans. It seemed I was always waiting for answers to questions I couldn't quite formulate. But at least I was his wife now.

We headed southeast toward Mexico D.F. where the weather was cooler. Allen always handed the federales our passports upside down and they always said ok. They couldn't read, I guessed.

Driving south, we started into the mountains, so high they reached up into the clouds. Then came Taxco, the silver city, and on down into the crater into Mexico City. We headed for the area around Chaupultepec near the statue on the famous Reforma, past Sandborn's and onto the Calle Nizza with all its fashionable couturier shops. I noticed the House of Henri de Chationne on this famous street. Not very far away was the Calle Atoyac, just one block from the Reforma in the American colony. This section also contained homes of a number of foreign ambassadors.

Our apartment house was situated on Calle Atoyac. Although not as grand as most of the other homes in this pricey area, our flat was a decently furnished two bedroom on the third floor. The first night there,

I was ready to turn in. Allen said he'd be out for a short time.

We'd made the last part of the trip with a gringo, his Mexican wife and baby. Every time we stopped for gas or food, the Mexican girl would point at Allen and say, "Diabolo." In bed with Star sleeping behind my knees, I wondered about this.

I fell asleep alone, waking at 8 am hearing music. Mariachis below my window were serenading and Allen was opening the front door. His breath smelled of liquor, but he was sober and smiling. The mariachis, he said, were for forgiveness. They were playing Spanish love songs. It didn't stop the sinking feeling in my heart.

Exhausted from his night on the town, Allen went to bed. I picked up his clothes. In his shirt pocket was a pack of dirty pictures -- men and women in all positions, three at once, two men, two women. It disgusted me and I tore them up, burned them, and threw the ashes in the commode.

Later I found out our gringo passenger minus his Mexican wife and baby had taken Allen with him to spend the night in a whore house in Lomas.

Somehow I must get back to the States. Who could help me? I couldn't ask my father-in-law, not after refusing his offer of a million dollars to sign papers to commit Allen. There was no one in the world I could turn to and I was terrified. I had only two phone numbers to call in Mexico, an attorney named "Frankie," and Marie St. Cloud, both friends of Dorothea's.

We phoned Frankie. A short while later, thanks to his arrangements, a maid, Teresa, appeared at the door with a grocery bag of food. She made coffee, offered us fruit and hard rolls called *bollias*. My stomach was beating like my heart, which had jumped into my gut. We settled in. Teresa unpacked for us. In fact, Teresa did everything, walked and fed Star, cooked, cleaned, washed and ironed, and on her day off, after church, she went to Xophamilleo and brought back tons of flowers.

Star understood Spanish at once. Unfortunately it wasn't that easy for me, but Teresa was simpatica, so we managed to communicate in spite of the language barrier.

Marie St. Cloud, Dorothea's other friend, gave a luncheon in my honor at the country club. Marie was the mistress of the President of Mexico and I'd been looking forward to meeting her. However, Allen had discovered that Rum Castillo was cheaper in the market than the coke he chased it with; he'd had one too many and I had to go to the luncheon alone. When Marie asked me where my husband was, I replied, "Indisposed."

She looked at me knowingly and said, "I see." A most perceptive woman.

The guests were all Mexicans who spoke perfect English but talked Spanish exclusively all afternoon. When I asked Marie about a position modeling, she offered to check it out and phone the next day.

Back home, Teresa told me "*El señor e muy boracho.*" Allen was very drunk. I was mortified and wished I knew how to make him stop drinking altogether. But I was nineteen years old and such weighty issues were beyond me.

Star was walked and fed and Teresa said she was going *ariba*. The Spanish-English dictionary said *ariba* meant "up". Did Teresa mean the roof? I went *ariba* to see. There I found wooden shacks with no insulation containing only a cot with no bedding and an outside community toilet and shower. This was where Teresa was living.

I moved Teresa and her few shabby belongings downstairs to the spare room and bath and told her to go to bed. She was only seventeen, just slightly younger than I. Teresa was happy in her own room with a comfortable bed now, and worked harder than ever for her $12.00 a month.

Marie St. Cloud phoned to give me the address on the Calle Nizza of the couturier Henri de Chationne, who made all the ball gowns for political wives. I was hired as one of their models. The work was hard, the pay meager, and the Mexicans were always patting my blond hair.

Allen stopped drinking for about six weeks. Weekends we went to Cuernavaca, where we visited Luis Sol Lande, whose family had a large hacienda there. Allen showed me the famous Border Gardens, the summer palace of Maximilian and then a tiny villa and bathhouse where he'd had an affair with an Indian girl.

Allen handed me a dime. "What's this for?" I asked. He had a devilish glint in his eye.

He said we'd soon be going to see the Hacienda Checomgoje, Tyrone Power's estate bought for Linda Christian, to further investigate the business deal that he supposedly had on the dockets. Linda Christian, Allen said, was widely known to possess the remarkable talent of being able to pick up a dime with her vagina. He wanted to see if I could duplicate that feat. Ever obliging, I attempted and succeeded on the first try.

The second oldest hacienda in Mexico, the Hacienda Checomgoje had been built by the Franciscan monks. Evidence was still there of how the monks Christianized the Indians -- chains on the wall and other instruments of torture. It was also a sugar mill, and had its own church within the walls. Allen wanted pictures of the inside of the church, the priest wasn't there to admit us, so Allen hung me by the ankles from an open window above while I shot the interior.

The history of the place was tragic. The Don had sent to Spain to get a new statue of one of the saints and the Indians went crazy. They made an entire family dance on salt and then killed them all and burned the main house to the ground.

I questioned Allen about the business deal to turn this place into a resort. He said while the deal had been on hold, it was soon to be reactivated. I desperately hoped for it to culminate soon, as I was more and more anxious to get out of Mexico and return to the States.

Allen wanted to show me the old palace of Cortez, and after that, we headed back to the apartment at a leisurely pace. When we arrived Teresa and Star were out, probably walking in the park on the Reforma.

Two hours later they still hadn't returned. "I think we should call the police," I said, concerned.

"No, no, I'll find them," Allen said, and started out the door. Just then, in came Star and Teresa.

Teresa said, "The señoras in the Calle call Star Lassie." Star had been visiting with the ritziest dogs in Mexico, the purebreds of the foreign ambassadors. I was relieved.

We'd spent months upon months in Mexico waiting for the hacienda deal to go through. During that time, it was my paycheck that took care of household expenses, while Allen's financial contribution was nil. He would make it up to me, he said, when the deal closed. However, it was official now. The plan to make the Tyrone Power - Linda Christian hacienda into a resort was off. Exactly why was vague.

Why were we hanging around? I finally talked sense into Allen and he agreed we could start planning a return to the States. Only a lack of funds was preventing our leaving.

Allen went to see Ambassador Hill at the American Embassy. He'd been phoning his father, who kept refusing to take the calls and informed the operator his son should stay out of the country as he was a constant source of embarrassment. Now Allen was hoping the ambassador could get better results.

Mr. Hill phoned Father, who said, "If my son is in trouble have him call me in person."

So it was a Catch 22. Finally we had to borrow money from the government to get back to the U.S., with the proviso that the funds would have to be repaid within six months or Allen's passport would be revoked.

CHAPTER NINE

We'd been in Mexico for almost a year and it had hardly been the bed of roses I'd so looked forward to in marriage. Illusions, delusions, dreams, call them what you will   I'd had a sobering dose of reality. All I could think of was if we could only get out of this place and back to our own country, then our lives could change.

It wasn't merely Allen's drinking, although he was doing a good deal of that. If only he had a real purpose, I reasoned, our marriage would be perfect. Each day, I rose with a place to go and a job to go to, whereas this vital element was lacking in Allen's life. He was merely waiting for something to happen; he had no focus. We'd expected the hacienda deal to culminate within days; days turned to weeks, weeks to months, and everything just kept dragging.

I was still madly in love with him but he seemed to delight in torturing me. For instance, one time I spied a letter, carelessly tossed in a place where I'd be sure to find it. Allen subconsciously wanted me to read that letter, and I obliged. The sender was Jean Ward Smith, the California sanitarium patient. She called Allen "darling," raved about his sexual prowess, said her mother thought she was crazy for having fallen head over heels for him, and alluded to his having cleaned out one of her bank accounts, "but it was worth every penny of it." She even sent a picture.

Allen claimed Jean meant nothing, but her letter upset me. I shared my anguish via mail with my mother-in-law. Anne, as usual, was full of hope and positive feedback: marriages all had their difficulties, nothing on earth was perfect, Allen and I loved each other and belonged together, in time our concerns would straighten out, especially when we set foot on native soil again. Anne's thoughts always warmed me, offering the sense of family and belonging that I had been so starved for. I clung to the ideas Anne's letters expressed: things would change. And it was true that Allen did have some very beautiful qualities when he was on his good behavior.

When things looked bleakest, freedom often exercised an appeal, and I fantasized life without Allen, striking out on my own. But I had no money. What else could I do but stay here? Where would I go? How would I survive? I was terribly afraid. Mexico was a foreign country, I didn't speak the language, didn't know my way around, and had no idea how to get out. My only option was staying with Allen ... he was all the security I had, and I was clinging for dear life. Besides, he was my husband, I definitely loved him in spite of the difficulties. Things had to get better!

Weekends were always pleasant in Mexico. We spent almost all of them at Luis Sol Lande's family hacienda in Cuernavaca. When other people were present, Allen was always at his best.

One night close to our departure, we attended a party given by an American named Catherine, a chubby divorcée nymphomaniac with two small children and a dog.

Catherine was what was referred to as a "remittance person." Remittance people are U.S. citizens whose families consider them such an embarrassment they are paid money to stay out of the country. The American colony in Mexico City was crawling with remittance people, and it wasn't hard to understand why Catherine was one of them.

Everyone was walking around with cocktails when I decided to have another Coke. I went to the kitchen to find Allen and Catherine in full embrace, kissing. I screamed and ran in the opposite direction.

Allen followed on my heels. "Troy! Baby wife! Where are you going? Come back! You don't understand!"

But I did understand. My husband had hurt and humiliated me once too much and I wanted to die. Hysterical now, I climbed up on a window sill, ready to jump, but Allen caught me and pulled me back. I was sobbing uncontrollably.

Later at the apartment, I was still inconsolable. I kept telling him, "I want to go home! I hate this place, and I hate what you've become! You're destroying me and I want a divorce!"

"Darling, you don't mean that. You're my baby and I love you truly. I'm absolutely mad about you and you know that."

"I can't believe a word you say," I cried.

"If you'd only let me explain. That woman means nothing at all ... honestly, she grabbed me and I was so startled, I ... "

The argument could have continued longer except that right then Star walked over to Allen and fainted. We took her to the vet at midnight. The verdict was she had fleas. My Star had never had a flea in her life! The vet said the reason Star fainted was because she couldn't understand what was wrong with her. He dipped her to get rid of the fleas.

The next morning when Teresa was packing our things she started crying because Allen had told her we were going to take her to the States with us. I tried to explain we couldn't, but Teresa remained distraught, and begged me to leave Star with her as a consolation. Teresa sobbed her heart out while I went to the phone to explain to Luis Sol Lande what Allen had done. Luis offered to take Teresa that afternoon to his father's hacienda in Cuernavaca where she'd become part of the family.

The following morning we were ready to start back to the U.S. Allen had sold the Jaguar, trading it in for an ugly blue Plymouth station wagon because the Jag needed rings and valves.

Luis came by to bid farewell. He told me Allen was a good man, just temporarily confused. Amazing. Allen had even fooled a man.

The journey to Matamoros Brownsville, Texas, was a bumpy, wearying experience, but we finally made it to the border. The first thing we did immediately upon entering Brownsville was to head straight away to a burger stand, where we both ordered huge hamburgers. Thank God for the USA. Now maybe Allen and I could at last have a real marriage.

Allen had decided the next stop on our itinerary would be Las Vegas, and we were pressing northwest toward Nevada on another long drive. We pulled up stakes at night and Vegas was a sight to behold.

The first thing I saw was Sinbad the Sailor standing on top of the Dunes Hotel. Sinbad never ceased to fascinate me. Allen headed the car to a place called Paradise Ranch. He said we'd be staying here in an apartment owned by his friend Jack Cannon, and that he had a job lined up as a 21 dealer. I didn't know exactly how the two were acquainted -- probably from the service.

We were so broke there wasn't even any tooth paste. I berated Allen for this and for all the past horrors that landed us in this tarantula filled desert. It was a bit rustic to say the least. My beige dress was sent to the 3 hour cleaner's and we went on to the Strip to the Tropicana, the closest hotel to the ranch. I thought the Trop was beautiful, and breakfast was only 99 cents.

I knew nothing about comping, gambling, hookers, everything I was hearing they had in Las Vegas. We looked around for the rest of the day, picked up my beige dress, and back I went to the Ranch and Star.

Allen and Jack now had to report for work, the swing shift at the Frontier Hotel, where Allen was slated to be a 21 dealer. This was supposed to be a very well paying position and only given to trusted employees.

Things were quiet and I had toothpaste again. I was calming down. There was a girl living in one of the apartments named Robin Criswell whom I got to know, a cocktail waitress at the Sahara Hotel whose boyfriend was an aging, married, prominent and respected Democratic United States Senator from California whose son had been arrested on dope charges. Robin suggested one Friday that I accompany her to work, and maybe I too might find a job.

I dressed in my beige shantung fitted dress, black high heel Herbert Levine pumps, dressed my hair, and tried to look calm and collected. Actually I was excited at the thought of working and being able to get a place of our own. Rents here were inexpensive, Allen was sober and working. I thought, oh, Lord, please let us make a home and a baby. I loved Allen, so I would even stay in this god forsaken place and forget about going back to New York if that was what he wanted.

Robin picked me up in her little Triumph and we drove down the Strip to the Sahara. It was 5 in the evening and the casino was crowded. When we walked in the door, a fat little white haired man grabbed me by the wrist and said, "You just stand here, Lucky."

He was shooting dice, everyone was shouting and he won every time. He started placing $100 chips in my hand, telling me to put them in my purse. Robin, dressed in her waitress uniform, came over to ask if anyone wanted drinks. Everyone did but when I asked for iced tea, Robin gave me a look of disbelief, shrugged her shoulders and went off to fill the order. The man was still handing me chips, insisting that I stand as I was because I was lucky for him. All the pit bosses were watching the one dice table. I didn't know why they didn't look very happy.

Robin took chits from everyone for the drinks, which were free when you were gambling. I had lots of chips in my purse and the little man, whom I had learned was from Oceanside, California, was still adding more.

About five hours later I had to tinkle and asked to be excused. The man looked relieved when I returned from the ladies'. He said he'd been losing while I was gone. I stood there again, he started to win again and put more and more chips in my hand. About midnight he began losing and quit. Robin came by dressed, took me by the hand and we left in her Triumph, back to Paradise Ranch.

When Allen came in later and I explained what happened, he took the chips and told me we must go to a casino and cash them in. We returned shortly $1200 richer. That should be enough to get a nice apartment, I said.

He said, "Tomorrow, my baby wife, we will have our own place."

We left Jack Cannon's early in the morning. I was beginning to think Allen had lived in Las Vegas before. Or maybe he'd asked one of the dealers he worked with where to find an apartment.

Our new quarters were located on Cleveland Street. The place was brand new nobody had ever lived in it. It had cheap plastic turquoise living room furniture and a pink bathroom. Even the tub was pink. It was $200 a month, it was air conditioned, had an all convenience spanking clean kitchen and no electric bill. It boasted a pink phone and we only had to pay for long distance calls.

I was almost relaxed and content for the first time in a year. Allen was sober and working. I took care of my beloved Star, and there was an empty lot across the street where she could romp. I looked after the apartment, did the marketing and Allen's laundry. Allen always had the car, so I walked everywhere. I even walked all the way to Saks, where I bought a grey and white cotton checked dress with rows and rows of narrow white lace that went round and round, as well as white pumps and purse.

I picked up a newspaper and went home. I hung up my new dress and unwrapped my Arpège perfume and other treasures and sat down to read the Las Vegas Journal.

Nothing looked very exciting until I spied an ad for pretty dancers at the Desert Inn. I decided I'd get dressed up and go there tomorrow afternoon. I took out my black leotard, shoes and hose. I told Allen when he came in and he thought it was a smashing idea. I never did anything without his approval.

When I tried on my new dress for him, he smiled and said, "You look like a breath of spring, darling. Let's go out for a bite."

We did the Sands for a light supper and then went on home. After a relaxing warm bath, I donned my shortie robe. Allen showered and came into the bedroom with the Nivea Skin Oil. We both laughed. It was getting to be a signal. He massaged me until my skin sparkled with Nivea and I lay in a cloud of Arpège . He stretched out beside me and began kissing me all over until I shuddered and drew him to me. He drove himself into me and I screamed with pleasure, scratched his back like a cat, bit his lips and could not be still. I'd become over sexed, I thought, but no, that couldn't be it. I loved him and he went wild too. We hadn't made love in nearly two weeks. Now we made up for lost time, going at it again and again until we were too exhausted to move.

That night Allen repeated Imsak, the sexual art he was so skilled at, which he periodically renewed at regular intervals. Imsak was always accompanied by the same hypnotic affirmations Allen asked me to repeat while staring in his eyes. Often he would ask me to tell him I would be his slave until the end of time, that I could not live without him, that I would do whatever he asked me.

I awakened in his arms with my face on his tan chest. He exuded an aroma of sun and sea, the way he always smelled when I slept in his arms. I was happy now. We would stay here until we could buy a ranch, maybe. I thought before I opened my eyes, I must be a pretty girl to have a man like this.

Allen was asleep, so I quietly went about doing what I had to do before dressing. I tiptoed to the kitchen to fix a tray, reached out the window for a yellow rose and placed it in a vase next to Allen's juice and milk. With a kiss on his forehead and one on his eyes, I awakened him. He smiled before he opened his eyes and said, "Oh, how I love you, my baby wife." He smelled the rose, kissed my hand, and drank his breakfast.

He retired to the shower singing "O Sole Mio" while I changed the bed. Then he took Star out while I dressed for my audition at the Desert Inn. When he returned with Star, he kissed me and went out again to get a paper.

Star had brought me a present, a big yellow painted desert turtle. I could see how much she loved that turtle. She was so gentle with him, the way she picked him up with her mouth ever so gingerly and laid him at my feet. I thought what do I feed it? Oh, well, Allen would know or find out. Star stretched out with the turtle between her paws and we watched television together.

God, I prayed, don't let it change. Allen is working, we love each other, he's not drinking. Please, God, help me keep it like this.

Allen came in looking sheepish. I giggled and asked, "What do I feed a turtle? You knew Star had it when you brought her back."

The turtle was eating Star's softened kibble and horse meat. We both laughed as the turtle helped himself to Star's water. We guessed we wouldn't have to worry anymore about turtle food.

Allen offered to chauffeur me to the audition at the Desert Inn, for which I was glad, since it was boiling hot, buses annoyed me, and I liked to have his moral support. Maybe everyone would see how beautiful I was because of our love. I prayed again and to myself said amen. The world was my oyster. I glowed and my happiness almost made me faint. I could reach for the stars now, I was in some heavenly place in my heart and soul. I was bonded to Allen now and forever with love. Once again I was walking on a big cotton candy cloud. God, let it be forever this time.

At the Desert Inn we parked in back, then walked around to the front entrance. Before reaching the door, I noticed a man heading in our direction. He was tall and nice looking, dressed casually in slacks and sport jacket. Approaching us directly, he introduced himself and handed me a card which identified him as Howard Koch of Paramount Pictures, Hollywood.

Up until that time I'd not heard of Howard Koch, although of course I knew Paramount. Later, I learned Mr. Koch was one of the most respected and successful producers in the motion picture business.

Now Mr. Koch was saying he wanted me to come to Hollywood so he could put me under contract. Then he looked at Allen and said politely, "and no hanky panky."

I dropped the card into my purse with a sense of anticipation and excitement. But putting an immediate damper on my enthusiasm, Allen told Howard Koch in no uncertain terms, "No wife of mine works in the motion picture industry!"

Mr. Koch turned to me. "You talk to him and call me collect in Hollywood tomorrow."

Allen was highly annoyed and acted as though I'd done something wrong. Saying he'd be back after the audition, he took off in a huff. I danced for the choreographer, Donn Arden, whose fabulous Las Vegas reviews were famous throughout the entertainment world, and was hired on the spot. I would start rehearsing on Monday next.

Allen picked me up outside the hotel. He was nasty and I could smell the rum. He dropped me off at home and left for work. He returned at about midnight when he was supposed to still be working to say he'd lost his job, he'd been fired for drinking on the job.

In the morning he said, "Sit down. We have to talk."

I told him I wanted to go to Hollywood and work in films. He said absolutely not.

I said, "Look, I don't even feel married to you. I don't even know if our Mexican marriage is legal."

With that I went to the dresser and pulled out a rolled up parchment document decorated with red velvet ribbons, grabbed scissors and cut it up. I put on a yellow dress and shoes to match, thinking I just wanted to leave.

He took me in his arms, said, "Marry me now? I love you."

I melted again and said yes. I said, "I'm ready. How do we do it here?"

"Come," he said, guiding me to the car. We drove to the Chapel of the Flowers on Las Vegas Boulevard South. There we filled out the papers. Allen bought me a tiger orchid corsage. We had two strangers for witnesses and were married once again, this time at least by a minister.

I felt content but at the same time anxious. Allen stopped to buy a bottle of Cordon Bleu champagne, a stuffed roasted chicken, caviar, crackers, milk and eggs, and we headed home.

I thought this time there could be no doubt, I was really married to Allen Topping now. It was May 18, 1962. Wedding days are not very happy, I thought. I had my first taste of champagne and caviar. I really didn't like either one, but they were so chic and expensive I thought I'd better pretend, and besides, I didn't want to hurt my husband's feelings.

There was no fireplace so we just sat at the kitchen bar. I was quiet, thinking. I had given up a movie career and potentially millions of dollars. Was I crazy?

"You call that producer and tell him you cannot come to Hollywood because your husband says no," Allen said, "and I am your husband. You're mine and don't you ever forget it."

Years later, I remembered those words. I had good reason to.

He was getting drunk so I said, "Let's go to bed."

I was not to make love on my wedding night, I thought. What a drag. I curled up, put my head on his shoulder and tried to sleep. Thoughts kept whirling in my head. Then I felt nauseated and ran to the bathroom and upchucked everything into the toilet. I brushed my teeth and washed my face, went back to bed. I still felt ill but couldn't vomit anymore. I guessed it was the champagne, never dreaming I might be pregnant.

In the morning he looked in on me to say he hadn't found another job yet but he would. He sat down on the chair next to the bed and asked why I looked so pale.

I was ill again. I didn't mention my faint suspicions. I'd get a better idea next week when my period was due. I wanted his baby so much, so it would be a happy surprise when I was sure. If my intuition was correct, I'd only be able to dance for a few months so he'd have to get another position.

I told Allen it was the champagne. He gave me two aspirins and a glass of water, climbed into bed, we cuddled and went to sleep for a while longer. Upon waking again I still didn't feel well, and could eat nothing but tea and toast. Toward late afternoon, I began to feel better. Yes, this did indeed have the earmarks of morning sickness, then. Dare I be happy yet? I wanted to be absolutely sure before I said anything.

My Desert Inn appearances would start the following week. I had to go to rehearsal so Allen did the chores, tended to Star and the turtle while I dressed. He drove me to the Desert Inn, said he'd be back later to fetch me after rehearsals. He was going to look for a job, he said.

Allen was drinking again. One night when he was sober, I told him I wouldn't be able to work very much longer. He looked at me with a puzzled expression and in an odd voice asked why.

I joined him on the couch, took his hand and said, "Allen, I have a surprise for you."

"What?" he asked.

"Darling, we're going to have a baby."

He didn't move, just kept staring at me. In a strange voice, he said, "Really?"

"I'm very happy about it, aren't you?"

"Of course."

He kissed me on the cheek, then got up and marched out the door. I went to bed and cried myself to sleep.

He returned late, intoxicated. I locked the bedroom door and went back to sleep. When I woke up in the morning Allen was passed out on the living room floor, his slacks all covered with damp, pungent smelling urine. Try as I might I couldn't wake him up.

Star licked his face but he remained motionless. I felt his pulse. Thank God he wasn't dead. Terrified, I grabbed the phone and called Sunrise Hospital for an ambulance.

Allen remained in the hospital for three days. When I went to fetch him the afternoon of his release, they brought him to me in a wheel chair. He was unshaven, grey in the face and wouldn't speak to me. We went home, he showered and shaved, fixed himself some eggs, drank some milk. I had paid the hospital bill with my paycheck. He was not working and his little government stipend just covered the rent unless he used it for drinking. What to do now, I thought? He said he was going out to find a job.

He asked, "Are you sure about the baby?"

I said, "Yes," and smiled, wishing my husband could share my happiness.

He went out and slammed the door.

I thought oh, my God, he doesn't want a baby but I do and I'll have to find a way. I remembered the old German doctor I had once consulted who warned, "You look like a very strong girl but you are not. Be careful." Now something in his words hammered home at me, in that if I was going to bring this child into the world, it would take all my strength, that I must remain as healthy and calm as possible for my baby's sake.

I took a taxi home from work. On the way, in the middle of traffic, I spotted our car. Allen was at the wheel, and next to him in the passenger seat, was a long haired blonde. I told the driver to cut them off and stop. Shaking with fury, I jumped out of the cab, pulled open our car door, yanked the blond out by her hair, and ordered her to get the hell in the cab and get lost. In a low, cold, furious voice, I told her, "You are in my car with my husband."

My entire body was pumped full of rage, as if I existed in another dimension. I started hitting Allen on the head with my purse. He stopped me with a kiss and a big laugh. Then he drove us home. I opened the car door and asked him for the house key. He said, "Why are you so pissed off, baby wife?"

I screamed, "You cheating bastard, you're supposed to be my husband, and you don't want this baby. Now will you please get the hell out of my life?"

What I didn't know was that the blond in the car with Allen, Rosamond Stone, had just married my husband.

CHAPTER TEN

Allen got the message and left. I was so upset I had some tea and toast and went to bed. That night I had the same dream again, dancing on the ocean liner.

Allen didn't come home for the next week.

About this time, I began to notice that my "boss of bosses" at the Desert Inn, Moe Dalitz, was paying me an increasing amount of attention.

I knew Moe enjoyed legendary status but didn't know the reason why. To me Moe was just a very nice older man who treated me like a lady. I knew nothing at all then about his background.

Veteran of Detroit's notorious bootlegging "Purple Gang" and leader of Cleveland's Mayfield Road bunch, Dalitz had been one of the select few gangsters present at Lucky Luciano's going away party when New York City Special Prosecutor Thomas E. Dewey had Luciano deported to Italy. Dalitz' cronies, like himself, were the biggest wheels in the highest echelons of organized crime in the country.

Although called in to testify by the Kefauver Committee, Dalitz had a big advantage over his cohorts: he owned investments in gambling joints and dog tracks in Kentucky and Ohio, where such activity was legal. Whereas fellow mobsters Meyer Lansky, Frank Costello and Tony Accardo had problems with the IRS, Dalitz, with his legit investments, could be out front with his money. Thus, in the late 40's Moe bought the Desert Inn with hidden mob investors behind him. Later, he took over other casinos, built the California La Costa spa/hotel, and also was the power behind Lorimar Pictures. (The front man at Lorimar, incidentally, Dalitz' protégé, was the future husband and ex-husband of Barbara Walters, Merv Adelson).

There was another Barbara in Moe Dalitz' life at this time, the lovely young actress Barbara Parkins, one of the stars of "Peyton Place." I got the gossip from Robin: Parkins was Moe's mistress, he financed her career, kept her in homes, jewels, furs and cars, put her with the best people, gave her the red carpet in Hollywood, and now she was off in London, sort of semi living there, although things were still amicable between Moe and her.

Moe must have known more about me than I knew about him. By some uncanny sixth sense, he apparently realized that Allen was away.

Perhaps some of the other dancers at the D.I. had revealed I was having husband problems. At any rate, Moe became extra friendly and in a subtle way seemed to be feeling me out.

When Allen put in an appearance again, Moe temporarily receded.

Allen stood at the door, looking contrite. "Please forgive me," he begged, a well practiced hangdog expression covering his face.

I said, "You'll only do it again."

I walked to the bedroom, stretched across the bed and cried till my eyes were practically swollen shut. That night I called in sick. I'll deal with this tomorrow, I thought, unable to think any more today.

After that I didn't hear a word from Allen for a month. He'd taken some of his clothes and split. Just like that, as if nothing had happened to me. He could just walk away. Perhaps he was enjoying a honeymoon with Rosamond, though I was unaware at this time he'd married her. I just worked, came home and did my chores, glad to have Star and the turtle to talk to. Phoning my mother in law provided moral support. It would be only a matter of time before problems were resolved; now that our mutual dream of a baby was imminent, Allen had to come back to me, Anne said.

I had lunch with Robin, who told me, "You don't need this guy." Where had I heard this before? I brushed tears away, saying a silent prayer because what I did need was a miracle. Robin and I walked around Saks for a while, I bought some Arpège, Lancôme face cream and lipstick. Robin dropped me off and left for her job.

Because of the problems I was having I was mostly keeping to myself, and I'm sure I must have had a forbidding, inapproachable look about me. When I walked through the Desert Inn, I scarcely noticed anything and seldom greeted anyone. I was just so miserable I kept my eyes downcast, hoping nobody would bother with me, and that I'd manage to get through it all. The only time I felt even half way human was when I danced.

Moe Dalitz was always smiling, and whenever I saw him, somehow that big smile of his cheered me, made my day just a little brighter. For Moe, I did stop to chat, and always came away feeling better.

Once Moe noticed I was wearing a strand of pearls Allen had given me.

"Pretty," Moe commented.

My hand went to my throat and my heart sort of caved in, thinking of Allen.

Moe said, "But a beautiful lady like you deserves better than that." I wondered if Moe was talking about the pearls or the man who gave them to me. Without saying a word more, Moe took my arm and guided me to the Desert Inn jewelry shop.

"Pick out something you like," he said.

I felt awkward. I didn't want to offend Moe, yet on the other hand, I didn't feel right about accepting his offer. I wondered why he wanted to buy me jewelry, just what he could have in mind. What about Barbara Parkins? What about Allen? What about my pregnancy? All sorts of thoughts like these were whirling around my head.

I tried to politely demur, saying I just couldn't and he shouldn't, but Moe was insistent. He said if nothing else he wanted to know my taste. Embarrassed and confused, I said I really didn't know what my taste was.

Then Moe said he'd select something himself. He chose a beautiful gold necklace with a series of large diamonds, designed and made in Italy. It was the most stunning piece of jewelry I'd ever seen. It cost $100,000. He said it was me.

And just who was I? Someone who believed in Prince Charming and in fairy tales and destiny. Someone a worldly, sophisticated, caring and charming man like Moe Dalitz respected and wanted to honor. Someone who'd been in a destructive co-dependent relationship for over four years and had kept hoping against hope it was all miraculously going to change. How many women would envy me for Moe? How many would shake their heads in disbelief over my relationship with Allen?

Could these women who would never understand my feelings for Allen possibly understand my mental and emotional conditioning? My lack of family ties, the rudderlessness I felt, the need for and sense of family Allen and his mother gave me? Could they ever grasp the deep impression Cook's prophesy with the shells had made on me?

Admittedly, fantasy played a large role in my life. In the face of glaring reality, I'd always envision things being otherwise ... yes, Allen could change, our whole situation could change. He didn't want babies but he could and would in the future. We had no real home but we would have in the future. He had no job but that too would change. He would give me the stability I so longed for. If I could just tough it out long enough, everything would right itself. Cook had assured me that it was ordained. Allen and I had to go through the fiery furnace, we had to weather the storm. One day, the dust would settle. It would all be worth it. How could there really be a place for any other man in my life, when I was so attached to Allen?

I felt wrong accepting Moe Dalitz's extravagance, and told him so. I explained I just could not erase Allen Topping from my mind and heart, at least not yet. I did appreciate Moe's kindness and regard for me. He said he hoped I'd resolve my problems soon.

Then the bomb hit. The doorbell rang, I answered, and there stood Allen. Shocked, I invited him in. What now, I thought.

He said, "Please let me come back. I love you."

I was shaking. He put his arms around me and I started to sob on his shoulder. He kept stroking the back of my head until I stopped crying. Then he said, "We have to talk."

He said he'd been in Miami, where he'd gotten a job as a desk clerk, but found he couldn't stay away from me. He wanted to get back together, he said.

I was pregnant. My baby needed a father. That seemed reason enough to say yes. Even so, I hesitated. Finally I said, "All right. But I want you to work."

He agreed. While he took Star out, I showered and washed my hair. I looked like a drowned rat with red eyes when he walked into the dressing room. He grabbed a sheet and towel to wrap around my body and I twisted another towel around my head, turban like. He walked me to the bed and tucked me in. He said, "You don't look good. Are you all right?"

"I'm fine."

We only slept in each other's arms that night. He knew me well enough to realize I wasn't up to lovemaking at that stage of the game.

Again and again I wondered about Allen's bizarre behavior, and about what his mother had told me about his war injuries. It had put things in perspective, but was there hope that his strange, often cruel actions could change? Cook's prophesy seemed to say yes. Through thick and thin, good times and bad times, if I loved him, it would be worth it. He was mine; God himself had decreed it. We were meant to be together. Oh, if only we could have a chance for a solid marriage soon. Now especially, with our baby on the way.

Considering what I knew about Allen's imbalance stemming from his war injuries, I often wondered if I'd made a mistake not to honor Mr. Topping's wishes to sign papers to commit Allen. It had seemed so crass to me, as if there were a price tag on my love, that my loyalty was for sale. Yet more and more I was entertaining doubts about my husband's emotional health. Could Allen and I survive without professional help? Was love enough?

The next morning he tried to make love to me but I was still too hurt and could only cry in his arms half the day.

The phone rang. Allen picked it up. He was talking to someone and I was curious whom, as we almost never received calls. Quietly, I lifted the extension and listened.

A woman was speaking on the other end. She said, "When are you coming back? After all, we're married, and we haven't been for very long."

From snatches of conversation, I gathered this woman lived in Miami, that her name was Virginia, and that she worked in the hotel business.

I hung up the phone. A buzzing went straight up my back to my neck and head. I walked to the bathroom, took his razor, leaned over the sink and slashed both my wrists. As the blood gushed out into the sink, I thought, now he can't torture me anymore.

It wasn't long before he was banging on the door. I didn't answer. He broke the door in, grabbed two large towels and wrapped them around my wrists. He was leading me to a chair in the living room, asking over and over, "Why? Why? Why?"

He called for an ambulance and opened the front door to wait. It was a very hot day but I was so cold. He kept repeating, "Oh, no ... why?" as if he didn't know, and I kept hearing his voice saying, "Oh, my God." I assumed he realized I'd heard the phone conversation with Virginia from Florida. I didn't know her last name. Later on, I would learn she was Italian when he would refer to her as "the Guinea," or "Ginny the Guinea." This woman's identity was remote from my consciousness now, as desperate thoughts raced through my mind. I believed in our destinies together, but despite my faith, this husband of mine kept on betraying and dishonoring me. Now everything was dashed to pieces. I couldn't change Allen. Would I go on forever dragging this corpse that was my love, buried deep within my chest? My heart was dead. I was only human, I could take just so much; my tolerance point had been reached. Now I wanted everything over and done with, this entire nightmare that was my life, ended. Prince Charming was a dead dream. Just let me out, out of this miserable planet Earth once and for all, now and forever. "Things gwang get bettah?" When? How long could I wait? No more. Finally it all must cease.

He was shaking his head and was so angry with me he refused to accompany me to Sunrise Hospital. As I lay alone in the ambulance, weak and bleeding, my last mental image of Allen was his turning away in disgust, walking back to the apartment and slamming the door.

Now I really wanted to die.

The doctor who sewed up my wrists asked me why.

I said, "My husband married another woman about six weeks ago and we aren't divorced." Of course, the irony was I didn't even know he'd not only married Ginny the Guinea but Rosamond Stone as well.

"Why didn't you kill him?" the doctor asked. "That's what you really wanted to do."

I said, "You see, I'm pregnant."

The doctor's voice was more sympathetic when he heard that. He asked how long we'd been married.

I told him. Then I said, "I don't feel very good." I had bad cramps in my stomach.

The doctor summoned another doctor to examine me.

The second doctor took my hand and said, "I'm afraid there won't be any baby."

I felt a gush come out of me, they gave me a shot and I drifted off to sleep.

When I awoke it was all over. I could go home the next day but I should rest.

The nurse said, "It was a boy."

I said, "I'm not pregnant anymore. I lost my baby. Oh, God, I wanted it so."

The nurse told me I was young; I could have other babies. She too asked why didn't you kill him, he's the one who deserves to die, not you.

"Wid piknie there is pain. ... avoid blood... be careful. I see blood wid piknie." Oh, my God. I heard Cook's voice, so long ago. "Keep strong, keep good, cause wid piknie there is pain... avoid blood."

What else was going to happen to me?

I stayed in bed for days, so heartsick I couldn't speak to Allen. The fourth day I awakened to find him gone, bag and baggage, including a Pan American pin that he prized highly. I assumed he had gone back to "Ginny the Guinea" in Miami.

He had no money. There hadn't been enough in my purse for an airline ticket, and his name was no longer on our former joint bank account. His new illegal spouse Ginny the Guinea must have sent him the money to fly to Miami, if that was where he went.

I thought I'd better look in my purse, anyway. It was empty. He'd taken my fifty dollars. I called in to work sick and then cried myself to sleep. My boss Donn Arden knew about my suicide attempt and sent a priest to see me. Moe Dalitz sent flowers and a kind note. Robin came over to walk and feed Star. My wrists and hands were bandaged so I couldn't shower or bathe.

Well, I thought, it's all over. I drifted off to sleep and dreamed my dream again on the ocean liner.

I decided to move to another apartment. This one was full of memories that I must forget. I found a place at the Baltimore Gardens, a new complex with a pool, where Star would be welcome.

I worked, saved money, and made friends with two neighbors, Hazel, who was married and very much in love with her husband, and Kathy Long, unmarried. Kathy was tough. She said her last boyfriend, a skim courier, was shot by the mob in a phone booth in Los Angeles. Hazel's husband Frank hailed from Miami and they were talking about moving back there.

So this was the independent lifestyle I'd been dreading so long -- lonely, empty, loveless. I thought a lot about the good times Allen and I had shared, and wondered if I'd ever in this lifetime find love again. A lesser love would be preferable; there would be less pain. Allen was my dream of perfect bliss. I had aimed too high. Now I just wanted a little peace of mind.

I swam a lot in the pool, got tan, shopped and did chores. I worked and stayed out all night playing dice. I never seemed to lose, but I never played it back either.

It was about this time that one of Moe Dalitz's associates, also named Moe, invited me out to dinner. He was a nice man and I was lonely, so I accepted his invitation. I knew he had no romantic interest in me, that this was to be just a friendly supper.

Actually, it turned out to be more than that. I soon understood that the purpose of the get together, as far as he was concerned, was to feel me out as to my receptivity toward Moe Dalitz at this time.

His conversation was largely a pitch for Moe. He told me things like, "Moe really likes you. He'd like to get to know you better. Moe takes a shine for a girl, he goes all out for her. You know, Moe's a very choosey guy, he doesn't go for many girls. He's selective. Moe likes you. He could do a lot for you. Look what he's done for Barbara Parkins. Moe would like to help you, to make your life comfortable. How do you feel about that? Do you think you'd like to let him take care of you? Do you think you could like Moe?"

I said, "I like Moe a lot. Who wouldn't? He's such a nice man."

"Then shall I tell him to call you?"

"I'm not sure I'm ready for any kind of commitment   I've been having a lot of personal problems."

Both Moes were aware of my suicide attempt, my losing the baby, and that I'd been having marital problems. "Why not get your mind off your troubles? Let Moe help you forget. He'll start the ball rolling in the right direction, so you'll put headaches and heartaches behind you. Get a new life going. You know, if you're interested in a career in Hollywood, Moe's the guy for it. And he'll be good to you. Moe is a very generous man."

"I like Moe, but I'm married and still deeply in love with my husband."

"How long since you've seen this no good S.O.B.?"

"Several weeks now   "

"A beautiful girl like you deserves far better than this loser. You ought to have a guy who treats you decently and who's good to you. Tell you what. Have dinner with Moe. Feel out the situation, the chemistry, see if the two of you agree on things, if you see eye to eye. I promise it'll be one of the biggest favors you ever did yourself. No obligation, just a friendly dinner between two people who have a high regard for each other. Some good food and wine, some pleasant conversation, and you two take it from there."

I said I would have dinner with Moe Dalitz.

CHAPTER ELEVEN

We dined in a private dining room at the Desert Inn. Moe could not have been more charming, discreet, or eager to please. He made it perfectly clear, without resorting to gaucherie or offensive statements, exactly how he planned on treating me if I would become his mistress. A master of finesse and delicacy, Moe never actually used the term "mistress," perhaps instinctively understanding that the word would turn me off, but of course we both understood that was what he meant.

Moe made a point of learning my taste in every department -- cars, furs, homes, furnishings, jewelry, paintings, travel, leisure, and so on. He declared he wanted any car of my choice, a Rolls, Maserati, or whatever I desired, delivered to my door the very next morning, and that the car would be registered in my name.

I confessed to Moe I didn't know how to drive, that I'd recently bought myself a navy blue Thunderbird with the idea of learning, but every time I tried, my knees knocked together and I couldn't hold the brake in. So the car just sat idle in the garage most of the time. I told Moe how Allen had steadfastly refused to teach me to drive, no doubt to gain yet more control over my life. Moe said that was going to have to change, I was going to have to start taking lessons. He laughed and said in the meantime he'd have to get me a chauffeur.

Moe went on about all the things he would do for me, the ways in which he wanted to help. A major priority would be to get me a nice place to live. He asked if I'd be interested in Hollywood. I said I'd had a chance in that direction and told him about Howard Koch's offer.

"I know Howard. What happened?"

I explained how Allen had ruined that. Moe shook his head in sympathy. To his questions, I offered honest answers. I described my current status with Allen, that although he was out of the picture now, I was still in love with him, that we'd had a stormy relationship with many separations, somehow always managing to get back together.

I couldn't fully describe my confusion. It was as if Allen were a concept I'd created in earliest childhood and could never let go of. Prince Charming, the recurring dreams and the subtle workings of my subconscious, the fantasies, the hopes, the chemistry, together with Anne's promptings and encouragement, to say nothing of Cook's eerily accurate prophesies had all been part of the fabric I'd woven around my love for Allen.

The case I'd built in my psyche was a strong one. We were meant to be together. The sea shells had predicted it those long years ago. All right, there were past mistakes, but there were also good times. Allen had made me miserable, he had also made me deliriously happy. That happiness could some day be ours again. And that longing for togetherness -- how I ached for that sense of belonging to a unit that the Topping family represented for me. How could I really explain?

Moe advised me like a father. "Look, Victoria," he said, "Obviously you know I'm very interested in you, and I'd like for us to get together. I understand you're still hung up on this guy and it's a tough transition to make. But regardless of what your decision on our getting together is, yes or no, I want to give you some friendly advice: get over this guy, get him out of your system for good, or it will destroy you. If you ever have a problem with him, if he pulls any crap on you again, come to me. We can take care of this guy so he won't be a problem to you again."

As delightful an evening as Moe and I spent together and as much as I wanted my life to change, I was hooked on Allen, and certain he'd come back into my life again. It wouldn't have been fair to encourage Moe under those circumstances. I had to tell Moe I really did believe in till death do us part and for better or for worse, and that I also had faith that in time Allen would mellow out. There was so much more I couldn't tell him, things that no one but I myself would understand.

Moe shook his head incredulously, and said if I changed my mind in the near future to let him know, that his offer was open as long as there was a place in his life   though he couldn't promise that would be the case forever. At any rate, any time I needed a favor, he wanted me to know that I had a friend for life and that I could always call upon him.

Three months had gone by and I hadn't heard a word from Allen. My thought patterns vacillated between hope and despair. I was on a solitary roller coaster, unable to give up the dream of perfect love and the man who had the power and capacity to bring that to life. I would face reality and then I would ignore it. I knew Allen was a lout but then I denied it. I stubbornly insisted he would change, and kept Cook's prophesy close to my heart as proof. I was trying to make a go of it on my own. Perhaps I would never see Allen again. I would try to forget him and the way to do that was to stay very busy. I put the baby out of my mind. Sadly, it just wasn't meant to be. A bigamist husband who couldn't stop drinking for the father of my child -- who needed that?

A visitor from the East popped in one day, Ruth Brady. It was comforting to talk to an old friend. We went out gambling after I finished work but never picked up any men. God knew enough men were trying to pick us up all the time. Ruthie stayed about a week and when she left asked me to think about taking a trip to Puerto Rico for Christmas. I needed a change.

I was bitterly unhappy about this marriage but I was learning to bury the memories deep in my heart. I just kept busy and smiled a lot so the world wouldn't know how humiliated I felt.

I made friends with a taxi driver named Bob, who drove me to and from work and around town. After a while he'd stop in and talk whenever he had a break. He was going to school to be a pharmacist, driving the cab to pay for it. We'd have long talks about my marriage and my feelings. Bob did his best to console me. He was concerned about my not sleeping well, and kept asking me, "Please, please don't smoke." Due to stress I'd taken up cigarettes and become addicted.

Bob was a nice man but it was the same story as with Moe Dalitz, albeit on a more modest scale. I was so emotionally involved with Allen I just never saw anyone else as a possible love interest. I didn't know then that one learns to love a man who is kind and caring, someone who knows how to be a friend.

I'd even started doing my own hair and nails, which filled in the time. I was thinking about that trip to Puerto Rico Ruthie had suggested, so I started planning my wardrobe and baggage. Shopping for the trip took up much of my time, for which I was grateful. I could spend hours at Saks and Nieman Marcus -- sheer escapism. I found some luggage I liked, and fantasized appearing in the various garments I purchased.

Subconsciously, my thoughts were about Allen all the time. Would he like this dress, those shoes, that nightgown? I even bought a mink jacket. A real bargain, it was on sale and I thought I looked smashing in it. Poor Star. She was alone most of the time and was so glad to see me when I was at home. Star was now on a special diet. She'd been getting too fat, the vet said, and she'd developed a kidney problem. I had to buy her food by the case and give her extra special attention. I'd never want anything to happen to my beautiful Star.

I had no really close friends here; mine were all in the East. Allen had taken me away from where I could have made a future, a proper marriage and a secure foundation.

It was very hot and I was in the pool swimming. The gate opened and there stood Allen. How he found me is a mystery still. He always managed. I climbed up the ladder out of the pool and sat on a lounge chair. No one else was at the pool. I'd make him come to me.

He walked around to where I was and sat opposite me. He said, "You look great. Did you have an abortion?"

I said, "You know I'd never do that, you flaming wart. I had a miscarriage. You don't have to worry about supporting a child now."

He said, "I know how you feel but please try to understand how I feel. I cannot give you all the things you deserve -- jewelry, clothes, servants, furs ..."

I said, "Oh, really? Is that why you married Virginia when you're married to me?"

He said, "I didn't know what I was doing."

"That's no excuse for bigamy. Bigamy's even worse than merely cheating on your spouse."

He said, "I'm so sorry. What more can I say?"

"Who the hell do you think you are? You can walk in here and beg me to forget your long history of cheating and drinking, and be oh so glad I lost the son you never wanted?"

"It was a boy? I fathered a son? How do you know?"

"They told me at the hospital."

"Don't for one minute think I wouldn't want our son. I didn't know it was a boy. Losing a son is a tragic experience for a man, Troy, particularly when he would have carried on the Topping line."

"Sure, another Topping skunk to go out and mess up every girl's life he could find. A great loss indeed."

"You're right to feel the way you do, and I'm so very sorry about your heartache, as well as my own, and about the loss of our son."

"Then why did you ask me if I'd had an abortion?"

"I don't know. I just thought you would, because you're such a child yourself, you wouldn't know what else to do."

"I should have called your father and asked him if he'd still consider giving me a million to commit you to an institution where you belong."

"What are you talking about? A million to commit me ..."

"That's right. Your father made me that offer, but I like a fool wasn't convinced you were certifiably nuts at that time. He told me he wanted to help you. I figured he was just angry with you and being spiteful. I loved you so I didn't believe him. What I should have done this time was call him to ask if the deal was still on."

He looked at me in horror and said, "You're right, my sweet baby.

I've behaved reprehensibly, and there's no excuse for it. I can only say I'll make it up to you somehow. We'll have another baby."

"Not on a bet. Given the kind of father you'd make, I don't want more babies. Don't you understand, Allen, you can never compensate for the things you've done?"

"Oh, Troy, honey, don't do this to us. I love you so. I'll do anything, if you'll just give me another chance."

"Another chance? How many do I have to give you?" I started to cry so I stood up and jumped in the pool, screaming, "I hate you, Allen, and I hope everyone hears me! I hate you, I hate you, I hate you!"

Fully dressed, Allen dove in the pool after me. He grabbed me by the neck, pulled me into his arms and held me until I stopped crying. We climbed out of the pool together and sat on the longues. Allen's clothes were dripping wet.

He said, "Troy, please try. You know I'll never love another woman as I love you. I'd lay the world at your feet if I could. It makes me sad that I can't. Everything would be different if I could."

"I don't need the world. I need one man who's there for me. Why do you run when I need you?"

"Because I'm afraid I won't be able to come through. I'm ashamed. I want to be everything you need, but something snaps. I start feeling desperate, like a failure, I know I've let you down and I panic. So I go off to lick my wounds. I can't face being such a disappointment to you. It wouldn't be this way except Mother and Father loused me up, they got the divorce, and the old man married Glad Ass."

"Divorce happens in the best of families. It's not the end of the world, Allen."

"In this case it is. A whole huge trust fund that would be the solution to my life is out of reach, because that cunt made him cut it off."

"All right, so your trust fund's inaccessible. Think how many people don't have trust funds to begin with. What do they do? They go out and get a job. They don't sit around moaning about not having free handouts from their family."

"You don't understand what my world is. I'm 40 years old. What the hell do you expect me to do? People in my world have trust funds, Troy, they don't have to rely on rinky dink nine to fives. It's humiliating. Get real, Troy. I couldn't get a glamorous, exciting job."

"Who's talking glamour and excitement? I'm talking self respect, Allen. Why can't you help yourself?"

"I get too angry about the unfairness. I feel so powerless I guess I strike out and you get the brunt of it. I know I've behaved abominably, but please believe me it was unintentional. I never meant to hurt you. I do want so to come back. I do love you so. I will try so hard to make you happy and be everything you need and want."

The conversation continued with Allen begging to reconcile and my resisting. He was so genuinely hurt and broken, so vulnerable and flat on his ass, I couldn't help feeling compassion for him.

We covered our usual territory, dredging up past hurts and misgivings. There were accusations, denials, affirmations, pledges, tears, laughter, anger, sentiment, and so on, the old familiar. The dialog continued for two hours, as negotiations heated up and quieted down in the old tug of war until finally, after much resistance, I began to relent again. Weakness was like a familiar friend now. But Allen appeared at a time when I'd been so lonely. Wasn't it better being semi-miserable and sometimes happy with a loved partner than being totally unhappy alone? Allen needed me, besides. I remembered Anne's words. What would become of Allen if he didn't have me? I was probably the only person outside his own mother who understood his affliction. More than adequate reason existed for his behavior. It wasn't directed at me. He couldn't help it.

A bestselling book I'd read recently, *You Are Not The Target*, by Laura Archera Huxley, the wife of British writer and philosopher Aldous Huxley, had made me view my relationship with Allen from a different perspective. Laura Huxley had explained how hostility we perceive others direct at us may very well not be the case at all, but rather stem from sources entirely unrelated to ourselves. Therefore, we shouldn't take offense, but instead should look to overcome our misplaced subjective judgments of being targets.

Surely, continued effort at building our relationship would be well worth it, for I had always known in my heart that Allen and I belonged together. Both Anne and Cook had said all would eventually be well.

But if we were to go back together, there were some things Allen would have to agree to, I told him. I didn't want to be pregnant again, to ever go through anything like that again. "It's up to you -- you see to it," I declared firmly.

"I will, I'll see to it," he promised.

"You'll work, you'll support the household, not me. No drinking, Allen. It's easy to say I love you but actions speak louder than words. So prove it or you don't get any more chances."

He leaned forward, looked me straight in the eye and said, "You got it, darling. I swear. I told you I'd do anything for another chance, so I'll do exactly as you want."

"You know, you really are a son of a bitch."

He laughed. "My baby wife has learned how to swear, I see," he said, and with that planted a kiss on the tip of my nose.

I was filled with conflicting emotions. I wished I could punish Allen but I was unable to hate him. I loved him, I felt sorry for him. I was angry with myself for letting him play on my sympathies, but I couldn't help it. I'd missed him, I was glad to see him again, imperfect as he was. Even the little girl inside had grown up. I was out of the hospital six weeks and felt I'd aged sixty years.

"Damn you, Allen, I still love you, you bastard. This must be pure insanity! Did Virginia divorce you?"

He said, "No need for it, it wasn't a legal marriage."

That was but one illegal union. The Rosamond Stone bigamous marriage didn't come up because I still didn't know about it.

"This is going to take some time, Allen," I said. "I'll try to forgive you, even though I can't forget."

"I understand you won't forget, but I'll be very happy if you'll try to forgive me."

I wanted to believe him. He'd come back to me, I couldn't send him away again -- where would he even go? He'd seemed so beaten down.

He stood up, leaned over and kissed me on the cheek. "Come on, let's get dressed, go out to dinner and celebrate. I've got my darling wife back."

"However, we'll drink soda water," I said.

"Where do you want to go? Your wish is my command."

"The Dunes. I want to see Sinbad."

"All right. But let's take a drive before dinner. The sunset is so pretty today."

After a spin up Hoover Dam, we dined at my favorite romantic haunt, The Captain's Table at the Dunes. The violins playing against the roar of the waterfall that was lit up like diamonds, the ceiling full of stars. Allen knew just how to get to me. We drank ginger ale in champagne glasses and I was so happy real bubbly couldn't have made me any higher. We held hands and he kept rubbing my knee with his.

Afterwards, the artist in the lobby did a color sketch of me. When I looked at it I saw to my chagrin that I no longer had stars in my eyes. The eyes were still green with flecks in them, but oh, so sad. I'd never realized this before just now. Surely Allen must have seen it.

We took a swing around the casino after dinner but I couldn't win when Allen was there. We lingered in the shops for a while before I agreed to leave. I wasn't fully convinced I wanted to start things up again, despite what I'd said. I was wary of being hurt and found it hard to trust Allen at this juncture. I wasn't ready to forgive him yet.

He said, "All right, let's go back and talk this out." He held out his hand.

At home, I went to the bath. "Shall I walk Star?" he asked.

"Go ahead. I want to soak in the tub for a while."

I relaxed, and after a long while put my entire head under water, so it was impossible to hear anything. When I raised up and opened my eyes, Allen was sitting by the side of the tub watching me.

He said, "I love you, darling. Why are you soaking your head?"

"To stop hearing and thinking. I don't want to distrust you, but damnit, Allen, I still hurt. I can't help it. I don't know if it will ever go away."

I stepped out of the bath into a terrycloth robe. At that moment Star walked in wagging her tail like mad. She was so happy to see us together again.

"See," Allen said, "she knows how very much I love you and her!"

I put on a shortie nightie. While Allen went into the shower, Star walked to the living room and positioned herself in front of the TV for the 11 o'clock news. Avid television viewer that she was, she would express frequent opinions by cocking her head and wagging her tail. She had brought her best friend Mr. Turtle to watch with her, placing him carefully by her side.

Allen led me by hand to the bedroom, where he had already set up his usual tools -- Nivea Skin Oil and a full bottle of Arpège.

"Did you go to the drug store?" I asked.

He said, "Why do you think I walked Star for so long?"

I smiled in anticipation as he poured the entire bottle of Arpège into the Nivea. He leaned over me, kissed me on the lips until I thought I was melting and becoming part of him. He whispered, "Turn over on your tummy." He dribbled the Nivea/Arpège on me and massaged every part of my back. He rolled me over and did my front. My nipples turned red and I stretched out languidly, enveloped by the fragrance, madly in love with this husband of mine, not knowing why.

He was good looking, sweet as an angel at times, and made love to me until I thought I was a piece of hot liquid gold. He kissed me over and over, all over me and then slowly melted into me. We both rolled and writhed until I went wild. He pulled my derrière closer to him, whispering, "I just can't get enough of you."

We made love repeatedly all night. When the morning came, I woke in his arms, my face on his chest. His body exuded the aroma of the sun and the sea. He smiled before opening his eyes, as was his habit.

"I guess I've forgiven you ... after last night," I murmured blissfully.

After bathing, we both repaired to the bedroom, wrapped in towels. He said, "Come on," picked me up and carried me to the bed. We massaged each other again and made love all over again.

I ran for the shower the next morning with Allen after me. He put his arms around me and said, "I love you so, and I love being in the shower with you, all nice and clean. How would you like to take a bath together after this?"

I laughed. "You're funny."

"This is just fun," he said. "Last night was heaven on earth."

Allen walked Star, and I was dressed by the time they returned. "It's Sunday," I said. "What shall we do, Allen? I know! We could get one of those 99 cent breakfasts at one of the casinos."

He said, "I'd rather be alone with you, but if that's what you want we'll do it."

After breakfast, we played in the pool for an hour like two happy kids. As we emerged, in the distance I heard the Mario Lanza rendition of "Be My Love," a song from the early 50's. I would never forget the past 24 hours, yet at the same time, I still couldn't forget what Allen had done. I loved him, but why couldn't I seem to really trust him anymore?

Allen rounded the corner on foot and came through the gate carrying a huge red rose and a big bottle of Arpège. I put the gifts in the house and we jumped into the pool again. We swam, floated and dove underwater. He took me in his arms again. He said, "Hey, Mermaid, come with me."

Back in the apartment we showered together again. He was so sweet I couldn't believe it. He held my hands continually, looked deep into my eyes, said "I love you" 100 times a day. I was in seventh heaven, but still in the back of my mind was the doubt   could I ever trust him again?

He got a job, night clerk in a hotel. I still had my job at night, so our schedules coincided. He sent me one red rose every night to my dressing room at the Desert Inn.

This must be what Cook meant in the prophesy of the sea shells... "You and him be one, two peas, one pod, batty and bench, one spirit ... " But Cook hadn't prepared me for how incredibly beautiful it would be. My Prince Charming was everything I had ever dreamed and more. The pain had been worth it.

Allen was sober, he was the perfect husband. I had it made in the shade. I was walking on air. Nightmares were a thing of the past.

CHAPTER TWELVE

Our second honeymoon continued for a few delirious months, then Dr. Jekyll turned back into Mr. Hyde. "Good times, bad times, thick and thin, when times is tuff, look black, you stick wid him, it gwang get bettah," Cook said. Once again, I prayed and waited. How much longer in darkness?

Perhaps predictably, now Allen was drinking again. He'd lost his job, and we were fighting more and more. I resented his not even looking for a new job but relying on my paycheck. Where was my life headed? Allen had stopped me from the careers I might have had; now he had me stuck in this blasted desert.

For some time I had again been victimized with my eating disorder. Nothing I ate stayed down. I was becoming more and more withdrawn and couldn't tell Allen how I felt. At bedtime I'd become anxious, never knowing when he was coming home. I wouldn't make love with him when he was drunk and he knew better than to come home unless he was sober. When would he reform? He'd proven he could be everything I wanted in a man and more, but why did it never last?

I still didn't know alcoholism was a disease; it would be quite a while and a lot more heartache until I found out. I still loved Allen no matter what he'd done in the past. What I'd told Moe Dalitz still applied: I clung to the hope that eventually Allen would mellow and settle down. The only time I didn't think about him was when I danced or played dice. I never lost. I was positive now I was unlucky in love. But it could change, it had changed in the past, it could change in the future. What marriage was about was weathering the storms.

Allen started hanging about at Foxy's, a little bar catty corner from the Sahara Hotel. I wondered what to do about my feelings of powerlessness. I spent hours swimming and floating. With most of my head and ears under the soothing water I could dream how it might have been ... and hopefully still would be.

I closed my eyes and floated on my back in the pool. I dreamed again the dream I always dreamed the ocean liner, dancing with "Mr. Wonderful," whomever he was.

I climbed out of the water, wrapped my head in a towel, stretched out on a longue to get some sun, then went inside, came out again to walk Star, and went back in to dress, set my hair and get ready for work again -- another day, same old routine. Allen was out, probably at Foxy's drinking again. I decided to put my pearls in the ice cube tray where he wouldn't find them. I'd won some money last week and bought them. They glowed pink around my thoughts. I wanted to keep these pearls, so I couldn't wear them lest Allen take them to the pawnshop, which he'd already done with some of my other jewelry. I dropped the pearls in the ice cube tray and put the container in the fridge.

Just then the phone rang. I picked it up to hear the voice of my sister-in-law Barbara, in tears, telling me that Father was dead. Barbara and Mother had read it in The New York Times.

Barbara was screeching how that bitch Glad Ass murdered him. Well, it did sound suspicious. It seemed Father died in London, there was no death certificate, only a pot of ashes was left of him, and the family wasn't even notified. Father had been complaining about being cold in the heat of summer out in Old Quogue, Long Island -- symptoms of slow arsenic poisoning, Barbara said. You tell Allen, and have him call me, please. I said I would.

Quickly, I dressed and walked the four long blocks to Foxy's, where I found Allen alone at the bar, nursing the usual glass of rum, chasing it with Coke. I said, "Please come home, I have something to tell you."

He said, "Why not here?"

"No," I insisted, "at home."

He got up, took my arm and guided me to the car. He wanted to know, "What is it? You're not pregnant again?"

"No, of course not. I have to tell you at home, inside and alone."

I thought about how many times he'd cursed his father and wondered now how he would react to his death. We walked through the gate, turned the corner and went on into the apartment. Lord, why did I have to be the one to tell him?

I was nervous. We sat down on the couch. I said, "Allen, your father is dead."

He said, "Can't be. He was never sick a day in his life, only had a trick knee from World War I. He was even a Bird Man, you know."

I repeated, "Your father is dead." I told him what Barbara had said and asked him to call her. He picked up the phone and dialed her number in New York.

Now he heard it from Barbara, screaming the whole thing at him in hysterics. He hung up the phone, came over to the couch, encircled me in arms, put his face in my lap and cried like a baby. My God, I thought, he loved his father. Why was he always cursing him?

He stopped crying long enough to get a sentence out. He said, "Father told me to leave the country, that I was a constant source of embarrassment." Then he cried for another hour. After that, he seemed better.

When the tears subsided, I put a cold compress on his eyes and he sat very still. I knew he was thinking about Glad Ass, as he called her.

I said, "I'm sorry, darling."

He shouted that Glad Ass killed his father and brought him back in a pot. "We have to be notified by The New York Times after he's nothing but a pile of ashes, scattered God knows where!"

He phoned Barbara back, got information he needed about the attorneys, the will, the ashes, other details. All the while he kept cursing his stepmother Glad Ass. "That bitch never was anything but a whore from the word go. She peed on Father's face, and now she's trying to shit all over us!"

When he calmed down a bit, he said, "Darling, go to work and tell them you're leaving. We have to get ready to go to New York."

"To New York? Why?"

"Listen, do you understand? They're trying to screw me out of my inheritance. Glad Ass got all the money, plus the homes, plus Mother's diamonds and emeralds. Well, she isn't going to get my paternal grandmother's inheritance, the Grace Bell Topping estate! That belongs to Barbara and me."

I didn't understand all the machinations that appeared to be taking place, so Allen elaborated. "It seems Father disowned Barbara and me, thanks to Glad Ass. She manipulated this whole thing, then she murders Father! She starts poisoning him in the Hamptons, then she takes him to London to finish the job undetected. And no death certificate! I have to get a lawyer tomorrow."

Again I thought Allen must have lived in Las Vegas before. Quickly, he looked in the phone book for the number of an attorney, John Gravenor, a very reputable mob connected lawyer I'd heard of. Of course, in Las Vegas, everyone you mention is accused of having mob affiliations, true or not. Gravenor, however, really deserved the reputation. His clients were all the top fronts for the casinos in town that were "mobbed up."

Allen made an appointment for the following day. He said, "Wait a minute, luv. I'll drive you to work."

In his grief he appeared to have done a turnabout. On the way to the casino, he said, "Don't forget, you don't have to work anymore. I'll make all this stuff up to you now." He kissed me and said, "I'll pick you up after work, angel. And I won't be drunk, all right?"

He opened the car door for me as he always did, and guided me out of the vehicle. I entered the Desert Inn to go to work.

I thought, I don't want to quit. If I do I can never come back and I never know what Allen will do next. But I had to quit, I guessed. Now I'd find out the true mettle of this man I married. I had to see it through. My head was spinning, thoughts going around and around.

I quit. Allen picked me up after work. He was sober and in good spirits, which surprised me. We went home and he again surprised me. The table had red roses on it, champagne, caviar and crackers.

I said, "What's this?"

Allen said, "My father's wake."

"He wasn't Irish," I said.

Allen laughed. "I know. I was kidding."

After a show I always felt hot and grimy. I said, "I want to take a shower."

He said, "I'll wait."

Clean and fresh now, I put on the turquoise satin kimono he'd bought me for Christmas, together with matching ballet slippers. Allen didn't like the fact that I'd grown two inches since we were married and now stood a full five foot eleven in stocking feet.

He had on a burgundy colored silk dressing gown, looking serene and elegant. I said, "To what do I owe this honor?"

Allen said, "Darling, I love you. I just got off track for a while, but believe me, I am in love with you, so, so in love with my beautiful baby wife."

He kissed the top of my head, then poured the champagne and served the caviar and crackers. We ate, drank and relaxed. He put on some soft music, took my hand and led me to the bedroom. I gasped. He'd made the bed with new turquoise satin sheets. Turquoise was my favorite color.

He removed my robe and reached for the Nivea Skin Oil. He poured a bottle of Arpège into the Nivea, shook it up and began massaging my body -- back first, legs and feet; then he turned me over and massaged from the front, covering my entire body.

I was in heaven from the champagne, the perfume, the massage, the satin sheets and my beloved husband. He kissed me from head to toe over and over, until I melted into him and he into me. We were as one. I had never felt closer to God than when in my husband's arms like this.

The slippery satin sheets made us slide off the bed onto the floor. We made love over and over on the floor. Now the pink carpeting would smell of Arpège forever. We made love until we dozed off, still on the floor. As I slept facing him, my head on his shoulder, I dreamed the dream of my childhood again.

I was on the ocean liner when I felt myself being lifted to the bed. Allen slid close to me, placed me in his arms and we went to sleep.

I awakened to see him staring at me. He said, "Did you know you slept with your eyes half open?"

"No," I said. "You didn't get me pregnant?"

He said, "No, I was careful. Relax."

I turned on the shower and stepped in. In a second he was there with me. He scrubbed my back and said, "I love showering with you. It's one of the things we do best together."

I giggled. We threw our heads back and laughed as we let the water drench us.

He dressed quickly, walked Star and said he was off to see the attorney.

Nothing to do now. I didn't have to work anymore. I arranged the roses, cleared the cocktail table and decided to do my nails. I was content for the present.

It will be all right now, I thought. I just wouldn't have a baby. He didn't want any. But maybe even that could change some day, I thought wistfully.

Allen returned from the attorney's office. I had completely forgotten it was my birthday until he handed me a long legal looking envelope with the words, "Happy Birthday."

I peered at the document inside. It was his last will and testament. I asked, "Are you planning on dying?"

"No, but I will inherit some money and I want to protect you."

He took out his wallet, handed me a $1000 bill and said, "I bet you can't spend this in one afternoon."

I said, "I bet I can."

He said, "No gambling. I mean shopping."

I said, "Wonderful! I love it."

He drove to the fashion mall. I kissed him as he helped me out of the car. Off I went to Nieman Marcus, feeling giddy and ecstatically happy for the first time in a very long while. I'd been almost afraid to be happy again.

I bought a pale blue wool skirt, a matching cashmere sweater decorated with blue and white flowers. Then I went to Saks for shoes and purse, with lingerie to match. I bought another pink silk shirtwaist dress with tiny rosettes, a black sequined gown (shades of my dream on the ocean liner), shoes, and vavroom, the thousand dollars had evaporated into thin air. I stopped at the perfume counter and bought Arpège and Reveillon perfumes, extra birthday gifts from myself to myself.

I arrived home to find our neighbors Hazel and Frank dressed and waiting.

Allen said, "Hurry and get ready, luv, we're going to supper."

I wore the black sequin gown, piled my hair up, and made my grand entrance. Everyone whistled. The four of us filed out to the garage, laughing.

Our parking space was empty. I said, "Allen, where's the car?"

"Over yonder," he grinned, pointing to the driveway.

There stood a silver blue Cadillac Coupe de Ville convertible. Had he chosen the color to tie in with my blond hair?

"It's lovely," I said, "but how did you pay for it?"

Allen said, "I traded in the Thunderbird and the estate in New York is paying for the rest. It's ours, baby."

He took my hand, beckoning, "Madame," and guided me into the luxuriously appointed new car.

Allen knew how much I loved the Captain's Table at the Dunes, the ambiance with its singing violins and waterfall, the fabulous food. It was an evening of dancing and laughter, a glamorous, fun night on the town, almost like my childhood dream, except we weren't on an ocean liner. I prayed silently that our life could go on like this.

I thought now maybe Allen wouldn't drink and get nasty anymore. He had promised that as soon as the estate was settled we'd take a trip to the Caribbean and on to Europe. We might even live there, he said. We'd have to see about the will business first, but after that, it looked like our lives could change drastically for the better. Another new chapter was beginning, and maybe my dreams would really come true now.

The next day it was decided we'd fly to New York to take care of settling the estate, come back for Star and our belongings, then drive to Miami. I wondered what was the magic of Miami. Allen had spoken of the Dinner Key Yacht Club in Coconut Grove. What plans he had in mind

I didn't know. I just wanted to build our marriage, hopefully even have a family and make him happy; that was my agenda.

During the few days before our departure, Allen was sweet, pleasant and very affectionate. We made mad love every night. It seemed like a storybook romance: every night, the house was full of flowers, champagne, and caviar; people came and went at cocktail time. He hired a caterer to do the hors d'oeuvres and clean up. After that we went out to dance and have a late supper. I thought I'd burst with happiness.

I packed a case for New York, including a sheer white blouse with ruffles around the neck and wrists I'd bought at Saks. I would wear that with a navy suit, I thought.

Allen planned to have five bespoke suits made while in New York at Witty Brothers. He'd been wearing a lot of grey slacks and navy blazers. He did need some suits.

We'd both need cruise wear but we could purchase that in New York or even when we returned to the desert. I was too elated, I thought my heart was beating too fast. I felt as though I could float to New York or anywhere, for that matter.

The time passed quickly. Hazel would come over and get both Star and the yellow turtle when we were ready to leave. In between my chores, Barbara was driving me bananas, phoning every hour, having one tirade after another, drunk as usual.

It now appeared that Glad Ass was trying to do Allen and Barbara out of their grandmother's estate too. I told Barbara I'd tell Allen and he'd take care of it when we got to New York. That finally seemed to satisfy her and I hung up to return to my packing.

I'd bought an emerald green satin shortie nightie and negligee with mules to match. I wished Allen would allow me to have my hair done back to its natural auburn. I never did like being blond, even though people said it looked chic. I thought again about my dream. I was coppery auburn on the ocean liner. My thoughts wandered to New York and my friends there. Hopefully I'd get a chance to see them before we left the city. I wished I could turn off my thoughts but they kept intruding, going round and round in my head.

Allen liked hosiery and black lace trimmed garter belts, a kick he'd first waxed enthusiastic about back in the early days in New York and which he was now coming on strong for since his return from Miami. He enjoyed watching me parade in this attire, wearing high heels. Strange. I wondered if any of his other women had ever worn this kind of getup.

He'd told me in no uncertain terms that the pantyhose I usually wore were singularly unsexy, that someone as tall, slender and curvaceous as I definitely belonged in these black lace garter belts and fishnet stockings. Ah, well, I thought, if it pleased him it was no big deal. I packed a few of these outfits as well.

CHAPTER THIRTEEN

As sweet as Allen had been over the past few days, a sudden ominous tension in the air warned me we were heading toward another bad spell. I could always feel it coming on, even if I couldn't identify the cause. Maybe if I ignored the symptoms they'd vanish. Allen was wounded. How to heal that wound? A part of me wanted to run away before anything terrible broke out again, but how could I? Allen's father had died. He was hurting. He needed me.

We left the next morning via TWA to New York, off to a poor start with Allen drinking all the way. The stewardess wasn't even pretty but he was flirting shamelessly. I stared out the window to avoid reacting.

Arriving in New York, after checking into a well appointed suite at the Drake Hotel and calling for a maid to unpack our clothes, we went down to the cocktail lounge and had a couple of drinks. I ate the unsalted almonds on the table hoping to avoid getting smashed. I still had never gotten used to cocktails. Allen, naturally, had his Anjao rum neat, chasing it with Coca Cola, making awful faces as he swallowed the rum. Why did he drink it if it tasted so bad, I wondered? Besides, the doctor at Sunrise Hospital, Las Vegas, told him he had high blood pressure and a duodenal ulcer to boot.

We sat in silence until I suggested we leave for dinner. At Pavillion Henri Soulé prepared us steaks and salad, then we walked back to the Drake. Allen dropped me there and took off alone.

Was his freezing me out attitude a reaction to his father's death? Nothing I said or did could snap Allen out of his dark mood, and he seemed to want to punish me. Why? I cried and cried. I phoned my mother-in-law who was, as usual, full of hope that problems would be resolved and that Allen and I could make it together.

Anne too, was grieving for Mr. Topping. "Troy," she confessed through tears, "I made a terrible mistake with the only man who ever meant anything to me. Allen Sr. was the love of my life, but out of stubborness and pride I threw it all away. I wanted to teach him a lesson, so I cut off my own nose to spite my face, and I've had to live out these long lonely years with regret. Now the only man I ever loved is dead, the father of my children gone forever. Don't let that happen to you, Troy. Take the bad with the good. Swallow your pride. We're all going to die some day and then it's too late. Darling, the years we're given on Earth can be precious ones if we only have the wisdom to understand. Don't make the mistake I did."

I thought about Cook's prophesy of the bad with the good, how I should "stick wid him" because "things gwang get bettah." When? When?

When Allen came in very late, I pretended to be asleep. I was in no mood to fight. The next morning I dressed in my navy suit with the white organza blouse under the jacket, the ruffle out over the collar. Allen emerged from the dressing room in a muted grey glen plaid suit. I had ordered room service -- fresh fruit for me, eggs benedict for him.

We ate breakfast in silence. Then, apparently seeing me for the first time, he eyed my blouse and blew his stack. He started shouting, "Take off that shitty looking blouse!" He reached out, grabbed the collar and ripped it to shreds.

I screamed, "You bastard, if you touch me again, I'll kill you!"

Furious, I changed into one of his Brooks Brothers shirts, confronted him and demanded "Is this better, my love?"

He glanced briefly. "Don't be ridiculous," he said, averting his eyes.

I took a pair of small scissors then and slashed the shirt to ribbons. "Would you like to select my wardrobe, too? You run the rest of my life!"

I turned on my heels, left the room and returned, still wearing the suit, this time with a plain high necked green blouse. He said, "You know I don't like green and blue together."

"Why don't you take a leap into the East River?" I snapped. "I'm not going to meet Glad Ass, as you call her, or the attorney. I don't need to go with you. Hell, I'm only your wife. I'll call Ginny the Guinea and have lunch with her. If you're not back by five, I'll find someone else who enjoys my company and wardrobe more that you do."

He smiled. "I'll be back by five, luv, I promise," he said with an air of contrition.

Allen returned at 4:45, of all things, early. He was depressed. I guessed it had been a difficult meeting. He said, "I had to settle for $250,000 or fight her in court for years."

I said, "If you start a small business we could live very nicely on that, if you'll stop this infernal drinking. Allen, I cannot put up with much more of your cruel behavior. It's got to stop. If you want a divorce, fine. It's not what I want, but I can't build a future without you doing your share. You promised you would, remember?"

"I don't want a divorce," he said. "I'm so ashamed of the things I've done to you. Will you try one more time?"

With tears streaming down my face, I said, "Allen, hold me. I hurt so inside."

He wrapped me up in his arms and tried to comfort me, but I was inconsolable. He held me a long time while I sobbed, then lifted my chin and promised, "I'll make it all up to you."

I said, "Please let's go home tonight. I miss Star and Mr. Turtle."

He agreed.

We traveled all night. About a week later, we finally entered Las Vegas at 6 am. As usual, it was like no other city. The concentration of people in the casinos immediately made me nervous. I was drained emotionally and physically, exhausted, depressed, and ready to collapse. We went home, having decided to pick up Star and Mr. Turtle tomorrow. We didn't make love, but merely drifted off to sleep. I dreamed my childhood dream again, my Prince Charming still had no face, but I danced with him all night long.

I woke early without opening my eyes. I was engulfed by all the pain Allen had given me in New York, and must put it in its proper place. My mind and heart were a file cabinet, so I would have to store away one more hurt with all the others.

When I answered the ringing phone, I was startled to hear a voice I hadn't heard in four years. Andrew Thompson, Jr. Oh, my God. Talk about burying the past. Hearing Andy's voice jolted me into a reality I'd wanted to forget.

"You don't know how hard I've tried to find you," Andy exclaimed. "Where did you disappear to?"

At that moment I wanted to sink through the floor. Allen would ask me about this call. He was lying right next to me in bed. What would I say? I'd kept this part of my life hidden. Now I'd have to confess to my husband the dark secret from my past that I was so ashamed of.

It sounded implausible. Married, divorced, and still a virgin at sixteen, all before I met and fell in love with Allen Topping? And yet it happened to me.

I'd been in New York only a few days, unable to find a job and feeling totally discouraged. I didn't want to phone my godmother. I started to panic. That was when Andrew entered my life for the briefest of moments. He was an older man of 22, a Chicago native and Northwestern graduate, spending the year studying in Manhattan, planning to return to the midwest at the end of the term.

Blond, slim, broad shouldered and a gangly 6'5 inches tall, Andy was all arms, legs and angles, a callow youth who hadn't grown into his body, mind or emotions yet. He was earnest, generous, impetuous, incredibly horny, a devout Catholic and a victim both of his religion and of the 1950's sexual mentality that was prevalent at the time.

We met in the park. Andy was sympathetic to my problems and promised to help, saying that if worse came to worst he'd bring me back with him to Chicago where I could stay with his parents. He wasn't going to desert me, I'd be ok. Having a supportive friend made me feel a whole lot better and Andy seemed like a lifeline.

It was eight fifteen p.m. After Andy had paid for my hamburger, Coke and fries in a coffee shop, it was natural to invite him back to my hotel room. Where else could we go? He had no money to take me anywhere glamorous or exciting. I expected we'd just talk a while longer before he'd leave. However, there was nowhere to sit in my cramped quarters but on the bed. One thing led to another, and soon Andy and I were in each other's arms, kissing passionately.

I was the proverbial naive "sweet sixteen and never been kissed," except Andy and I didn't stop at mere kissing. Since I believed "above the waist" was safe ground, I enjoyed preliminary making out without worry. Aroused, I gave into pleasurable sensations after Andy unhooked my bra to caress my breasts and suck my nipples.

"You're so hot," Andy muttered in my ear, "oh, God, you're hot!"

As his hand reached inside my panties and found my clitoris, I moaned with pleasure. My whole body shook and I cried out. Nothing had prepared me for this; the powerful feelings were new and totally overwhelming. I wanted to keep on, but became frightened.

"We better stop!" I whispered, removing Andy's hand as my Nana had instructed me it was proper for a well bred young lady to do when a boy tried to go too far.

"Please! I love you, Victoria! Oh, God!"

Andy had unzipped his fly, exposing an enormous naked penis, a sight that made me gasp out loud. Everything was happening so fast. My confused feelings were an admixture of desire, curiosity, wonder and terrible, earthshaking fear. Fear ultimately won the battle that first night.

"I can't!" Breaking loose, I turned away, my body wracked with nervous sobs. Andy, shaking too, a tortured expression covering his face, immediately got up and made a beeline for the bathroom. I heard a few muffled grunts, the sound of water running and the toilet flushing before he emerged, wearing a dazed look.

He apologized profusely for losing control. Believe it or not, despite being a few years older than I, Andy wasn't much more experienced than I was. He'd been so conscious of wanting to obey his religion, had never had a real girlfriend before, and although it was torture, he too was still a virgin. Remorseful, Andy wanted me to know how much he cared for me and respected me.

"Not only do I respect you completely, Victoria, but I'm also deeply in love with you," he said. "Even though we only met a few hours ago, I believe in love at first sight, don't you?"

Was Andrew Thompson, Jr. my Prince Charming? I was confused. Cook had said Prince Charming's initials were A.T., that father and son had the same name. So far so good: Andy's dad was Andrew Thompson, Sr.; this part checked out perfectly. However, there were questions. For one thing, although Andy had blue eyes, he didn't fit the description, "but one eye is no good." Both of his eyes were fine. His father owned no airplane but he did have a Chris Craft. Nevertheless, his father had been a pilot in World War II, he knew how to fly, so it was conceivable that some day in the future he might buy a plane. I gathered Mr. Thompson, Sr. was well to do.

Yes, I supposed, Andy could be Prince Charming. He was sincere. He said he loved me. The only thing was, I'd always imagined that meeting Prince Charming would be like rockets going off, and although I enjoyed Andy's company, a certain magic was missing. Still ...

The following night, our necking and petting went even further than the previous time. We lay semi naked on the bed. Andy had removed my blouse and bra but I was still clad in a skirt and half slip as well as my thin, skimpy panties. More daring than I, Andy had pulled his trousers and jockey shorts down to his knees, exposing his genitals. One thing led to another, and soon the situation was really getting out of hand. I became even more frightened than I had the first time and sobbed in Andy's arms.

Andy assured me of his love, saying he'd never felt this way about anyone in his life. After a long, heartfelt soul search, Andy came to the conclusion that before we were heedlessly swept into committing a sin against God, it seemed our best option, in light of all the givens of our situation, was to get married. Did I agree?

"We only met yesterday. Are you sure, Andy?"

"Absolutely. I couldn't possibly feel this way about anyone but the girl of my dreams," he answered. "I always knew it would happen like a ton of bricks falling and I'd know it was real. I don't have a single doubt in the world."

At this point, I was really counting my blessings. The few days I'd spent by myself in New York City had more than convinced me I was incapable of making it on my own, so Andy must really be Prince Charming because he was such a godsend. If it didn't feel like we were "two peas, one pod, batty and bench, one spirit," as Cook had phrased it, maybe after we were married that would change. Really, as Nana always said, things do work out for the best. I'd have a husband to look after me. All my problems would be solved.

"How do we go about it?" I asked.

Since I was underage, marriage presented a problem. Andy said he could get me a fake i.d. that would say I was 18. Then we could go to Elkton, Maryland and elope. We could do it tomorrow, Friday, after his classes ended. Right after we were pronounced man and wife, we'd head straight for a motel. Just think what lay ahead for us! No more having to hold back. We could go all the way, once we had that license we could do it as many times a day as we wanted. It was going to be incredible to be married.

The next day, I waited anxiously for the appointed hour when my fiancé would knock on the door. This really was for the best. Andy was a great guy and I liked him. Still ...

Maybe I was getting cold feet, maybe that was normal, but I did wonder if all this mightn't be happening too fast. Was I really making the right decision? Was this was what I wanted for the rest of my life? Only a few hours ago I was sure, now I was doubting. Andy returned with the fake i.d., then with Star in tow, we walked the dozen or so blocks to Penn Station, where we boarded a train for Baltimore. Star was curled up in a mandatory traveling case, placed on the unoccupied seat opposite us.

Andy held my hand the whole way and talked a lot about how great it was going to be to have sex. "Tonight you lose your cherry," he promised. "You'll be a made woman tonight." He could hardly wait.

The thought filled me with a strange dread, as if I should know this person better to be marrying him. Oddly enough, as sexually turned on as I'd been, I was having second thoughts about that side of things now too. Maybe I was scared, but the thought of going all the way with Andy no longer seemed as tantalizing as it once had. Something in me was turning away, and I didn't know why. What was wrong with me?

Our conversation took other directions, one of which was Andy telling me about the extreme measures he'd resorted to to get out of serving in the Army.

He'd put soap under his armpits and walked around with wet blotters in his shoes for days. He'd also claimed to be homosexual and as if that weren't enough, had faked a form of insanity. Andy laughed when he told me this, but it turned me off. I thought it was dishonest and morally reprehensible. Only in later years could I realize Andy did no differently than scores of other young men, and who knows if I were a male I'd feel the same, but at the time I judged him harshly for it. Or maybe I was looking for an excuse.

The seriousness of what we were going to do kept entering and leaving my head. I didn't want to focus on it, but I just had the creeping feeling something was wrong and I was making a bad mistake. But what else could I do? And soon we'd be in bed together. What then?

At two in the morning, the three of us, Star, Andy and I, stood on the doorstep at the Justice of the Peace in Elkton, Maryland. Andy rang the doorbell. I had butterflies in my stomach and was shaking like a leaf. With a sinking feeling I realized I was doing this for all the wrong reasons.

Andy filled out the forms while I stood back, feeling guilty, praying no one would guess my real age and report me to the police. I was wearing a picture hat Andy said made me look more mature, but was still fearful of being exposed as an impostor. I wondered if the Justice of the Peace could see through our motives for matrimony, if he could tell how horny Andy was, see the erection sticking up in his pants and know we were getting legally hitched so as not to risk sinning outside of wedlock. Would he know Andy was Catholic, which made premarital sex a mortal sin, so we were saving Andy's soul this way? At least, that was Andy's reason. As far as I was concerned, at this point I guessed I was going through this ceremony mainly because I didn't know how to get out of it.

I'd rushed out of panic. Andy was a desperation measure, but it was too late now to turn back the tide. Besides, I didn't want to hurt his feelings. No, there was no way out. I had to say. "I do." I was still thinking how in a short while we'd be in bed together. I was sure now Andy definitely wasn't Prince Charming, coincidences aside. My throat was dry and parched and I had a stomach ache.

As we stood there in front of the Justice repeating our vows, to my relief, I got a small reprieve in the form of my menstrual period, which I hadn't been expecting. It came on a full week early, and since I was regular as clockwork, I can only guess it must have been caused by stress.

I thanked God silently that I wouldn't be able to go the limit with Andy that night.

Alone at last in our motel room, I told Andy I had the curse. Needless to say, he was crestfallen. He'd been thinking of nothing else but fucking his brains out, and already had such a giant erection it was practically busting through his pants. He was so horny he asked me to jerk him off.

I obliged, but midway Andy took over himself, since he knew how better than I did. I'd learn this art soon enough, he promised.

I watched as his hand moved faster and faster up and down the shaft of his penis. His face contorted and his teeth gritted, his breath escaped in rapid hisses, as his whole body writhed and pounded toward release. The rapid thrusting and the contortions turned me off. Desire and curiosity had deserted me. I felt increasingly reticent, even repelled. This wasn't what I'd been expecting. From what I'd fantasized and seen in movies and read in books, sex should be a beautifully soft, melting sweetness of two bodies joining together in oneness. I became increasingly withdrawn, brooding because the magic I'd expected in my Prince Charming just didn't seem to be there.

Over the next few days, Andy wanted me to jerk him off innumerable times, sometimes up to ten times a day. I'm afraid my performance was lackluster, given my increasing apprehension. Was my period killing sexual desire, or had I really lost all feeling for Andy? Would the excitement I had initially felt return? Or had I made the biggest mistake of my life?

We'd been married four days. Andy emerged from the bathroom with the all too familiar noticeable bulge in his trousers.

"When does your pip end?" he asked.

"What?"

"I mean, how much longer before we can do it?"

"A few more days," I said cautiously.

"A few more days? God, I don't know if I can stand this!"

When my period ended, I was still feeling reluctance, so I manufactured one phony excuse after the next ... I have a headache, I feel nauseated, I think I have a cold coming on ... Frantic, Andy was pushing hard, putting me on the spot. His mania only made me more convinced I couldn't go through with it.

He couldn't figure it out. When? Why? Why not? You weren't like this before ... what's got into you now? We're married. Isn't this the reason we got married? You were so hot before, and so on.

I couldn't describe my emotions, but this feeling of being obligated to come across alarmed me. How could I keep refusing? I was building to this terrible fear that was all consuming and irreversible. I'd break out in cold sweats. And Andy had thought I was hot! Andy was such a nice guy, but God help me, I just couldn't bring myself to sleep with my husband. I liked him, I appreciated his devotion, but his desperate urgency to have sex with me was offputting.

He kept the pressure on. I felt cornered. By now I knew I'd done Andy a terrible disservice and I was sick at heart. How to explain? How had I ever gotten myself into such a mess? I wanted to run, but to where?

I had to summon the courage to tell the truth. It had been a mistake. Andy was crushed. "I guess we did rush into it pretty headlong," he conceded. "But if we hang in there ..."

He hoped maybe in time I'd come around. I had to assure him there was no chance. It just wasn't there for me and it never would be. I knew that now. He wasn't Prince Charming and we didn't belong together. In my life, I don't believe I ever felt worse about being more rotten to a nicer person who didn't deserve a such a raw deal. If I hadn't been looking for a blond, blue eyed prince with the initials A.T. whose father had the same name, if I hadn't been so alone and frightened, if, if, if ...

"Do you want a divorce, Andy?" I asked in a small voice.

Andy swallowed hard and actually looked like he was going to cry. He said right now he didn't have the heart to go through all that red tape. He still hoped time could make a difference. We'd stay in touch because he still loved me, and maybe I was just too young.

"The marriage probably isn't really legal anyway," Andy said. "We lied on the certificate, the i.d. was a phony, you're underage, there was no parental consent, and the union was unconsummated. I'm sure I'd never have a problem with the church. They wouldn't consider us married. We'd easily get an annulment."

After Andy left, I wept, even more for him than for myself. I was alone and scared, and had never felt more remorseful or totally ashamed in my life. Andy deserved so much better. As I buried the experience deep in my heart, I just prayed all my nightmares would vanish and that I could soon find my Prince Charming for real and solve all my problems then.

What was I going to do? I had no job prospects nor any idea of how to start again. That was when I phoned Dorothea. And the road had led me to Allen.

Three and a half years ago, prior to marrying Allen, I'd received a communication from Andy announcing the end of our marriage. I'd filed it away at the back of a drawer thinking it was over and Allen didn't have to know it ever happened. I wouldn't be hearing from Andy again. But now he had contacted me.

"I've combed the earth for you," Andy said. "Am I glad I've found you!"

Aware of Allen's curiosity, I nervously continued chatting with Andy for several minutes. He now had his own jewelry business, Andy said, and was doing very well. About us, I said, "Andy, I'm sorry about everything. I guess I was frightened. I didn't mean to hurt you."

"I know. I've put it behind me now. And I've found someone I want to marry."

"That's wonderful. Congratulations!"

He didn't sound too enthusiastic about it and I wondered why. Then he asked me, "I'd like you to do me a favor. As you know from the letter I sent you back a few years, I took the liberty of getting a civil divorce on grounds of desertion. I thought it was best for both of us. But what I really want is the sanction of the Vatican. I want to be married in the church. My future wife is Catholic and it would mean a lot to both of our families, hers and mine."

"No problem, Andy," I assured him. "How can I help?"

Andy said he wanted me to talk to a priest and describe the circumstances of our unconsummated marriage. There was an urgency, I learned, because the girl Andy wanted to wed was pregnant.

When Allen heard I'd been previously married, he cracked up.

"This takes the cake!" he exclaimed, roaring with laughter. All along I was thinking he'd be upset if he knew. Now he was telling me it was the greatest joke of the century. Troy Topping, married to another man. Hilarious. He'd never known I was a fallen woman.

"Some marriage," I sniffed. "I never even took my underpants off!"

"Oh no? That's not what I heard." Allen was enjoying this immensely. "My gossip says you were quite the scarlet woman in your day."

"You know perfectly well I was a virgin when we first made love!" I retorted. "Some things can't be faked."

"And you were worried about my past," Allen persisted, "about my divorcing Trudy. Ho, ha ha, this is hysterical! What did this ex-husband of yours want? Why was he calling?"

"He wants an annulment from the church and I said I'd help."

"Why? You're not Catholic."

"Andy is."

"So that's his problem. Let him worry about it."

"I told Andy I'd do as he asked, talk to the Catholic hierarchy and explain everything. They're waiting to hear from me."

"Why the hell should you have to put yourself out for a bunch of eunuchs or homos or whatever the hell these sick Church bastards are?"

"Allen, it's a favor to Andy. It's the least I can do. It's asking nothing."

"Why should you? It's ridiculous."

"You don't understand. Andy's a really nice, decent guy and it was all my fault. I misled him."

"So now he's knocked somebody up. Well, at least the son of a bitch finally lost his cherry," Allen said.

I met with the Catholic dignitaries Andy had arranged appointments with. After I described the circumstances of our pathetic fiasco of a "marriage," the church granted Andy a quickie annulment, and now as far as they were was concerned, Andy was free to marry his pregnant girlfriend. It was as though he and I had never been married.

Even though I wasn't Catholic, I felt washed anew, as if my sins, along with my ex-husband's, had been forgiven and I was ready for a clean start. In a way, I was envious of Andy's wife. She had a responsible man for a husband. He would provide everything a woman needs for happiness in life -- a beautiful home, lovely children, devotion, security, stability. Andy was the kind of man a woman could always count on.

I was filled with strange regrets. Allen was my Prince Charming, the love of my life. Our destinies were bound together, "two peas, one pod, batty and bench, one spirit... no matter how fah, always cam bak togetha...caant live one widdout da otha.. you and him are one..."

All that was true. But what was the special magnetism that insisted I should love Allen, despite all his shortcomings?

And would he ever give me what I wanted?

CHAPTER FOURTEEN

Another day, time to get up and get dressed. We'd soon be leaving Las Vegas, perhaps in the next forty-eight hours. Allen was already packing our things. Star was walked, fed and watered. He turned to me and said, "Darling, I'm sorry but we can't take Mr. Turtle. Hazel wants him. He's hibernating on her couch. You know how much she loves animals ... she even has three snakes now. She'll take good care of Mr. T. She really loves him."

I'd grown so fond of Mr. Turtle it made me sad to lose him. Turtles weren't as demonstrative as dogs, but nevertheless, this tortoise had endeared himself so that he was a part of the family. I brushed tears off my cheek, turned to Allen and agreed about Mr. Turtle.

We'd be heading east again. Where to now? I knew it would be Miami first, but then what? Why did I feel so frightened and insecure? Well, I wouldn't think any more about the past today. Concentrate on the future. With $250,000 we could start a business, buy a home, maybe even have horses so we could both ride again. Our life together was just beginning and now we could build our marriage on a solid foundation -- love and money.

We'd decided to leave the following day so Allen put our belongings in the trunk of the Cadillac, everything with the exception of what we'd be wearing and our toiletries. I dreaded the trip, remembering the drive from New York to Mexico City, but maybe this would be something to look forward to. At least I hoped it would.

We said our goodbyes to all our friends -- Hazel, Frank, Kathy, Robin, Jack Cannon, and Mr. Turtle, and took off in a cloud of dust. Allen headed right up over Boulder Dam to 40 East.

As I looked out at the flaming desert that I so disliked, I hoped this would be the last time I'd have to live on it. We stopped most of the time at Best Western motels because of Star. The trip was boring.

Finally the landscape changed. At last we were out of that infernal scrub country, I thought, out of Texas, finished with any and all manner of arid deserts. The scenery was starting to become emerald green with lush foliage. As we entered Louisiana I saw once again the beautiful weeping willow trees I so admired. We stopped a lot to water Star, who'd already had one accident in the new car and seemed to need to go a lot more than usual.

Reaching Mississippi, we checked into a motel in Handsboro, outside Biloxi. I was very tired and poor Star was looking ill. She had to go out every five minutes, it seemed, so I left the sliding glass door of our room open to allow her to come and go as she pleased. I didn't want her to be uncomfortable. Her muzzle was turning grey and she didn't play much anymore. She was 13 years old, after all. The vet said she'd be all right as long as she was well cared for and with her mistress.

Allen, as much as he loved Star, seemed to grow impatient with her kidney problems, since it slowed down his projected schedule, schedule for what, I didn't know. But he did take time out to shoot innumerable rolls of film on her.

"How come you've been taking so many pictures of Star lately?" I asked.

"Because I love her, darling, and I want us to remember her as she is always."

"You really do love Star, don't you, Allen?"

"I love that dog as if she were my own flesh and blood."

Allen had stayed out late the previous night, I'd gone for a swim in the dark, taken a shower and turned in early.

When I woke that morning, Allen was already dressed and was packing our suitcases. I jumped out of bed to get ready. Allen said, with detectible signs of uneasiness, "I've called a vet named Dr. Duncan. Star's acting funny, so I phoned for an appointment. I want him to have a look at her. I'll take her. You stay here."

I agreed.

He said, "I'm really in a rush to get to Miami."

I kissed Star on the top of her muzzle, never dreaming it would be the last time I would ever see her.

Star went willingly with Allen; she loved and trusted him. Two hours later, Allen came back alone.

I asked, "Where's Star?"

He looked at me very seriously and said, "Sit down. I have something unpleasant to say to you."

Worried, I did as he asked.

He said, "Star had kidney disease, for which there's no cure, so I had the vet put her to sleep."

I shot up like a ramrod, then immediately went to the phone and called the vet.

He told me although it would have required time and treatments, that he could have cured Star. I hung up the phone and screamed at

Allen, "You son of a bitch! You had to kill her so you could get to Miami quicker. She could have been helped here."

My heart was now in pieces. My sorrow was bottomless. I wept and wept. Allen left. He returned at around five, sober, and said he'd made "arrangements" for Star, a copper coffin encased in cement and a grave in the yard of the Baptist church near the vet's office. He would show me in the morning.

It was a terrible day and night. He tried to make love to me; I curled up in a ball and cried myself to sleep. I had lost my best friend, my childhood friend. I dreamed only of Star when she was a little puppy.

I woke at daylight when Allen brought me a tray. I pushed it away, rose and dressed.

"Allen, take me where you buried her, you bastard. What is so wonderful in this Miami of yours?"

He took my arm, guided me into the car and headed toward the churchyard cemetery. Already a stone marker and flowers covered Star's burial site. He straddled the grave and took photos of it from every angle.

"Wait, wait, I've got to shoot this with my 28 millimeter wide angle lens," he exclaimed, leaping across the other side of the grave and hunkering down.

I screamed at him, "Walk on it, Allen, you can't hurt her now."

He said, "Now, now, you must understand that she was suffering."

I turned away weeping, my face to heaven, asking why, Lord, why?

I got back in the car and thought, Heaven's Blazing Star is gone. I will never see my sweet, beautiful collie dog Star again in this lifetime.

I would have to send a note to the AKC in New York.

CHAPTER FIFTEEN

We were packing up back at the motel. I said, "Please throw away Star's stainless steel feeding and watering pan, her collar and lead, and the case of canned food. She won't be needing them now." I was crying bitterly. He obeyed my wishes and then loaded the car.

The whole trip was a nightmare. I just couldn't bring myself to speak to him. I looked up into the clouds and every cloud looked like Star. I hoped Star was in collie heaven. Over so many years and through so much, she'd been such a good pet and devoted friend. She was such a part of me.

I wondered how I could survive without her. I was afraid. Life seemed so desolate and empty now.

I remembered when I'd taken the trip to Puerto Rico with Ruthie. Bob, my friend the taxi driver, had cared for Star while I was away. When I returned Star was so overjoyed seeing me again she knocked me to the floor and held me pinned down until she'd "washed my face" with her tongue. I had the sinking feeling maybe she thought I'd deserted her, that I was never coming back. I sat up and held her close to me and told her how much I loved her and always would.

Star was one of the happiest things in my life. She held me together when Allen was breaking me into pieces. And now she was gone from the earth so suddenly, utterly, and unnecessarily. I wondered if I could ever forgive Allen.

Three days later we arrived in Miami. Allen had a suite reserved at the Four Ambassadors Hotel on Brickell, convenient to Coconut Grove and his Dinner Key Yacht Club, nowhere near a beach. He dropped me off to attend to some business.

Returning three hours later, he said he'd sold the Cadillac.

"What do we do for a car now?" I asked.

He said, "We leave tomorrow for San Juan, Puerto Rico. I've made reservations at the Condado Beach Hotel."

I turned pale and in a second my heart started to beat 100 miles an hour. I went in the bedroom and lay on my back, but my heart kept going faster and I couldn't breathe. Allen took one look at me and picked up the phone to call for a physician.

The doctor arrived with some kind of a monitoring machine. He put one hand on my chest and with the other punched me hard, trying to stop the fast heartbeat. It only got worse. He kept saying I should go to the hospital, but I refused. The doctor took Allen aside to talk. I was cold and clammy.

Damn Allen and his second rate hotels with second rate air conditioners. My status continued unchanged for seven hours until I finally agreed to go to the hospital in a taxi. As usual, Allen left me alone. He always ran when things were unpleasant. The hospital gave me shots to stop the palpitations, then I called a cab and returned to the hotel.

Of course Allen was nowhere to be found. I decided to have my hair done at the beauty salon, which beat sitting around alone. After that, I went back to the empty suite. Once again, my husband was not coming home tonight.

I stayed up till one a.m. sitting on the balcony watching the lights twinkling on Biscayne Bay before finally deciding to turn in. I had no more illusions about my husband. He was rotten to the core and I must learn to face it. Why did I love this man? I drifted off to sleep. Strangely enough, I felt more warmth tonight sleeping alone than if Allen were there.

When he showed up in the morning I was ready to leave for the airport. I didn't like Miami, I was anxious to escape this place. I mentioned nothing to Allen about his absence of the previous night. I felt calm and collected now, but not in any mood to bring up issues past or present. I had thought and thought till I was numb.

The flight to Isla Verde Airport in Puerto Rico took three hours. It was hot and humid but there was a soothing trade wind blowing. I sniffed the salt smelling air with pleasure.

A taxi sped us to the Condado Beach Hotel. The room was crummy and the air conditioner didn't work.

I picked up the phone and rang Pepe Diaz to ask about a suite at the hotel he managed, the La Concha. Pepe was an old friend I'd met in Vegas.

Pepe, surprised to hear I was in P.R., said, "What are you doing over at the Condado? I always have a suite for you here. Come on over at once."

At the La Concha, Pepe ushered us into the hotel's Penthouse Suite. It was cool and large, with a fabulous view on three sides of the ocean and beach, and at night, the lights of Ponce.

I hung up my clothes and drew a bubble bath, ready to loll about in the tub of fragrant bubbles and dream a happy dream. I was so alone with my thoughts I didn't hear Allen leave the suite. In the warm bath, I drifted off to sleep, my head turned to the green tile wall. I again dreamed my ocean liner dream, the dream of my childhood. The water was almost cold when I woke.

I stepped into a long terry cloth robe and slippers, and for a while merely walked around the suite, my mind a blank. I just kept looking at the El Mar Caribe, the turquoise sea, the waves coming in and going out. The surf was so soothing to my ears and my broken heart. It was still early, so I donned a bikini, grabbed a shortie robe and went down to the beach.

I ran toward the surf and dove in. For a long time I swam and swam; then I floated, allowing the waves to carry me back to shore. The beach was deserted. I spread my towel on the white sand and lay down in the sun. Behind the hotel glass doors guests lay in deck chairs by the pool. There was a pool bar. If Allen were here, that was where he'd be, I thought. What kind of a monster had I married? He was the devil himself. I strolled down to the water again and picked up a tiny shell that looked like a human face, exactly the same kind Cook had read for me so long ago, when she'd given me my life's prophesy about Prince Charming, A.T., the man who would bring me "good times, bad times." I remembered Cook's words now: "When times are tuff, look black, stick wid him, through thick and thin ... you give him your heart and it work out fie you. It gwang get betta."

Behind me I heard the splash of a horse's hoofs in the surf. Astride his mount, a security guard approached. Horse and rider stopped in front of me. I reached up to pat the animal's muzzle and mouth and the horse put his head down to nibble on my fingers with his lips.

"What's his name?" I asked.

"He is called Pablito," the security guard answered.

"Pablito?" I laughed at the diminutive. "He's so big!"

"Yes, but he is gentle and sweet as a little lamb."

"I can see that," I said, stroking Pablito's neck, wishing I had some carrots to offer him. My hand went back to his face and he lipped me again and nickered. I asked if I could ride him. The security guard, whose name was Marcos, said, "If you come early in the morning you may ride him. Do you need a saddle?"

I said, "Not for this sweetheart. I'll ride bareback. I won't jump him."

I bid the two adios. As I watched them disappear down the beach, I was thinking about how a mutual love of animals was an important bond Allen and I shared. Allen loved horses as much as I did; in fact, he was an expert rider who'd won many ribbons at the National Horse Show in Madison Square Garden. One of my great dreams for us was to own horses, to ride together all the time. And of course Allen was a big dog lover as well; he and Star had adored each other, something I could never figure out!

I went to the shower to wash off the salt and sand from my body. I rinsed my suit, washed my hair, and returned to our suite, where I blow dried my hair and did makeup. If Allen didn't show by 8 p.m., I'd have a cocktail on the roof, order the "El Mirador" dinner at the El San Juan, and as long as I was alone, I'd go to the casino and shoot dice. Maybe I'd win enough to have some money of my own.

I might even go to the El Convento, the hotel and casino where all the politicians and presidents stayed. It was a chic, beautiful, historic establishment in Old San Juan. I thought if I was ever lucky enough to meet anyone again like Don, the man in New York who owned the airline, I'd leave Allen. Then he'd regret not treating me right. No woman should have to put up with what I had, Prince Charming regardless.

Alas, the door opened and there stood my husband, grinning from ear to ear. He said, "How's my baby wife? You look lovely."

He handed me a gift wrapped box. Inside were two diamond rings. Removing my plain gold wedding band, he placed a diamond studded wedding band and a 5 carat emerald cut diamond engagement ring on my finger. They looked fantastic, I thought, on my long slim sun kissed fingers with their hot pink nail polish. I was glad I'd waited for Allen and for the first time in weeks I leaped into his arms.

I was wearing a gold lame gown. He said, "You're gorgeous!" I kissed him. He changed into white slacks and a navy blazer and said, "Let's do the town."

I asked him for my gold wedding band back. After all, I said, we did marry twice with it, and I slipped it into my gold purse.

Allen ordered his usual drinks one after the other, grimacing every time the rum splashed down his gullet. We did go to the El Convento for dinner. The food was excellent, even though I hardly ate. I was too elated to feel hungry. Allen didn't eat much either, busy as he was with his Cuban rum.

I kept gazing at my diamond rings. As ecstatic as I felt, was I happy? Happiness was like broken glass, I thought. Once in a while you could pick up a piece of it but it was only partial, never thorough. I had so believed that one day my happiness would be complete. All evening long, pictures flashed through my mind and heart, scenes of moments with Allen from when we'd first met up till the present. We'd been through so much together, and yes, I did have a number of pretty pictures for memories, but an awful lot were ugly. I did my best to ignore the latter. It was with a sinking feeling I confronted the realization that Allen Topping was not a man I could trust anymore.

After dinner we went to the Flamenco to dance the merengue. Allen knew what a great dancer I was and it fed his ego to see the other men eyeing me enviously. This guy Topping was a lucky man to have me, but I doubted he realized it.

We did make a great looking couple on the dance floor. He whispered in my perfumed ear, "Your gown is wonderful on you. You're my beautiful wife and I'm very proud of you. Let's go back to the hotel. It's late and I want to show you El Junkie tomorrow."

He called for the limo we'd hired for a few days. Drinking had perhaps made him amorous. He started kissing me in the limo, becoming increasingly aroused. The driver couldn't see in back. Allen locked the doors and windows. He removed my gown carefully, then ripped off my panties and kissed me thoroughly all over my body. When he knew I was ready, he entered me. I moaned and writhed like a snake in his embrace. He spread his hands on my buttocks to pull me yet closer to him until he held me so tight I gasped and moaned. He whispered hoarsely in my ear, "I can't get close enough to you."

He made me wild. He said, "I love everything you do to me."

I rearranged myself in case anyone should see us on our way up to the suite. Allen had my panties in his pocket. We took the elevator up to the penthouse. No one was around.

"Good lord," I said, "we made love on the floor of the limo."

He laughed, grabbed me and pulled me toward him and unzipped my gold gown. He said softly, "Step out of it."

I stood half dressed in a gold bra and garter belt, hose and gold sandals. He said, "My golden goddess."

Taking me by the hand, he led me to the bedroom and lifted me onto the bed. He undressed and joined me, and again we made love, wildly, for hours. I woke up in his arms, both of us still nude; I was remembering how in passion he had ripped everything off me.

That morning the limo driver rang us up. We were dressed in casual attire, I in Banana Republic khakis and a straw pith helmet.

Our driver had placed breakfast consisting of fruit and coffee on little tables in front of us. Off we went to see Puerto Rico's famous incredible rain forest, where the flowers and trees seemed to rise to the clouds. We were surrounded by wild orchids and strange birds I'd never seen before. Allen pointed out the scenery. He was attentive, held my hand, whispering words of tenderness in my ear.

After we came down from El Junkie, he wanted a drink so we took off for a famed restaurant, Bollo's in Myaguenez City for a lobster dinner. Later, we drove back to our penthouse, where Allen called room service for more drinks.

I showered and changed into a white cotton jumpsuit while he drank. When I came back to the living room, he was looking sheepish. Out of the clear blue, he said, "I want a divorce."

Mouth agape, I studied his face, not believing what I'd heard. All I could say was, "Are you kidding?"

He said, "No." He sounded emphatic.

"After last night?" I said. "What kind of animal are you?"

He said again, "I want a divorce," mumbling it this time.

I wouldn't dignify his statement with an answer. Avoiding his eyes, I turned toward the guest bedroom. Hours later, dulled with pain, I finally fell asleep.

I woke up the following morning to find him gone. I ordered breakfast and waited. Was he with another woman? Thinking about the whole situation was making me angrier and more confused. I wished I had a mother to run home to, someone I could talk to about it. I wanted to call Anne, confide my troubles, ask her advice, but I just didn't dare. Somehow, being in this position made me too ashamed. Would things ever straighten out? What alternative did I have? I had to do something. But what?

It was two p.m. when I heard Allen at the door. He had a small package in his hand and was grinning from ear to ear. I was aghast. What was his game?

He said, "Should I throw my hat in first?"

Bewildered, I shook my head. "You're impossible," I concluded.

Allen handed me the package. Inside was a velvet box containing a 35 karat emerald cut blue aquamarine, set in a heavy solid gold mounting. It took my breath away, and it fit perfectly.

"What's this one for?" I asked. "Were you out with another woman last night?"

He answered, "I was not with anyone else. You know I'm mad

about you."

"I thought you wanted a divorce?"

"I was just kidding. You know how I feel about you. Would you like to go to Nassau?"

I nodded, feeling numb.

CHAPTER SIXTEEN

A private plane flew us to the Bahamas, where we checked in at the British Colonial Hotel, Nassau.

On one occasion there Allen presented me with another small velvet box. Laughing, he said, "Look what I have for my darling wife." On my right pinky finger he placed a gold signet ring with the Topping family crest. He then picked me up and headed for the bedroom saying, "Now we shall have a baby, baby wife."

I jumped out of his arms in protest. "No way! I won't do it!" He argued but I refused to give in.

One day it would be gifts and lovemaking, the next: bizarre behavior. Anne Topping's evaluations of her son's problems seldom left my mind. Allen's actions had a cause and he could not be held fully responsible for his behavior. But at the same time he was destroying my sanity. I felt shell shocked, helpless. I was in total denial, trying to tune out reality, hoping against hope to still salvage something. Mr. Topping had been right; his son desperately needed the help of a competent professional. How much longer could we go on this way? Allen would have to snap out of it or I would have to find the courage to end this once and for all.

Allen's drinking had gotten way out of control. One alcohol hazed afternoon in the bar, he banged his fist on the counter, asserting to all strangers present, "I am a man, damn it, I am a man!"

This brought to mind another incident, back in the beginning of our relationship when we were living in New York at my apartment. There was a gay bar on 3rd Avenue we used to walk by with Star. Every time we passed it Allen became infuriated and wanted to turn a fire hose on "the fucking faggots" inside. I asked him why; they weren't bothering him.

Now I told him, "Look, when you're through proving things to yourself, I'll be at the Pilot House Club."

I moved my belongings out of the British Colonial into the Pilot House, and cried all night. In the morning Allen appeared at my room. We made love all day and all night.

The next day, following brunch, he said we'd be returning to Puerto Rico and had to pack. At the La Concha penthouse suite, Allen was oddly quiet and I sensed something was up. I donned a bikini, we went down to the pool bar and he ordered two La Concha specials, 180 proof rum.

I swam a few laps, then climbed out of the pool. We had the place to ourselves.

Allen turned to me and once again, he said, "I want a divorce."

I couldn't believe it. After the twenty-four hour session of lovemaking, now this again? Would Allen's games and torture never cease? Why was he doing this? The terrible thing was it was all so unpredictable yet so horribly predictable. Everything could be going swimmingly, when without warning he'd ruin it; nor could I ever understand the reason for this self destructive course my husband seemed so bent on.

All of a sudden I thought, I can take no more, I've had enough of living. Why must my love always demand such a heavy price? Prince Charming was my life's dream, but this was a losing battle. I still believed with all my heart and soul Allen and I were meant for each other, that it was written in the stars, just as Cook had said. But maybe our rightful home was not of this earth, rather in some other part of the universe where life was different. Why couldn't we be happy? Why was everything torture? I couldn't handle it anymore. Living with Allen was beyond my capacity, living without him was impossible. I loved him beyond measure but oh, God, I'd been through the fiery furnace too many times, and now I wanted out.

Very quietly, I said, "All right. Suit yourself. I'm tired. I'm going upstairs for awhile. I'll be down later." I asked him to order me another La Concha special to take upstairs with me. I heard my voice saying, "You can have your bleeping divorce. I hate you."

I picked up my drink and returned to the suite. I tried to think sanely because I was beginning to believe I was going mad.

Then I went to the bathroom cabinet and took out a bottle of 50 Nembutal sleeping pills. I changed into a cotton jump suit, swallowed all the pills and chased them with the La Concha special, which I drank quickly in its entirety.

I climbed into bed and said a prayer asking the Lord to forgive me, that I could stand no more, amen.

Everything was becoming dark. Then I fell asleep.

When I woke, I was in a white hospital room with two I.V.'s in my arm. A short, squat, black haired nurse was peering at me. The uniform clad nurse smiled. Her name, she said, was Pica.

"You very sick," she said. "*muy enfermo.*"

"How long have I been here?" I asked groggily.

"*Quatro dias*, four days. Only sleep."

"I want to leave," I said. "Please call the doctor."

Pica left the room briefly. When she returned, I asked her to call my husband.

"Later," Pica promised. "The doctor he comes pronto. *Ajora*, I help you take bath, then you eat ... *comida*."

I was unable to bathe without help. I asked for my clothes. Allen would bring them tomorrow, Pica said. I started to cry hysterically. Pica ran into the hall.

A doctor came in, put his hand on my forehead, and in English with a thick Spanish accent said, "Señora, you must have been through hell to want to die. Your husband has told me some of the things he has put you through, but I can imagine the rest. Please do not cry. I will be able to send you home tomorrow if you stay calm. I will send Pica with you to care for you. You are too weak to walk, so you will go in an ambulance. Now please eat something to help your strength. I will see you in the morning."

Pica smiled at me and brushed my hair, calling me "Señora Blonda." She told me el señor, my husband, was *muy feo*, very ugly. I thought, I will not cry anymore. Allen isn't worth my tears. I wished I didn't love him. God help me, I was in love with the devil himself. I'm damned, I thought, heaven help me. There was no way out. I had no money of my own at this point. Allen was blowing his inheritance. What could I do? What was going to happen? I fell asleep after managing to eat some soup and pudding.

I woke at 10 in the morning. Pica had taken the I.V.'s out the previous night, and I now had band-aids on my arms. I climbed onto the gurney that would take me to the ambulance. When I arrived at the La Concha, a private elevator whisked me to the penthouse, thanks to my friend Pepe Diaz.

As usual, Allen was nowhere to be found. The bastard couldn't even put in an appearance to say I'm sorry. I was weak, overwhelmed by a sense of dread. Every day, the only thing I wanted to eat was steak.

Pica came at noon, which always made me feel glad. She prepared my bath, rinsed my lingerie and massaged my back and neck. She told me she hailed from the island of Vireques, off the coast of Puerto Rico. I had another nurse for half of the day, a woman who just sat silently with her arms folded across her chest and never smiled.

Pica remade the bed and asked if I'd eaten anything, then told me to rest. I asked when my husband was coming home.

Pica said, "*El señor* is *muy boracho.* Doctor say no come. Come tomorrow. Is better. *El doctor* say *el señor* very bad man."

I turned on the "tele" and we looked at "Soap" in Spanish. It seemed amusing to watch American actors in Spanish. I laughed a lot but at the same time I was bored, simultaneously heartbroken and also worried that my suntan was fading. I was weak and pale. Pica gave me a pill with a glass of water. I went to bed. How alone I felt. It seemed I was always alone or Allen was threatening me with being alone. I fell asleep with Pica rubbing my neck.

I opened my eyes at 9 a.m., checked my surroundings, ran to the shower and went through the motions of dressing. Pica was gone and the other nurse was on duty. The doctor finally arrived with Allen. It was obvious my husband didn't want to be alone with me. The doctor asked a few questions, then examined me.

He told me Allen didn't want a divorce. I must be strong now and not cry. To Allen he said. "She is still very upset, her nerves are bad and she is weak. You should be very gentle with her. Maybe a trip somewhere else?"

Allen nodded and promised to take care of me. He asked where I'd like to go.

I answered, "Jamaica."

The doctor left, the nurses were dismissed, and we were alone. Allen gave me that oft assumed hangdog expression I knew so well and said, "I'm sorry, baby. I don't want to hurt you. I've done enough to you."

He reached for my hand but I drew away from him. I said, "You can't make it all right with lies anymore and then ask me for a divorce. Why did you bring me here? Why did you put my best friend to sleep? You have a lot to answer for. Tell me. I want to know."

Allen put his arm around my shoulder and said, "I love you, darling. You should know that. Star was very ill and I didn't want her to suffer. I don't want you to suffer either."

He's a demon, I thought, he's conning me again. What was the use? I couldn't go on with one heartbreak after another. He thought all he had to do was make love to me, say he loved me, give me another jewel and when all was presumably ok then ask for a divorce again. I couldn't stand it. What caused his unpredictable behavior? Would he ever stabilize? Was there anything I could do to change the pattern?

He said, "What do you want to do? When do you want to go?"

I said, "I don't care."

"I'll book us a flight on B.W.I. to Kingston," he said. "After that, how about a trip around the world? Then we can decide where we want to live."

I shook my head incredulously. "At the rate you're spending your money, we won't have to be concerned where to live. We won't have any options left."

He reached into his pocket. Surprise, surprise! Another present, a long thin gold box containing a solid gold watch. I put it on, fastened the safety clasp, and walked to the bedroom to find my three rings. He followed. I said, "Now what, darling? Do we make love again, and then you want a divorce again? You've got to talk to me. You make me feel like I'm used and then thrown away."

Tears stung my eyes. "I have nobody to go to," I said. "You even took my Star. You seem to enjoy torturing me and then you run away. Every time you make me ill you run. Do you shrink and fall in a bottle, or is it women?"

He said, "That's your imagination."

Bringing up the past never helped. I wished the sleeping pills had worked, God forgive me. I thought, this time, Lord, you've got to help me fight this devil or take me away from him or let me die.

The Manor House in Kingston, Jamaica, stood high atop Constant Spring Road, past the botanical gardens. It was a very old establishment owned by a British couple. There was no air conditioning, no beach, no pool, about the only amenity being mosquito netting around the bed. The dining room was pleasant, the hotel well staffed, which, I supposed, was meant to compensate for its lack of amenities in other departments. Bugs, heat and humidity constantly intruded. I was assailed by a sense of *déjà vu*, at the same time I was now seeing Jamaica from quite a different perspective than that of my childhood. I thought about Cook's prophesy of my Prince Charming and impulsively, thinking she could help me, I made an effort to locate Cook, but it was no use; our old Cook had vanished from the earth.

I'd make the best of it. It wouldn't be long, I thought. Of course the rum flowed in abundance. Allen took me to lunch at a quaint British pub in downtown Kingston, which, like the hotel, lacked air conditioning. My hair and clothes felt wet all the time.

At Nelson's statue in Kingston Harbor, it was so infernally hot and miserable I just wanted to be at a beach swimming in the cool sea.

Nevertheless, I kept misgivings to myself. As always, I was patient and cooperative, while Allen kept shooting rolls of film -- full lengths, long shots, closeups with his 80 millimeter portrait lens, wide angles while I posed in front of all the tourist attractions. If Allen got nothing else out of this marriage, he got a model available on 24 hour call, ever ready to help him indulge his obsession with photography, and at no charge. He even taught me a few rudiments about photography and frequently would ask me to take his picture; but I did often wonder why he never asked anybody to snap a photo of us together.

Jamaica was a bad scene. My Nana's plantation had been sold and was full of lean to tenant farmer shacks. I was disgusted and never wanted to go back there again.

After three days of the oppressive atmosphere I told Allen I wanted to leave. I'd already fainted twice and to stay here any longer might be risky to my health. So we checked into the Emerald Beach Hotel in Nassau, where for a change of pace, everything was luxurious and lovely. I swam, played tennis and volleyball and lay in the sun trying to recapture my suntan. I'd lost too much weight but a tan would at least make me appear healthy again.

Allen was carousing around drinking all the rum he could find and I thought I was being pretty smart to treat him the way you would a wild stallion -- give him enough rope and he'd hang himself.

At least there was no more talk about divorce.

I did my eye makeup and lipstick, dabbed on Réveillon perfume, dressed myself in a copper colored form fitting lame gown slit to the hip on both sides and slipped on copper pumps to match. I had a sunburn now. Admiring myself in the mirror, I thought I looked fantastic.

Seeing me, Allen whistled. I smiled. "Get dressed," I told him, "I'm ready to go out for dinner."

He selected a beige suit so that we blended in color. Nobody would ever guess how unhappy I was, and I'd never let on. How I wished we were back in the States, but I had no control over that. I had relinquished any and all power that should rightfully have been mine, turned myself body and soul over to the man I loved.

From the start of our relationship, I'd allowed him to make all decisions. Food, lodging, transportation, travel plans, money, including my own earnings, were his jurisdiction. I thought a man was supposed to handle these things and had no faith that I could be remotely capable. My self image was that of being helpless and dependent on

Allen. The thought that I might be able to take charge never crossed my mind.

So I was limping along, playing the same games with the man I couldn't live with and couldn't live without.

Allen lined up an evening of dining and dancing, then later, back in the suite, he made love to me all night long. I couldn't resist him. It was no use. I did love the guy. He went out of his way to please me, to give me one orgasm after another. We napped, and then came another perfume-laced Nivea massage with lovemaking again. He kissed every part of my body before entering me and he stayed inside until I was wild, time and time again. When we fell asleep he was still inside me. Again the following morning we made love yet another time.

We lunched in the hotel. He smiled a lot but I couldn't. Despite being relaxed I was unhappy. Allen was up to something again, I knew it.

He paid the luncheon tab, saying he was going to take care of the hotel as we were leaving today for Miami. He didn't come back.

I cried all day and half the night. I was a victim again, crying those angry tears that made me hurt so, unable to deal with the truth of the matter. This time, I wouldn't wait, though. He'd left $500 in my purse. Well, at least that was something. I packed, dressed, phoned B.W.I. and left for the airport. I'd check in at the Ocean Ranch Hotel in Miami Springs, the only place I knew to go. He'd taken me there when we were in Miami last.

It was a three hour flight. My room at the Ocean Ranch was tacky, but now I had less than five hundred dollars, no job, and a husband who was nowhere to be found. The hotel had a pool so I decided to swim my head off into oblivion. It would be easier to sleep later if I wore myself out.

I swam every day and slept all night. I didn't know what to do next. Where could I go? The thought frightened me to death. I'd paid the rent for a week. I'd try to put off making a decision. Right now, I just couldn't face any more.

I'd been here about three days and was sunning myself at the pool when I heard the desk clerk's voice paging me. I stepped into my sandals and robe and went to the lobby desk.

"You paged me?"

The desk clerk looked serious. He said, "I have a registration of some people who checked in last night." He handed the card to me. It read, "Mr. and Mrs. Allen S. Topping, Jr., 8 Elmsmere Road, Half Way Tree, Kingston, Jamaica, B.W.I." The Toppings had been assigned room

105.

I had to read the entry twice. Jolt turned into fury in my heart. I thanked the desk clerk and went directly to my room, where I showered and dressed. Then I called a cab and told the driver to take me to the District Attorney's office in Miami.

There, I swore out a warrant for Allen Topping's arrest. The charge was bigamy. I returned to the Ocean Ranch, gave a maid $5.00 to open the door of room 105. Inside, I found a marriage license which stated that three days ago, a marital union between civil engineer/"bachelor" Allen Stewart Topping and "gentlewoman/spinster" Grace May Davison had been solemnized "on said Island of Jamaica, Parish of St. Andrews." Ms. Davison, aka Mrs. Topping, was a Canadian citizen resident of Toronto, Ontario. A further search provided evidence that Grace flew as a stewardess for Air Canada. There were several pictures of Allen and his new bride together with a collection of her correspondence to and from Canada. Judging from the photos, this gentlewoman was no prize. I took every document I could find.

In one photo Allen appeared to be wearing swim trunks, but on closer inspection I recognized it was a panty girdle from my modeling days in New York. Rummaging in my suitcase, I found the item missing, along with a few of my bikini panties. What in the world did Allen need with these?

I called the D.A., John Tanksley to inform him that I'd mailed him evidence taken from room 105. I would have to identify Allen when the police came to arrest him.

At about ten that evening, I met two detectives in the lobby. They flashed their i.d.'s, took one look at me -- eyes red and swollen, teeth chattering, body shaking -- and said I wouldn't be required to identify him.

They arrested Allen that evening. He spent exactly one night in jail. My only consolation was the witch he married in Jamaica was weeping and alone too. I hated Allen and I hated Grace, the ugly woman he married, as well. To kill time, I went to the hairdresser. After a leisurely afternoon of beautification, I stopped in the lounge for a cocktail, had dinner and returned to my room. Suddenly I was very tired. I undressed and went to sleep. No dreams came that night.

The next morning, many questions were still circulating in my mind. Why had Allen married this Canadian stewardess? She wasn't young, just a few years his junior, which made her no chicken; she wasn't attractive -- large nose and deep set eyes; her body was nothing to write home about; she was flat chested and built like a cow from the waist down. She had long dark grey streaked hair and a sallow complexion. Where did he find this woman? Was she, like Allen, a drunk?

I felt smashed to smithereens. I couldn't stop asking myself endless questions. This had to be the end. I couldn't allow him to hurt me further.

Best I return to New York and try to get a job. That would keep me busy and take care of my money problem. I'd stay here a few more days and then fly out. I phoned my friend who owned the cocktail lounges in Manhattan who'd been so kind to me before. She said a job was waiting for me and I could have my tiny sublet back when I arrived on Monday next.

When I opened the door to exit my hotel room, whom should I discover but Grace, the gentlewoman herself, standing there staring me in the face. I was surprised how tall she was, just an inch or so shorter than I. But God, was she homely, with skin the yellowest I'd ever seen on a Caucasian. I wondered if she might be infected with hepatitis? Or perhaps drinking too much carrot juice.

"Please take him back," Grace begged, her jaundiced skin crinkling into furrows. "He's broke, you know."

I looked at her with part pity, part disgust, and in a controlled, angry voice said, "Get away from here! If you know what's best, you'll go back to Canada before I call Immigration and Air Canada."

The gentlewoman picked up the suitcase at her side and left.

This ugly wench was what he wanted a divorce for?

When I returned to my room a few hours later, I found a note on the door. Allen wanted to talk with me. Please phone him when I got in. What was there to discuss? What could he want now? He'd blown his inheritance with the help of his new found Canadian love. He made his bed. So be it.

I would think on it. Probably, I would not be capable of talking with him, anyway. I was far too hurt and angry.

CHAPTER SEVENTEEN

What could he want from me now? He'd destroyed me and he knew it. Could he possibly expect I'd be able to forgive him for this fiasco? Maybe it was a ploy to get me to drop the bigamy charge? Whatever it was, I doubted I could bring myself to talk to Allen this time. Probably the ugly bitch from Canada had left or was unable to pay the hotel bill. Maybe she was divorcing him. Why? It was an illegal marriage. Why be bothered?

Although I felt like ignoring him, at the same time I was curious what game he'd play now. Surely not sex. He couldn't pull that number, because no way would I ever sleep with him again. No harm in a callback, though, so I ultimately told Allen he could come over if he wanted, only no funny business. I was holding the cards, wasn't I?

I dressed in a plain dark blue sailor dress and navy high heeled shoes. He wouldn't like the shoes, as they made me taller than he was. I wore all the jewelry he'd given me, the gold watch, the aquamarine and the diamond rings. He'd never get his hands on those. He'd sold all my other jewelry and pissed away the money.

I piled my hair on top of my head. No need for makeup; I had a suntan. I put on some bright coral Lancôme lipstick that matched my nail polish. I'd lost more and more weight as the days went on, but I looked chic, definitely New York in the spring. I wasn't hungry or thirsty but ordered Cokes, cheese and crackers from room service. He wouldn't like that either.

When he walked in the door, for some unknown reason he had on his cashmere topcoat. This was Florida in September. I didn't ask him to remove it, either. I wanted to cry when I saw him, but refused to let myself. I just wanted to die from humiliation. Inviting him in, I pointed to a chair across from the couch where I sat.

His face was sunburned, as usual. Allen had that florid year round alcoholic's coloring, and I must say he looked none the worse for having spent the night in jail. Oh, I wished they'd kept him there. Maybe the D.A. thought bigamy was a joke. Most all the men I'd spoken with did.

Neither of us said anything. I asked him to turn on the TV and get the news. He sat down again, still without removing the coat, and I still didn't ask him to either. We just sat in silence.

Ultimately politeness got the better of me. I offered him a Coke, some cheese and crackers. He accepted. It appeared he wasn't too hungry after his night in the slammer.

I finally asked, "Allen, what do you want?"

He said, "I love you, baby wife. Please forgive me?"

I said, "Did you call Grace baby wife too?"

"I did not," he said, "and she's gone from our lives."

"She's gone from my life," I said at the top of my voice in almost a growl, "I know that."

"She's gone from mine too," Allen said. "I don't know what got into me."

I said, "Did you know she confronted me this morning and asked me to take you back because you were broke?"

He shook his head. "No."

"I told her to hightail it back to Canada before I called Immigration and her employer, Air Canada. She left in a hurry, the ugly bitch. What do you see in these women?"

He put his head down and nodded from side to side. I guessed he really didn't know. Or was it another con of his?

What manner of man was this that I loved so? At present I was very angry but needed to keep it in check so the rage wouldn't overpower me. All I knew was that I was feeling irreparably broken into pieces. Lord, I thought, tell me what to do now. He was begging me to take him back and I said, "Look, Allen, I'm tired, I hurt, I'm humiliated and my only escape from this agony is to sleep. Please leave."

He managed to get me to agree we could continue the discussion the following day. I knew arguing with Allen was useless: adept at verbal manipulation, he always managed to control the direction and flow, making me the underdog. You couldn't win with him. Best never to open the door a crack, never give him an inch or he'd take the proverbial mile. I knew better.

Nevertheless, I agreed now mainly in order to negotiate a bit of temporary space for myself. And we did need to wrap things up. I told him, "We do have a lot to discuss, since you mucked up my whole life. You cost me a modeling career, a movie career, a few million dollars, a baby, and then on top of that, all this. All right, phone me tomorrow, even though I'm off my rocker to give you the time of day ... our union has been such a farce. And you'd better have some great answers lined up for tomorrow. Good night, you bastard."

Allen left with a grin, obviously thinking he'd conned me again. I did my ablutions and went to bed. Perhaps at last I was changing, and had discovered the secret of how to deal with Allen. As long as I was on top, I wasn't going to get hurt. I was in the driver's seat now. With satisfaction, I noted the glimmerings of a bitch with the upper hand coming alive in me now. Hopefully, this would make a difference.

I was depressed the next morning. I wondered whether the pain would subside, or if I could ever bury it deep enough so it wouldn't seem like pain anymore.

I took a long bubble bath and tried to relax. I had a sunburn so I couldn't swim today. I patted myself dry, then covered the burn with Baby Magic and put on a cotton robe, slippers, and wrapped my head in a turban.

I wrote a letter to my godmother but was careful not to tell her about the horrors that were going on in my life. You couldn't say Dorothea hadn't warned me.

I didn't want to appear anxious to please when Allen came calling. Preparing for the occasion, I chose a black, high necked fitted dress with long sleeves, black hose, and black high heeled pumps -- widow's weeds, I thought. I dabbed on lipstick and perfume, and combed my hair high on my head, entwining it with pearls. Once more, I put on all the jewelry Allen had given me, and was ready to do battle with him.

I really will let him have it this time, I thought. Night two coming up. The ruckus of all ruckuses. I planned and connived in my mind how to hurt him, destroy his ego, shame him and anything else I could do to hurt him -- not physically, of course, that wasn't my aim. I really wanted to dump all my hurt on Allen and not feel anything about him ever again.

He had destroyed my dreams, my trust in him. What kind of a cat and mouse game could I play with him? Sex? No, then he'd trap me again, and I wanted to trap him. Well, I'd think of something. I'd get him back and give him hell on earth. I'd come up with a way. I was a grown up woman now. The little girl inside hurt too much for me to be anything else. I must ever protect that little girl. It was war with Allen now. I put my hand up to my hair and felt the pearls in it, wishing they were black. Black was bitchy and that was the way I'd be tonight. I'd drag this out till he pleaded like the cur dog he was.

Why even play a game with Allen? Why not just dump him once and for all and have done with it, hurt him as he'd hurt me? Wouldn't that be a better form of revenge? The thought occurred to me that I had the power to make him suffer. But it really wasn't a consideration. I wanted to see him squirm. Allen had gotten the better of me so many times, he had controlled me and won out. I was determined to be in charge this time.

I lined my eyelids with green, adding green mascara, which brought out the devil in my eyes, the devil I intended to be tonight. Allen would rue the day he ever met me and be sorry he'd made me grow up hurt.

The phone rang at 6 p.m. Allen asked if he could come over. I told him I'd like to go out to dinner before we went to war. We both laughed. He took me to the hotel dining room -- rotten fare, but nevertheless, I had his nerves in an uproar. He didn't order a drink; I ordered a martini on the rocks. Courage, I thought.

It was a strained dinner, neither one of us wanting a public scene. After coffee, we repaired to my suite. As before, I took a seat on the couch; this time he sat down next to me. He reached for my hand, which I pulled away at once.

"You make me feel like a piece of chewing gum that someone else has chewed. What is it you want of me now?" I demanded, rising to face him. "You betrayed me. But what's the use of repeating what you already know?"

"You're right," he agreed.

"Allen, where would we begin?" I asked. "You can think of starting over again when I feel like this? I wouldn't know if we could. You tell me, you poor excuse for a husband."

He winced, then composed himself and posed a profound question. "If I go to work, work hard and take care of you like the precious jewel that you are, will you at least try?"

"I really don't know if that's possible," I said. "Your psychological bent is to create crazy making circumstances in people's lives that can only lead to agony and humiliation. Can you change all that's happened?"

He dropped his eyes. "No, of course not," he said, "nor do I expect you to change your feelings about me all at once. But I do want another chance to build our marriage, I want it very badly."

"Just look at the record, Allen. How can you make me believe again, based on the record?"

"That was before. This is now."

"What you do, each time, is to create new hurts that aren't any different from the old ones. If you were me, would you want to leave yourself open to more of the same?"

"I hurt too, you know. I didn't want that ugly Grace. I just got drunk and didn't know what was going on. So I must never drink again, and then it won't happen again."

"You're the only man I've ever known, Allen. I was barely seventeen when we got together, but I'm an adult now, twenty-one years old. And maybe it's time for a change for me."

"What do you mean, a change? What are you talking about?"

"I've been told I'm desirable and that any number of other men might enjoy being with me. So perhaps I ought to start looking in other directions."

Allen scoffed at my remark. He said, "You don't know what a jungle it is out there, Troy. Do you have any idea how many sexual degenerates are running around? Half the men out there in the singles marketplace can't even get it up. You'd be lost. You don't know what a good deal you have in me. I'm normal!"

"To give credit where credit is due, you're the world's greatest lover, Allen, but that's not reason enough for me to endure the rest of your torture. Some people like grapes so much they don't mind spitting out the pits. Other people like grapes but just don't go for the idea of being forced to spit out those pits. Well, I think I may have come to the point where I'm ready to give up grapes, Allen, because the pits are making me sick."

"Just let me show you it can and will be different," he persisted.

I said, "How can I be sure of anything you promise now? You'd have to keep on proving it forever. Are you able to do that? I mean, do you think you can even try?"

"I can, of course I can."

"You're capable of such dangerous, cruel, inhuman actions that I'd be taking my life in my hands. I'm afraid you'll dishonor me again. I'm your wife, but you never treated me with the respect I deserve. Honesty, integrity, and deep love build a union, and it can't be one sided. Can you do it? No more lies?"

"I know you have doubts, but believe me ..."

"My wounds haven't even begun to heal yet. You know, all I ever wanted was you, to have your baby and to live behind the little picket fence ... and my Star ... "

"I loved Star as much as you did. You don't understand about Star ...."

I held my hand up to silence his objections. "Now Star's gone to collie heaven and I want no baby because of you. But do you understand I want more than you've ever given me? You blew your money with that Canadian so called flying whore, and God knows how many others you bedded and wedded illegally. And you have the unmitigated gall to ask my forgiveness? I'll never forget this nightmare. But God help me, I'm ashamed to admit I do still love you, if that isn't pure insanity."

I turned away, sorry I'd allowed myself to get this emotional. "Listen," I said, "no more talk tonight. I can't. It'll have to keep while I see how I'm bearing up. Phone me in a couple of days and we'll see then ..."

"All right," he said, knowing he couldn't push me further. He kissed my cheek and looked deep into my eyes. "What have I done to you, my love? I wish I could undo it. How about my phoning you tomorrow? We could walk on the beach, maybe clear our heads. Mother would like to come down and visit with us."

"That's nice," I said, "but not Barbara. Your poor mother. I love her dearly but I will not put up with Barbara."

He agreed.

"And by the way, my love, booze and women are out, understand? I won't mention these things again unless they bear mentioning, but don't for a moment think I'll forget them."

"Don't worry, I won't," he promised. "You've taught me that much."

I smiled a phony smile and said in a sick, sweet voice, "Good night, darling. Be a love and don't call me. I'll call you."

He grinned that devilish smile of his, kissed my hand and left.

I was utterly exhausted now, so I climbed into a hot tub full of bubbles and began my game of dreaming. The cassette player was playing one of my favorite recordings, "Please Believe Me." If only I could believe him. I almost fell asleep in the tub. Would I have dreamed my childhood dream? I wondered if my Nana in heaven knew what Allen had done. I cried, Nana, Nana, I need you. I hurt so.

How could I forget what he'd done when I didn't understand him or his motivations? I mused over what Anne had said about wartime injuries causing the erratic behavior, about Cook's sea shell prophesy, and how bonded I was to Allen. Yes, despite it all, we must keep trying. It was an attachment that wouldn't die. I had too much invested in this relationship to walk away -- and walk away to where? What would life be without Allen? I loved him, damn it all. Maybe I still could drag some semblance of happiness out of this marriage yet.

The pattern was fixed, it was absolute. Cook had said to stick with him because eventually things would get better. It was written in the stars. I'd always known that. But aside from all this, I had to prove something to myself. I was going to get the upper hand with Allen Topping if it killed me. Grace was not going to have him. I'd have my payback. I'd make this husband of mine tow the mark if it was the last thing I did. Maybe after that I'd cut him loose. Then he'd be sorry.

I wrapped myself in a robe and turban and cried myself to sleep.

Waking late, I donned a bikini, sandals and a robe, called for juice and coffee. I'd swim off some of this anguish, maybe. After a long time in the pool, I decided I needed a new dress. Allen had phoned for a dinner date, and I wanted him never to forget the upcoming experience.

At the mall, I bought a long white silk gown that offset my tan. With its slit dolman sleeves, high neckline ending at the throat, its low back and body slit to the left hip, it would make just the right statement. The dress would look smashing tonight with my dark mink jacket. I'd force Allen to take me to the yacht club.

Once more, I'd wear all my jewelry. I bought a large bottle of Arpège, white satin panties and bra, a garter belt and gold lame hose. All this would knock his socks off. I sprang for a pair of long gold earrings, then went back to the hotel to dress. I spent a long time on my toilette, noting the smirk on my face with satisfaction. Prior to dressing, I'd bathed in Arpège, and now I was walking in a cloud of it.

The phone rang as I was fastening my new earrings in place. I let it ring five times before picking up. Allen, of course. Was I ready? I said almost, but come on up anyway.

He knocked and entered. I handed him my fur, observing that his eyes were almost popping out of his head. So far so good. He said, "You look like a dream walking."

"Wasn't that an old time song from your era, darling?" I purred, hoping he'd feel as ancient as I was trying to make him seem.

"Where are we going?" he asked, swallowing.

"Your favorite hangout, Dinner Key Yacht Club, so all your broads can get a good look at your wife."

"I'd rather not," he said. "But if you insist."

"I do insist, darling," I said with sarcasm.

"All right," he agreed reluctantly.

I said, "If you ever look at another woman, Allen, I will make a scene you won't soon forget."

He smiled. "You look so gorgeous, how could I?"

I said, "With you, one never knows."

He helped put my jacket around my shoulders and we left, I slinking in my traffic stopping white gown, he decked out in black tails. What a couple we made. One would never know what a mess we were in.

A cab whisked us to the yacht club. He checked my mink and we walked arm in arm to the cocktail lounge, where he ordered me a vermouth cassis on the rocks and a Coke for himself. The lounge was loaded with women -- dowagers no doubt scouting for a roll in the hay. This place must be a hangout for gigolos and horny over the hill erstwhile bimbos.

Allen was very jumpy, I noticed. Was this where he met Grace? I fingered my glass with my left hand, displaying my diamonds and a polished platinum fingernail. I was waiting like a lioness ready to pounce.

Several women were looking over at Allen, giving him filthy glances. Why, I wondered? Like I didn't know. I smiled through half closed eyes. I wanted him to be a nervous wreck, and for all the bitches here to die with envy.

Somehow I couldn't really hate him, so I had to hate the women. What an evening this would be. I rubbed my gold clad leg against his. He looked up surprised. I smiled and said nothing. This was getting interesting.

I said, "Allen, I'm rather famished."

He ushered me into the dining room. I ordered chicken Kiev and salad, followed by coffee and a brandy. Allen, good boy that he was currently playing, remained abstemious.

"Well, sweetheart, talk to me," I said.

He looked at me and said, "You're beautiful and I'm a jerk! But I won't be again. I promise you with all my heart and soul."

It sounded like he really meant it, but I cautioned myself silently not to be too sure.

Just then who should walk in ... alone ... but Grace. Allen pretended to be oblivious while Grace stared at us.

My eyes, focused on Allen, were level and cool. "Tell her to leave."

He whispered, "I can't."

"Do you want me to?"

He looked at me, disbelieving. I could read his thoughts. I've turned this sweet darling into a bitch, he was thinking. He said quietly, "Please?"

"If you even look at that ugly witch I'll make her even uglier, and then you can have her for good," I warned.

Grace had turned away and was no longer peering at us. I had a good look at her as she ambled over to a table. Her skin was almost Grey Poupon mustard yellow against her navy Air Canada uniform. She looked tired, old and unattractive. I wondered whose husband Grace would sleep with tonight. It wasn't my problem, anyway, so the hell with the ugly pill.

Allen was acting nervous and guilty, trying to compose himself. I thought, I must torture him for a while more. He's still acting, but I'll teach him a thing or two about acting.

I said, "Allen, I want a Chartreuse on the rocks."

"You'll be ill," he warned. "You're not used to drinking."

I said, "I feel rotten anyway, and maybe this will help."

He ordered it. I drank it. Then I decided now it was time to parade, to slink past Grace on Allen's arm. Laughing, I tossed my head high, nose in the air, and uttered some nonsense about a Todd Raleigh joining us tomorrow, then giggled as we glided by Grace. Allen didn't dare feast his eyes anywhere but on me, while I was looking down my nose at Grace, enjoying this rarefied moment of being the only female in the world.

I thought I still don't want to make love with him, but I will, like he's never had it before. He was sober and was going to have to be extremely patient because I'd take my bloody time. I'd keep him up all night, I decided.

I said, "I feel you've been walking on my love for you with dirty feet."

He said, "No, not at all. I love you madly and you know it."

"You never loved anyone in your life. I do hope you'll be able to one day, but I doubt it."

He said, "Let's go home and I'll prove it."

"One night in the sack proves nothing, or even every night when you're not taking on your responsibilities."

"I will take care of you now. I realize what I've done to you, and I'm really ashamed."

"Horse pucky," I said. "But we'll go home anyway and see if you can make me believe you ... again."

In bed, several hours later, the sex was getting wilder and crazier, but I wouldn't let him have an orgasm even though I'd had a few. He made love to me all over my body. It was strange, strong, animalistic, but incomplete. I wanted more and more and he was very patient. He now knew what an unbelievable creature he'd created.

I bathed and perfumed after each Big O, forcing him to start all over again. He finally couldn't control himself anymore and I knew from now on he was mine. He was going out of his mind and I went with him to some place we'd never been before, somewhere not of this earth.

Finally we both fell asleep in each other's arms, but I still dreamed my dream and the prince still had no face. The dancing dream on the ocean liner -- what did it mean? Maybe it was something I'd never find. However, when I slept in Allen's arms, my face on his chest, I was happy. He always smelled the same, like the sun and the sea. I'd remember that fragrance all the days of my life.

When I woke, he was kissing me, saying we must make plans. I agreed. We couldn't go on dining in the hotel and Florida itself gave me a bad feeling. I had no idea where I wanted to go other than sleep in Allen's arms, to live with him in splendor, somewhere and just be happy. I was hooked again. Allen had a lot to make up for, but he knew it. Now maybe he'd grow up. He had to get a job, I didn't care what kind; however, I didn't want to go back to that bloody desert Las Vegas.

It was Sunday. Last night was a new adventure, but today was reality. I didn't want to bear the brunt of financial responsibility in this marriage anymore. I had no babies, Star was gone, so it was starting from scratch. There should be enough money from Allen's inheritance left for an apartment and a trip to Europe, but I wanted a home.

I dressed in a silver lame robe with matching silver hosiery, underwear and shoes. I drenched myself in a new perfume, Diva. Maybe I'd dance again professionally just for fun, or maybe even sing. Just as long as Allen was the real breadwinner of the family.

He joined me on the patio for brunch, wearing white slacks and a blue shirt that matched his eyes. He seemed quiet, nervous, concerned and tired. I couldn't care less if he was tired. I'd make him forget his fatigue. Besides, like his father, he had the constitution of a horse. His father was no longer around to support him. What would he do?

He suggested that Monday he'd look for a job in contracting. A good beginning. After all, he had studied architecture at Yale. He could build me a home. He had destroyed my childlike ways. I'd become a woman and I'd learned to handle him.

I sat on his lap, played with his ear and said, "Let's go to bed. It's Sunday, anyway."

He smiled and said, "You're difficult to resist."

Bed lasted for seven hours and was as wild and incredible as the previous night. I woke him up at 6 a.m. Monday.

"Rise and shine, darling," I cooed in his ear. "Time to go job hunting!"

He smiled before opening his eyes. I handed him a newspaper and coffee. I was wearing a bright printed short robe and my hair, longer now and the color of burnished gold, dusted his lips.

He downed his coffee quickly, hit the shower, dressed in casual Miami style attire, kissed me and left to begin his job search.

The District Attorney's office phoned. I told the D. A. I hadn't decided whether or not to drop the charges. Changing into a swim suit, I headed for the pool to meditate. The ripples in the water lulled me to a soporific state as I lolled in the sun till I felt all golden again. I turned over on my stomach, then drowsy as I was, I felt Allen's hands on my back, rubbing me with lotion.

He said he'd found a job, but it was in England.

I said, "You have to be kidding."

"I'm not."

"You'd better find something here." Then I thought of two friends of ours, Ellen and Keith Larson, who by coincidence happened also to be friends of Hazel and Frank, our friends from Las Vegas. Keith was a builder. "I'll call Ellen. Keith is working on bridges down in the Keys around Marathon. I'm really not ready to go to England, luv."

"Why not?"

"Its too cold there. And besides, with your Yale degree you can get connected here."

He loved to hear me say that. Somewhere in the distance there was the sound of "Lara's Theme," one of my favorites. The music switched to "Killing Me Softly," causing me to shudder.

I made the phone call the next day. Coincidentally, Ellen told me that Hazel and Frank were moving back to Florida from Vegas, and that Frank would be joining Keith in the construction business. I arranged for Allen and me to have dinner with Ellen and Keith the following evening.

We dined aboard a yacht owned by Joel Henderson, an investment banker from New York with whom the Larsons invested money. Joel lived in Locust Valley, Long Island, but kept a yacht and some condos he rented out down in the Keys. As luck would have it, there was a vacancy, a small 3 bedroom place that Allen and I could lease for a reasonable price.

Allen's position was agreed upon, and things were looking up. The Keys were lovely with turquoise blue waters, and I liked swimming in the Gulf of Mexico. I'd make it work, somehow. Maybe my godmother, Dorothea del Drago, would know some social people down here and we could have some fun for a change.

CHAPTER EIGHTEEN

The five years in the Keys were sheer happiness. I now believed I had reached the point Cook had described: home safe. "Caant live one widout de otha. You and him be one. Two peas, one pod, batty and bench, one spirit. Go through thick and thin, live it out ... when times be tuff, look black, stick wid him, it gwang get bettah." It was exactly as Cook said; we'd weathered the storm and now we had our beautiful life together.

Allen was on the wagon, always the perfect angel when he didn't drink. Wonder of wonders, he went to work every day. I redecorated the condo, we gave small dinner parties, we had many friends and a good social life. We enjoyed the beach and frolicked in the surf together like two kids.

Our love grew stronger, as I became more trustful and we had the beginnings of a true friendship. We didn't discuss having another child; Allen knew down deep I couldn't forget what had happened in Las Vegas.

We took short trips to the Caribbean, played volley ball at the El San Juan in Puerto Rico and swam at the La Concha. We'd dine at the El Convento and dance the night away. We revisited the Fortalenza and El Junkie, the rain forest. I never tired of being in these beautiful places with him.

He was attentive, considerate, a great dancer, acted the role of the Prince Charming I'd always dreamed about. He dressed well, he was gallant and protective, and to me the best looking man in the world. He saw to anything I wanted and sometimes told me how much he loved me every five seconds.

As a lover, he was patient, sometimes gentle, sometimes wild, and he took me there with him. The magic, the spark was always alive, and we never became bored with each other.

For a change, I was really happy. I supposed this was what love and marriage were all about, getting through the tough times, emerging with a fresh perspective, something meaningful, lasting and wonderful. The pain had been worth it. It was exactly as Cook had predicted so long ago.

When we gave a dinner party he was the perfect host. He drank ginger ale from a champagne glass. Sometimes he'd wink at me from across the room, I'd float over, take his arm and gaze up at him, awed by love. I was telling the whole world what a lucky woman I was to have this man and I was going to keep our marriage this way.

I'd be in the pantry getting some more wine for the guests, he'd follow me and crush me in his arms. "I love you so," he'd say. I'd even let him mess up my lipstick.

Weekdays when he was working, I shopped, rode horses on the beach. My dream remained a country estate with horses and collies.

Anne came to visit us now and then and he knew better than to be cruel to her. Or maybe there was no reason for the cruelty anymore. Maybe he'd outgrown the resentment he'd always had for his mother. I'd really miss Anne when she left. Barbara came too occasionally but embarrassed me, so I'd told her unless she could change her behavior, she and her lover Art Smith would not be welcome again. Allen put his hands over his face and laughed his head off. He too was relieved when they left.

On shorter holidays we went sailing. I hadn't done any sailing since I was 12 and it was fun with Allen.

He never forgot a birthday, an anniversary or just for no reason at all, he'd come home with flowers or a new Parisian perfume.

Sometimes in the middle of the night while I was dreaming, he'd awaken me for a bath oil massage, and he'd ask, "Has that prince of yours got a face yet?"

I'd reach up and pull his head down to kiss him over and over. We'd make love, my skin sparkling in a cloud of perfume.

I said, "No face yet, sweetheart. Maybe soon."

He said, "I must think of something fantastic, love you more or do something for you so I can get my face on that prince you dream about every night while you're in my arms."

I'd awaken in the morning in his arms and the odor of the sun and sea was on his chest, that wonderful fragrance I'll never forget.

Some winters at Christmas we'd go to New York, where we'd stay at the Carlyle with Anne. One time I suggested to him, "Let's ask your mother if she'd like to go to midnight mass at St. Patrick's or the one at the Actors' Church."

"I'm not a Catholic."

"I'm not a Catholic either."

As it turned out Anne had chills and didn't want to go out.

We never stayed very long because Barbara would arrive with Art Smith, whom she now referred to as her husband. I was civil to her but she'd get Allen so angry so we'd decide to go home.

He'd grab me at odd moments and say, "I'm such a lucky guy. I love you so."

I used to tease him about letting his hair grow long, and he'd say, "I'm no fairy, no way."

"I love you with short hair, darling. I was just kidding."

He said, "Sweetheart, how would you like to have short hair?"

And he ran after me with a pair of scissors in hand. I screamed as he grabbed him hair, but he just pulled my face up to his and kissed me. "Silly girl," he said. "I love to bury my face in your hair. Come on, let's go upstairs."

I used to beg him, "Please, can I have my hair done back to the auburn color?"

He'd say no. "I love you blond, with that golden tan and your satin skin."

I did what he wanted and he was willing to do what I wanted. We were working on this marriage, and it was coming out right.

I even bought a cookbook to try to prepare fantastic dinners, but I really lacked an aptitude for cooking, so Allen would take over and finish for me. He always laughed at me trying to cook.

He always hit the shower when he arrived home, and then come down to dinner. He'd always kiss me, pull my chair out at the table and bury his face in my hair. We'd dine slowly, make small talk and sometimes in the middle of dinner he'd get up, take me upstairs to bed to make love.

He was spontaneously romantic at a moment's notice. At such times, we wouldn't bother to go downstairs again to finish dinner. I always fell asleep in his arms and when I'd wake, his fragrance of sun and sea was always there.

I'd rub my face on his chest and he'd smile before opening his eyes.

One Sunday morning he said, "Let's take a bath."

I laughed. "How? This tub is smaller than most of the ones we've used."

He said, "I'll get in and then you step in front of me."

We faced each other in the tub throwing bubbles at each other, laughing. God, I was lucky. I loved him more and more every passing day. He was so sweet and angelic those whole five years.

For a birthday gift he bought me a silver blue Eldorado convertible. I was overwhelmed. "Now you'll have to teach me to drive," I said.

He said he would, starting in a couple of weeks. In the interim he drove the car. I didn't care, I'd wait. He loved the car, let him drive it. Maybe I'd call a driving school and learn when he was at work to surprise him.

I didn't think anymore about what he'd done to me in the past. I was just busy being happy with the love of my life.

On one of our trips we went to Santo Domingo and perfected our meringue. The dance had an interesting history. It was invented by a Dominican general with a wooden leg, so it was danced with one leg stiff. It was almost like a march. I picked it right up, but Allen was so silly. He was afraid of stepping on my toes. I wore white satin shoes trimmed in rhinestones.

We finally got it down pat. Everywhere we went, people admired the way we performed the meringue. One year in Puerto Rico, Miguel Babachono, a big politico from Mexico, was entranced with us. Miguel used to call me "Svenska" because he thought I was a Swede. That blond hair!

At the end of the evening someone taught me a Puerto Rican folk dance, which I performed barefooted. I was tired and Allen knew it. He said, "Come on, lover, it's late, and we have plans."

He picked up my shoes and purse, said our goodbyes to everyone, and caught our flight home from Isla Verde.

We arrived home in 3 hours, exhausted. I bathed and went to bed. Allen showered. He said, "You look like a flower I haven't figured out which one yet, something exotic and wonderful."

He climbed into bed, took me in his arms, let out a sigh and we both went off to dreamland.

He had the charm, charisma, a fantastic way of keeping me happy. I never asked for anything material but it still bothered him that he couldn't give me emeralds and diamonds. I always told him I had more than any woman could ever ask for.

I asked him to teach me to play chess. He said, "It's a bore. Let's play lovers instead."

"Allen, it's two in the afternoon."

"So? Let's go up to heaven." Heaven was one of his euphemisms for the bedroom.

He had ordered some roses for the bedroom. He scattered the petals all over the bed, then massaged me with Nivea and Moment Suprême. He sprinkled more rose petals all over me, put one rose in my navel and another in my mouth, stuck between my teeth. Then he leaned over, buried his face in my hair and murmured in my ear, "God, how I love you."

He made love like never before, never as gently as this in the beginning, never as wild later on. He was whispering words that I couldn't quite make out but which excited me beyond measure. I wanted it go on forever.

He put both his hands around my jaw and kissed me until I went crazy with him. Later he put a rose on either of my nipples and one on my `rose.' And then he kissed me there. We slept until dawn. Again it was the sun and the sea on his chest I smelled mixed with the rose petals and Moment Suprême, that divine fragrance issued by Jean Patou in 1929.

That did it. This night was our moment supreme!

He looked so angelic when he was asleep. Lord, I thought, there were no words to describe how I loved him. I would keep this man happy, as happy as he was keeping me.

I was now fully aware of Allen's drinking problem, and tried very hard both to understand and to help. We were going to AA meetings together. Everything seemed to be under control.

Then one day, something set him off again. I had thought our union was strong enough to withstand anything. Apparently I was wrong.

I came home mid afternoon to find the shades drawn, the house in darkness, and Allen pacing with a rum and Coke in his hand. He seemed agitated. I knew something had happened.

"What's wrong, Allen?" I asked.

At first he wouldn't talk about it. Finally I discovered he was brooding about Glad Ass when he blurted out, "The cunt's got herself a stud, an aspiring young actor. She's staking the son of a bitch to a career, same as Father did with Joan Crawford. Bitch! The whore's doing it on my goddamn fucking millions that I'll fucking never see!"

The actor was Richard Anderson, who would later become known as one of the stars of the television hit, "The Six Million Dollar Man," and would also make an auspicious marriage to Katherine Thalberg, daughter of two Hollywood legends, Norma Shearer and Irving Thalberg.

Allen had done a flip flop. He quit going to AA meetings and went back to drinking with a vengeance. I tried to understand, but my attempts to help were fruitless. I couldn't make him listen to reason, couldn't get him to allow his fellow AA members to intervene, couldn't stop the destructive downward course he had, without warning, landed in. It was as if he had simply snapped overnight.

Throughout our relationship I'd seen the two sides of Allen's nature, but had come to believe that with love, his dark side had been transformed. Now this Jekyll and Hyde again. How long could my patience hold out? Things were rapidly deteriorating. As blissful as our life had been, we started arguing again. Allen's nasty streak came to prevail.

I was bitterly disappointed by this turn of events, and I was beginning to believe nothing could be salvaged anymore.

After that, it was all downhill. One day I returned from shopping, parked my Coupe de Ville in the garage and went upstairs. Hearing a noise in the guest room, I opened the door to look inside.

Grace the gentlewoman was in bed with my husband next to her, passed out drunk.

All the old hurts Allen had put me through seemed to converge at once. Furious, I rushed at the sleeping stewardess and yanked her by the hair, ordering her out of the house before I called the police. Allen didn't move a muscle.

Grace hugged the sheet to keep me from seeing her shapeless, sagging body and said, "Please, Troy, try to understand. I ran into him accidentally in a bar and we --"

"You mean you ran into him with your crotch and took him to a bar because that was the only way you could get him stoned and into my bed, you bitch. Do you hear me, I told you to get the hell out of here!" I pushed and pulled at her, while Allen still slept, dead to the world.

Grace ducked my punches and grabbed her stewardess uniform, still clutching the sheet to her body. I got hold of the sheet and pulled it off, shoving her out the guest room door into the hall. I went after her, scratching her back hard, and was surprised to find out how tough her skin was. She kept protesting her innocence and was still trying to dress as I ejected her out the front door.

"Don't ever come near my husband or my home again!" I shouted after her.

She ran up the street half naked, this unmitigated hussy who had the nerve to call herself a spinster and gentlewoman.

It was the end. It had finally fallen apart. I couldn't go on being torn apart, never knowing when the worm would turn. I was still frightened of being without Allen Topping, but nevertheless, I now wanted this relationship over and done with no matter what.

I called Hazel, who after a few years of living in Florida had transferred to California with Frank. Ellen and Keith had moved there as well, and as a matter of fact, Keith and Frank were now partners in a motion picture production company.

I told Hazel what had happened, confessing I feared Allen was incapable of really quitting alcohol, that this time, after finding him in bed with Grace, I'd really had it.

"At least it was in the guest room," Hazel observed.

"Be thankful for small favors," I nodded ruefully.

Hazel asked why didn't I come visit in L.A. while I decided on a course of action. The west coast might provide a good change of pace for me.

But I'd already decided on another course of action. I was heading back to New York.

Allen was still out cold as I began packing my suitcases. Then I thought of the funds I'd invested with Joel Henderson. It was my money, held in joint account. Grace helped Allen blow his inheritance, but she wasn't going to get her hands on the money I'd saved and invested with Joel that Allen didn't even know about.

I called Joel in New York and arranged to have Allen's name taken off the account, with a new account opened in my name only. I said I was leaving Allen, and warned Joel that since Allen was drinking again, I didn't have much faith he'd be responsible about paying the rent. Joel thanked me for telling him and promised to take care of everything.

I stretched out on a chaise longue and waited for the bum to awaken. As usual, just before he opened his eyes he smiled.

"Good morning, you bastard," I greeted him.

Allen said, "What am I doing in the guest room?"

"What you do and where you do it is no longer of any concern to me," I said. "As of tomorrow, I'm out of here. You had the nerve to bring your beloved Grace here, and don't tell me you blacked out again. You've insulted and humiliated me one time too many."

"Sweetheart, please ..."

"I dropped the bigamy charges five years ago because I thought you'd reform. I believed in you, Allen, but my faith was misplaced. You can drink yourself to death and you can have any woman you want now, I won't stand in your way. You always wanted to know how far you could push. Now you have the answer. This is it for you and me."

"Please, I didn't know what I was doing. You know what happens to me when I get crocked."

"Your bizarre behavior since I've known you disgusts me and I want no more of it or you."

Allen said, "You knew it's always been a joke, a farce with Grace, but she begs and pleads, and when I'm drunk, what the hell. She's a lousy lay, anyway, she's flat chested ... and that ugly face "

"Some magnetic attraction, huh, Allen? What does she do, suck toes?"

He said, "The marriage to Grace was never legal, it was bullshit. I never loved her! You're the only love in my life. You're my legal wife and my only heir, you know that."

I laughed in his face. "You're so tenacious I can't believe it. You need to see how much you can get away with. You actually think you can worm your way back into my good graces after this, don't you? Well, you can't con me again. Just go to your crotch Grace. Maybe you can con her."

Allen shouted, "Wait, luv, you can't just walk out like this. Please listen."

"I've had it, Allen. And there won't be a divorce. I don't need one."

"Baby! Baby wife! No, don't do this to me," he implored, a panicked expression on his face as reality started sinking in.

"You don't need me any more. Go make your new wife miserable."

CHAPTER NINETEEN

Starting over again without Allen was about the toughest thing I ever did in my life. I was terrified of being alone and didn't think I could handle even the simplest decisions. All those years together, Allen had seen to everything. I hadn't minded handing over my paycheck, because he took care of things I didn't think I could begin to understand. I'd always felt inept and helpless, always had the feeling of needing someone to take care of me.

On my own now in New York, I tried to revive my modeling career. Granted, I was too old to start in the high fashion field again, but I visited agents listed in the Madison Avenue Handbook, made rounds, saw photographers, did bread and butter jobs, trade shows and industrials, record album covers, romance magazines, runway and showroom work, and managed to pay the bills. I enrolled in acting classes, went out on commercial auditions and readings for legit productions. I answered every ad in Back Stage and Show Business, did some summer stock in Maine and even some gigs in the Catskills. I lived from job to job, like everybody else. I survived. But I was emotionally unfulfilled. Was this all there was?

I hated coming home to an empty apartment, waking to face the void, wondering if I'd ever find love again. I dated, but the magic was always missing. I was invited to parties and openings, nightclubs and to weekends in the country. Nothing brought a sense of a belonging. Would I ever fall in love again?

It didn't look promising. Was every man in Manhattan either married, gay, sick, a lech, or all of the above? Or was it just my luck?

Until Denny. Denny Slater, the only man who could have made me forget Allen Topping.

We met at the Colony Club. I was chatting away with an old friend, Mary Lee, when all of a sudden Mary Lee looked up and said, "Victoria, here's the guy for you."

The person coming toward us was very good looking indeed, tall, dark and handsome, as the saying goes. Denny Slater had just returned from Europe. Right away he asked me to dance, then when I was in his arms, he wanted to know if I liked candy. I said no.

"Too bad," he said. "My family owns Fannie Farmer."

"Really, Denny? What else do you own?"

He said, "The New York Jets. Want to meet Joe Namath?"

"I do not. I'm very happy to meet you, Denny."

He said, "Never mind what I own, let's just dance the night away. I love to feel those long slim legs close to me."

"Wait a minute. Is that a way to speak to a lady you've just met?"

"Sorry, but you really are a turn on."

My heart was banging away at my chest as he held me closer.

Denny and I had a wonderful long flirt, as the Europeans call it, and we talked a lot about a future together. He said, "I want to get a divorce. We should be married. Will you wait?"

"I'll wait, but I don't like lonely weekends and holidays."

He promised, "Won't be long, luv." He had to run. "Have to take her to a ball."

"Her" was Anne Slater, his Locust Valley socialite wife, known for her trademark blue frame, blue tinted glasses.

The Sunday papers had a picture of him with her in which Denny had a dark, heavy beard, a five o'clock shadow that really showed. Poor lamb, didn't have time to shave for that ball, we'd stayed in bed too long having a ball of our own. When he phoned again, I asked him what his wife had said when he came in late. He answered, "`Hurry and dress, we'll be late.'"

"Denny," I said, "are you all right? You sound hoarse."

He said, "Just a sore throat. I'll be over later."

Denny Slater was not only the one man who made me forget past miseries, he incidentally also happened to be Chairman of the Board of Warner Bros. and in a position to do me a lot of good career wise. I really wanted to marry Denny. I loved the guy!

However, fate is not kind. Three months later, at a very early age, Denny died suddenly. That sore throat he had was the beginning and it killed him. I mourned him for a long time. After all, he was Denniston Lyon Slater, and we loved each other. It was finished but I could remember Denny with love.

Denny and I used to go to El Morocco quite a bit, which was where he introduced me to friends of his like attorney Roy Cohn. Frequently, Denny would bring along another friend, his Yorkshire Terrier, "Dreadful." We had so many big plans.

Hearing about Allen's bigamy antics, Denny roared with laughter. When it was time for me to testify against Allen in the Miami bigamy suit, Denny was about to embark on a business a trip, but left an envelope for me at the Essex House containing a good deal of money, airline tickets and a note.

It said, "Go somewhere after it's over and have some fun. I'll be back shortly. Love, Denny." This was typical of the sweet man who was so unhappily married to Anne Slater.

When Denny died so suddenly, a light went out. I really didn't want to stay in New York anymore. Hazel and Ellen talked again about my coming to California. A visit to the west coast might provide a change of scenery to help me get my mind off the past. I had no idea a new life and career awaited there.

A chauffeur driven limo whisked me straight away to an estate in Bel Air. Both Keith and Frank had made it big in a short span of time as successful film producers. They and their wives were close mouthed regarding specifics of how this career boost came about. I gathered there was a connection of sorts, an investor or group of investors behind them, but I didn't know who. Truthfully, I couldn't help being a bit envious and only wished their good fortune could happen to me. I was curious to know more, but since no information was forthcoming, I didn't want to pry or appear nosy about my friends' business affairs, particularly when one day Hazel asked if I wouldn't like to play a part in a motion picture myself!

"Just like that?" I asked.

"Sure, just like that. Of course, it won't be a major role, and you could end up on the cutting room floor, but it will be a credit. If nothing else it will give you `current footage,' and maybe it'll get you an agent, possibly even a whole new life."

"Wow! Sounds great to me! I accept."

CHAPTER TWENTY

Hazel was a prophet. A whole new life did indeed open up for me. Money, career and social life took decided upturns. I settled down to enjoy California living. By the time I was thirty, I'd worked in ten motion pictures and numerous television shows, I owned my own home in Toluca Lake and had a house full of animals -- five collies and a horse named Duke whom I stabled in neighboring Glendale.

When I was working, I woke at 5 am and sometimes didn't return till 9 p.m. Weekends, friends in Bel Air and Beverly Hills were forever inviting single men for me, hoping the relationships would take.

Allen kept phoning, begging and vowing the usual promises over and over. Every once in a while I relented, usually when I wasn't working, especially at Christmas; then Allen would fly out to spend the holidays with me. It was no use, though; he still drank. I was wary and found it impossible to trust him any more. Prince Charming was a beautiful concept and I would never really stop hoping it could come true for me, but right now I couldn't bring myself to reconcile with Allen.

One year during a small party I gave on Christmas Eve, Allen had passed out in the guest room.

I was kneeling on the floor in the den picking up discarded wrapping paper and ribbons, when Hazel, Ellen, and Frank, who were helping me, all surrounded me chanting, "Keep on cleaning up, honey, and don't look up." Then all of a sudden I heard Allen's voice cursing like mad. I stood up. He'd come out of the guest room in a t shirt minus boxers. Oh, my God, I thought, he's lost his mind. This was more than I could stand.

He wasn't going to rain on my Christmas party. I picked up a golf club, chased him back into the guest room and locked him in.

After this he returned to Florida. I had no idea then that during this time period he had wedded a series of other women without benefit of a divorce from me. Nor did I yet suspect how many undissolved unions there had been previously; Grace was just the tip of the iceberg. It would be a few more years before I'd find out the full scope of the situation, that Allen wasn't merely the careless bigamist he appeared at first glance, but a genuine hard core polygamist, no accident intended.

Time passed, our lives continued on separate courses, I heard from Allen sporadically. At one point we had a phone conversation in which he claimed he'd not seen Grace in a matter of several years. He said he was doing horoscopes for a living, which made me laugh.

"What's so funny about that?" he asked.

"Allen, you could never sit still long enough to put up a chart. You always paced like a lion when you were home. In fact, I can even hear you pacing right this minute while we're talking on the phone."

"I swear."

"Sure. So how about our charts, Allen, yours and mine ... July 31st and November 19th, Leo and Scorpio. What have you got to say about that subject?"

"We're very destructive for each other."

"Tell me about it. Must be that deadly Scorpio sting. Too bad you didn't take up astrology sooner. Think how much grief could have been spared."

He mentioned he'd been having heart trouble, for which he was taking prescriptive medication.

"Does it help?"

"It eases the pain."

"I guess it would have that effect, when you're chasing it with rum," I observed dryly.

I never got caught up in the tinsel town politics and parties scene, but sometimes, viewing the Hollywood game from a distance, I'd long for the familiarity and simplicity of my old life with Allen. I tried to make a go of it with others, and sometimes even managed some semblance of a relationship. But always, in my heart of hearts, I knew I couldn't really get behind it. Something was always missing.

Allen really was my Prince Charming, but in my youth, I'd lacked the wisdom to know how to deal with him. Perhaps if Allen and I had been able to spend more time in a family situation it all could have been different. I often longed to talk with Anne about her son, but sadly, she had passed on. Her death came as a terrible shock, as if a part of my life were gone with her. Barbara too had died. Sadly, my family, my only family was dissolving. I wept for these two unhappy women. Now Allen was all that remained.

Sometimes when Allen would call, I'd really be tempted. No matter how bad it had sometimes been, with Allen I had connected. We'd had an intimate, close relationship. I missed that, and there were times I thought I'd do almost anything to have it again.

So I kept renewing the tie with Allen. He represented roots; I couldn't pull away from him altogether, couldn't totally relinquish my dream of us as one soul, one being.

Once again, I'd neither seen nor heard from Allen for some time when he phoned out of the blue to say he wanted to come fetch me so that we could go to Europe to live. He began ringing every morning at 9:30 and we talked for hours, making plans, laughing, joking. I began to look forward to the daily calls. He swore up and down he hadn't set eyes on Grace in eight years. Somehow, I felt he was my old Allen.

One of the last conversations I had with Allen took place toward the end of February, 1989.

He said, "I'm so ashamed of the things I did to you. You're the only woman I've ever truly loved. I'll always love you, Troy, now and forever. You're my one and only heir and I really mean that. Whatever I have is yours, always, and that's the way I want it. That's why I had John Gravenor write the will the way he did."

"How do you mean, Allen?"

"I mean that I denied any past or future heirs for good reason. I want you to be my heir. When I'm gone everything will be yours. When we were together I went through a lot of financial problems, but everything's ok now, and I want to make sure you'll be taken care of. I'm in good shape, not like I used to be."

"No?"

"You see, Mother and Barbara, when they died, both left everything to me, and I didn't piss it away. On top of that, I just settled a lawsuit, a car accident, somebody plowed into me head on, and I collected two hundred and fifty grand. I want you to have everything when I'm gone."

"Allen, why are we talking about the will and your dying when you're telling me you're coming to fetch me and we're going traveling again?"

He said, "I just want you to know how much I love and adore you."

"You're not thinking of checking out, are you? You're not ill?"

"I'm in good health, Troy. Would I be planning to drive all the way to see you if I were sick?"

"Allen, you're telling me this for a reason."

He said, "I just know that I love you and always did, and again, I'm ashamed of what I did to you. I remember every inch of your pink and white body, inside and out. Remember how you used to parade for me in black lingerie and bend over when I asked you to? I can still see it, like it's going on right now. Lord, you're gorgeous. I'm going to fetch you really soon. Remember, I love you and you're my heir."

The conversation continued. Allen told me he'd run into our old friend from Las Vegas, Jack Cannon, and "Guess what? The old fart's had a pump put in."

At first I didn't know what Allen meant by a pump. He explained a pump was a penile implant. When men started getting past their prime and developed erective problems, the surgical "pump" came to the rescue. I cracked up at the mental image of a preparing to get laid Jack Cannon standing nude by his bedside, inflating this thing he'd had planted in his pecker, probably with the aid of a contraption one uses for bicycle tires. Was it a hand job or did it have a foot pedal? Or maybe the pumping up was achieved using something similar to a blood pressure monitoring device? At any rate it gave me a good laugh.

"How about you, darling?" I teased. "Swordsman that you always were, are you ready for a pump job yet?"

"Not on a bet. The day any broad tells me I need help is the day I give up living."

"So you're still going strong, eh? The old cocksman hasn't faded yet?"

"Not yet, baby, and I'm just waiting to show you what I mean by that."

I chuckled. Allen hadn't changed much. I guessed he never would.

"Allen, when did you see Grace last?"

He said, "I haven't seen or heard from the ugly witch for eight years and I hope I never do again."

"Honey, when are you coming to California?"

He said, "As fast as I can drive it. Just let me clean up some business, and I can probably leave in about 4 or 5 days, ok?"

"Please hurry, Allen. I've missed you so."

"I will, baby. See you soon, and I love you, Troy. Bye."

He hung up the phone.

Then one morning the phone rang and a woman's voice on the other line inquired, "Who's this?"

I don't like rude people who phone, then ask whom they're calling. Don't they know? I answered with a question. "Who is this?"

"Grace Topping," came the reply.

I slammed the receiver in her ear.

Grace even had the audacity to phone back. It was apparent she was calling from a public booth in a restaurant, with people talking and music playing in the background. Above the din, I thought I heard Allen laughing, but I couldn't be sure. Once again, Grace asked, "Who's this?"

"This is Mrs. Allen Stewart Topping, Jr."

Grace began shouting about bigamy, polygamy, immigration and so forth. Again I slammed down the receiver.

The next day, March 3, 1989, Allen phoned to say he'd be leaving Florida the following morning, arriving in L.A. to fetch me in five days. Did I want to sell my house, because we'd be spending most of our time from now on in Europe? Wary because of the calls from Grace, I said I'd keep the house, but I was looking forward to our trip.

As was my custom, I marked the date and time on my desk calendar. In addition, I made a notation that Allen would be arriving in five days. Needless to say Allen never showed. Not in five days or five weeks or five months or five years.

I never saw him again, never heard his voice again.

In the weeks that followed Allen's final phone call, I did a lot of thinking. I remembered how I used to pray: Lord, please either make him able to love me as I love him, or make me stop caring. I never got an answer. Was it all for the best? Was this the way it was meant to be?

I still dreamed my childhood dream of Prince Charming who still had no face. I danced my life away with that faceless prince and forever wore a black sequin dress on an ocean liner going nowhere. In some respects it was no longer merely a dream, but had become a nightmare.

A part of me would never stop loving Allen.

Four months went by. It was July, 1989. Since Allen phoned no more, I wanted to call him, but I didn't have his unlisted number. I rang the apartment house he lived at on Bayshore Drive in Coconut Grove.

"This is Victoria Topping," I told the secretary at the management office. "I need to get in touch with my husband, Allen Topping, a resident of your building. I wonder if you could give me his number?"

"Just a minute, please."

I was put on hold. Several moments later, a man identifying himself as the manager came on the line. "How can I help you?" he asked.

I repeated my request. He said, "I'm very sorry, ma'am, but there is no number for Mr. Topping. Mr. Topping is deceased."

"Deceased? No, I don't think so. There must be a mistake."

"There's no mistake. Mr. Topping formerly lived here, but he died."

"When? How?"

"Oh, let's see now ... it was back last winter. Yes, I remember exactly when, because the rent was due March 1st and that's the very day he died."

That couldn't be! March 1, 1989? I'd spoken with Allen on the 3rd, hadn't I? That was two days later! Already, I was suspicious. Already I didn't believe Allen could be dead.

I asked, "What did he die of?"

"I'm not actually sure, though I heard he was admitted to the hospital with an ingrown toenail."

"Strange." Incredulous, I kept shaking my head, as if feeling sorry for the manager who was deluded enough to call Allen Topping deceased. Of course Allen couldn't be dead, though I couldn't figure out what in blazes his game was this time.

For Allen to have died on March 1st was an obvious impossibility, given our conversation of the 3rd. Just to prove I wasn't bonkers, I consulted my calendar, and sure enough, there was my entry verifying it: "March 3, 1989, 9:30 a.m., talked with Allen. March 8th, Allen arriving (5 days)." Yes, our conversation was indeed two days after his alleged "death." Something didn't jibe at all.

But even apart from this, I knew absolutely that Allen wasn't dead. My reaction to his "demise" added up to something like a flash, an insight, a form of intuition, if you will. I've always called this "off the top of my head." I'd had many experiences of just knowing things "off the top of my head," and been right. I suspect everyone has such instances in which a still small voice reveals something about which there's no doubt as to authenticity. How do we know these things? We just do!

Instead of the shock, disbelief and sadness that one might expect from being given news of Allen's "death," I had a calm sense of understanding that the man I had loved and married was still very much in and of this world.

Ok, he was alive. But officially he was dead. To get to the bottom of the confusion and penetrate the mystery, my first step would be to play the official "death game." I was Allen's legal heir, he'd told me so.

I dug out the last will and testament he'd signed in Nevada naming me as his sole heir. It sounded irrevocable. I'd fly to Florida, file Allen's will, then learn what happened. First I sent for the death certificate, Allen's driver's license, and other documents.

When I arrived in Florida I'd probably retain a private detective to find out all I could.

CHAPTER TWENTY-ONE

I was prepared for war in Florida.

I'd spoken to Eleanor Chapman at the Veteran's Hospital in Miami, where Allen supposedly expired, and I had such medical reports as were legally issuable. The story was Allen had been admitted to the V.A. hospital complaining about a painful ingrown toenail. The death certificate stated the demise to have been caused by multiple organ system failure due to renal failure and sepsis hephrectomy.

There had been no autopsy.

From the information I'd gathered, the following picture emerged of the departed: he had heart and kidney trouble, diabetes, and cirrhosis of the liver; he was blind, sterile, and had had a penile implant. The above information hit me wrong.

Blindness, for one thing. Allen was blind in the right eye only. He had a valid Florida driver's license (# T152 017 21 415 000). How could he have been blind in both eyes if he'd been contemplating driving from Miami to Los Angeles to see me? How had he managed to operate a vehicle and have had a recent auto accident? How had he been able to read, as he'd done to me over the telephone?

The deceased was sterile? (How did they determine that about a corpse, anyway?) Allen had made at least three separate wives pregnant. Penile implant? He'd been adamant he'd never had one and never would. Most notably, there was no mention of the crescent shaped metal plate in Allen's head, the result of his World War II battle injury. Wouldn't a Veteran's Hospital include that in a medical history? And how about Allen's ulcer that didn't appear in the medical reports?

Perhaps the cadaver that had been placed in the crematorium wasn't Allen's? Now there was a thought.

The body that was allegedly Allen's had been whisked to the Van Orsdell Funeral Home, 4600 S.W. 8th Street, Coral Gables, and given a hasty cremation ten hours after being pronounced dead. The mortician taking care of things was one Mr. Grady Hinton. I thought about my telephone conversation with Mr. Hinton. He told me Grace had brought the body there without documents and ordered the cremation.

"You mean you performed a cremation with no papers, no death certificate, nothing?"

"What was I to do when this pathetic, grieving skinny creature arrives with the body?" Hinton whined in his unctuous manner.

It was hard to believe that the V.A. had released the body to Grace so unceremoniously. Did they just let her haul it away in her car? No ambulance? No hearse? It didn't seem right that Grace would be carrying that corpse in the trunk of her car. I wanted to know more specifics, but Hinton refused to supply further information, except to say that someone -- he wouldn't say who -- had purchased an urn, and that "we had a very nice service for him. He wasn't present, of course."

This was just one more of a series of circumstances that didn't add up.

To my surprise, the courthouse was filthy looking. The last time I'd seen downtown Miami, the city was clean, a series of pink and white buildings with flowers blooming everywhere. Now the town looked like a ghetto slum area. I wondered what had happened here ... Little Havana, dirty buildings, crowded streets, pushcarts with fly covered food and fruit operated by scrungy looking ruffians.

How depressing everything was -- death certificates, hospital records, insurance companies, lawyers, private detectives, funeral directors, everyone I had to deal with and didn't want to. It seemed overwhelming, all the legalities and procedures.

Allen Topping, my Prince Charming, was a son of a bitch; nevertheless I felt like I'd lost my soul. He wasn't dead, yet sometimes I was thinking of him as if he were. The attachment wouldn't die. I would bury him deeper and deeper in my heart in order to remember him without pain.

I drew a tub, climbed in, sipped my morning juice there, thinking again of Allen. I dozed off for a moment, in which I saw Allen standing beside the tub saying, "Come out. I need you." I awakened with a gasp. His figure was disappearing and I could see through him. It wasn't he, of course, only another one of my stupid dreams. And yet, despite the ectoplasmic quality, I knew now on an even deeper level that he wasn't dead.

What was the point of Allen appearing to be dead if he wasn't? Why had the body cremated so quickly? Why was there no autopsy? At first it was just a split second picture that flashed through my mind, but gradually, that picture began to fill in.

Either Allen was in trouble and staged his own "death" to escape the consequences, or else the motive was money, to collect on an insurance policy. I felt the latter was the case. He'd changed his identity. Someone else, perhaps someone Allen found in a bar, a drunk, a drug addict, a derelict, could have been admitted to the hospital under the name Allen Topping, given all Allen's i.d.'s. This man died. Nor was it as far fetched as it sounded. Allen Topping as I knew him was both diabolical and sociopathic enough to be capable of such a bizarre scheme.

The thoughts whirled around in my head. This couldn't be done alone. He would need accomplices. And the logical chief accomplice was Grace. Allen and Grace had perpetrated a scam.

Allen would need a fresh identity, of course, which was easy to arrange. I'd seen such advertisements in the newspaper; for a few dollars you could buy yourself a new birth certificate, marriage and driver's license, even a Social Security card. Or if you wanted to assume someone else's identity, all you had to do was watch the obituaries, then get a hold of that person's old credentials and become him.

I retained private detective Frank Ybarra of the Florida Investigation Services on Southeast 1st Avenue. Hoping to find out more on what happened to Allen, I accompanied Frank to the address where Grace was allegedly living, the Jamestown Apartments on Tiger Tail in Coconut Grove. It was a quiet, residential area, the building pink stucco.

Frank rang the bell to apartment 1C. The front windows were shut tight, protected by white jalousied shutters. No one answered at first. We rang again. There was the sound of shuffling feet inside. I thought I heard the muffled sound of a female voice. Then louder, a woman called out, "Who is it? What do you want?"

"Ma'am," Frank began, "if you don't mind, we'd like to talk to you. It's about Allen Topping."

Silence, dead silence. Frank repeated the request. At this point, I noticed a finger had lifted one of the wooden panels on the louvered shutters. For an instant, Grace's face was visible. Then she hid behind the panel once again.

Frank said, "Ma'am, we'd appreciate it very much if you'd open the door."

"I will not open the door! Go away!"

"It's a matter of great concern regarding Mr. Topping."

"Mr. Topping is dead." I picked up a note of fear in Grace's voice.

"With regard to the death of Mr. Topping --"

"Who is that lady with you?" Grace demanded suspiciously, sounding like a fishwife.

Frank answered, "You know who the lady is. She is Mr. Topping's wife."

Grace screamed, "No, no, no! I'm his wife!"

Something had set Grace off, and obviously that something was both my curiosity about Allen and my being referred to as his wife. Grace began yelling that she was calling the police, for what reason I couldn't surmise.

"What do you people want?" she raged, crazed and paranoid.

"Mr. Topping's wife wants to know what happened," Frank began, but Grace would listen no more. Frank asked me, "Do you want to wait for the police?"

"No, they can't make her talk with me, or give up the ashes or the gold Rolex watch I gave him for Christmas that I'd like to have back."

"I think you'll have a tough job recovering it," Frank agreed. "I don't think we're going to get anything at all out of this bitch."

"Why was she so afraid of me?" I wondered, when Frank and I were driving back to Miami.

"She's hiding something, that's for sure," Frank said. "Did you ever think it might be Allen?"

"Allen inside with Grace?"

"Can you think of a better reason why she'd be so nervous?"

No, I could not.

A hearing at my request was being held at the Department of Social Security, I wondered if Grace would show her face. The past decades hadn't been kind to Grace she was older and homelier than ever, with reddish pinkish white hair now. Although I hadn't been able to tell much about her from the split second glimpse under the jalousied shutters, one day recently I'd spotted her getting into her car when I passed by the Jamestown Apartment building, so I knew how she'd changed.

Whatever I'd hoped for in a confrontation with Grace failed to materialize when she didn't appear at the hearing but sent legal representation to plead her case. Grace's side claimed Grace was in Canada, which must have been a quick exit, since I'd seen her the previous day at 3 p.m. in Coconut Grove. The judge noted having received a letter from Grace on her whereabouts stating she was in Toronto, but postmarked Miami. I also learned that Grace had a phone which accepted no incoming calls, and that she had a problem with Immigration.

I'd brought along several official documents, including one from Washington that was sent to me unsolicited by the White House. Engraved on thick parchment, it bore the official gold leaf seal of the United States, an eagle with a crown of stars on its head, two different kinds of branches clasped in either foot, with "E Pluribus Unum" tacked on over the spread out wings. The document read:

The United States of America
Honors the memory of
Allen Topping, Jr.

This certificate is awarded by a grateful nation in recognition of devoted and selfless consecration to the service of our country in the Armed Forces of the United States.

George H.W. Bush
President of the United States

Now if the United States of America and its President, George Herbert Walker Bush, considered me Allen Topping's wife, wouldn't you think Judge Solomon of the Social Security Department would have seen fit to give me a fair hearing? But no, I sat waiting while the judge chit chatted with Grace's legal counsel and everybody shuffled papers.

I had retained an attorney to represent me in the will proceedings as well as in several other areas, but had come to this Social Security hearing alone, sure it would be cut and dried enough for me to take care of myself. I regretted that decision.

I'd no idea what was going on or why I had yet to be acknowledged by the court. Then oddly, Grace's paralegal, a woman named Anna Baum, jumped up and declared, "Grace marries Judge Branson." What did that mean? Why the present tense? It wasn't "Grace married Judge Branson," or "Grace is going to marry Judge Branson," which would have made more sense, but "Grace marries Judge Branson." And who was Judge Branson?

Curious when I would be called on, I politely tried to ask the judge, but he glared at me and announced I could speak only when spoken to. Angrily I thought, for Pete's sake, I was the one who asked for this special hearing, yet this paralegal gets to disrupt the proceedings, and I'm told to shut up. What a farce.

The hearing dragged on, with my being questioned on Allen's divorce from his "second marriage." Of course, they had it wrong. Grace had filed a false statement claiming I was Allen's second wife, Trudy his first. I had proof to the contrary.

The court itself had requested that ad litem attorney Mr. Dunleavy research Allen Topping's marital unions, and Mr. Dunleavy had uncovered a number of hitherto undisclosed ones, however, the judge ruled that these numerous marriage certificates, ordered by the court itself, were not to be admitted as evidence. So the court was throwing out its own evidence, which would have clearly disputed Grace's allegations and proven my case.

The judge was referring to our union as Allen's "second marriage," whereas it was in reality at least his sixth or more.

The jury is still out on the complete list of Allen Topping's former wives, but from the "short list" of U.S. Attorney Robert Senior, ad litem attorney Mr. Dunleavy, the State of Florida, and other sources, my own efforts included, we can at least ascertain Allen to have wed the following list of women:

Minnie Mae Walker, married on the Fourth of July, 1942, Walker County, Georgia, (no divorce on record); Milly Ownbey, also married in 1942, possibly divorced 6/7/42; Minnie May Walker, (remarried in Chattanooga, TN, 1944); Marnie Phillips, Oklahoma, 1945; Mariana Townsend Look, 11/49, Palm Beach, divorced 10/16/52 ("the cause from which it appears to the Court that the defendant, Allen Stewart Topping, Jr., has been guilty of such cruel and inhuman treatment that it is no longer safe for the petitioner to live and cohabit with him or remain under his dominion or control;" Gertrude Secomb Monson, 1952, Savannah, GA (has daughter by him, Georgianna Topping; divorced him 3/14/68. (This was Trudy, the one he told me he divorced when we were in Tijuana, '59). Allen and I were married in Mexico 8/31/59, again in Nevada, 5/18/62.

Contrary to Grace Topping's allegation, Allen and I were never divorced. However, were we ever married? He wasn't divorced from Trudy till '68, and probably was never divorced from a bunch of the others either.

Additional wives included: Rosamond Stone, Nevada, early 60's, no divorce on record; Ginny the Guinea, (née Pistelli) 1961, Miami; and of course Grace May Davison, 9/29/62, illegal marriage ... Allen was still married to me as well as to Trudy and probably to a few others; Grace again, 2/18/72 ... illegal; (furthermore, Grace lied on this marriage license by claiming she was born in Oregon, USA, when she was actually hatched in Canada); divorced from Grace, 1/20/80, married Grace again 5/27/87.

Allen also married a person named Cheryl Ann Bradshaw, and another party called Pat (probably a New York model, early to middle 1940's), as well as somebody with the surname Solomon. In addition he entered into the state of holy matrimony with: Amanda Burkhart, Suzanne Beers, Emily Owens, and the following group of women in California: Valerie Chute, (I believe she was a French tourist passing through), Jane Hammond, Janet Ziegler and Melissa Ann Towne.

Heaven only knows how many others there were. The search team did only a desultory scan investigation, covering but four or five states in the process, concluding there was more than enough evidence to prove that Allen was a bigamist and there was no need to delve any further. And of course there was no mention of the duchess, his alleged first wife. If they overlooked her, how many more didn't they know about? Couldn't wartime Europe have yielded more trophies than merely that one? Speaking of which, how did Allen manage to seemingly be in two places at the same time, i.e, serve in the army in Europe (which his medical records attested to) and yet be available to marry so many women on home soil (which the collection of marriage licenses proved he had done)?

At any rate, it was another piece of the puzzle, another part of Cook's prophesy come true: "and a high whole heap o' wedding ring." I wondered if Cook had any idea how many wedding rings there were (or how much gold went into the wedding ring fiascos).

I tried raise the matter of the inconsistencies on the three Topping/Davison marriage licenses. Evidence showed Grace had lied. Would this not constitute fraud? Should such a person be entitled to an illegal spouse's U.S. Social Security benefits? Again, I got nowhere. Later on, the appeals judge did not want to upset Judge Solomon's verdict, and the matter was slated for a federal court.

Perhaps the trouble had started with the will. Grace had actually filed her will several weeks after I filed mine. A hearing had been set before Judge Christie in Probate Court, but I was never notified. In my absence, Judge Christie ruled in Grace's favor. I requested a second hearing to challenge this decision. However, the presiding judge, Judge Newman, did not want to rule against another judge's decision. My 1962 will was sealed and I would have to petition the court to change this.

On top of that, Grace had the balls to sue the U.S. government for wrongful death.

But the big question that perplexed me as I left the fiasco that was the Social Security hearing that day was: who is Judge Branson?

CHAPTER TWENTY-TWO

I told the driver to head away from Miami as fast as possible. I was glad I'd decided to stay at the Boca Raton Club, close to the ocean where one could still smell the air once in a while from one's balcony.

Reclining in my seat, I watched the ripples on Biscayne Bay as we traveled north on South Bayshore Drive. As usual, the weather was blazing hot and humid. Florida had even developed a lousy climate, and its ocean was polluted. In summer there were sea lice from the Portuguese man o' wars, sharks of all kind, and now they were talking about radioactive seaweed.

Having dozed off, I woke to discover we were back at the Boca Raton Club. I was tired, disappointed about the hearing. I went to my suite and tried to stop thinking. Another hearing was scheduled in a few days. Would Grace appear for that?

What havoc Allen had left in his wake. How often, waking from my recurring dream, did I hear the shuffle of Allen's footsteps as he approached. How well I knew that step. I jumped up suddenly, almost anticipating he'd come now. But of course, there was no sign of him.

I was thinking about Star. Star, why did you have to leave me? For some unknown reason, my mind flashed to a "60 Minutes" broadcast with George Burns on one of his monthly visits to Forest Lawn, talking to his wife Gracie Allen, who was interred there. I said, well, if it works for George Burns, maybe it will work for me. Like George talking out loud to Gracie, I started talking to my beloved collie Star. I needed answers and didn't know where to get them. I asked Star to help me find out.

It seemed almost like a prayer. And as if an answer to that prayer, my hand felt guided to pick up the newspaper. My eye caught an advertisement for psychic readings by telephone. Maybe Star was trying to tell me something. I dialed the number, and a soft voice answered, "Hello? This is Magda, the psychic. How may I help you?"

I said, "Hello. My name is Victoria Topping, and I believe you may be able to answer a problem I have."

"I'll try," Magda replied, "but first I'll need some information from you, yes?" She had a slight accent, Hungarian, no doubt, as her name suggested. "When is your birthday?"

"July 31," I answered. "I'm a Leo. Do you need the year as well?"

"No, but I do need the birth date of the person you have this problem with, and his name."

I said, "He's my husband, was or is -- his name is Allen Topping, his birth date is November 19 -- Scorpio, third decanan."

"You say this man was or is your husband?"

"We were living a continent apart," I explained, "but were in touch by phone. Then suddenly the calls stopped. I heard Allen was dead, but for a number of reasons I think there's been a mistake. So I decided to enlist your talents to help me find out the real story."

"I'm seeing a death certificate, and it's very, very clear, the mental picture I have of this certificate," Magda said. "The cause of death listed on the document I'm seeing as I speak to you is -- yes, kidney and liver malfunction."

"That's exactly right!" I exclaimed. "Magda, you're extraordinary!"

"You see, I knew this. They -- my guides -- were telling me these things as I spoke to you, but I did need you to confirm that for me. I thank you."

"That's incredible, Magda. You say `they told you.' Can `they' tell you anything else?"

"I see a military hospital. Yes, it's the Veteran's Hospital in Miami, and this is the strange part. I'm not sure how to explain. Someone was in this hospital and died, but it was not your husband! There was a replacement here. Hmmm, very strange."

"And my husband? What about him now?"

"Well, right now, I'm feeling a warm glow as we speak. I believe your husband is very much alive."

I gasped. Magda had given me the confirmation I'd hoped for. She could see that Allen was still alive and that he had indeed perpetrated a scam.

The psychic continued, "He is out of touch with you because someone is standing in the way. I don't know who. As yet, I can't see the person."

I asked, "Magda, does the name Judge Branson mean anything to you?"

Magda was silent a moment, then said, "It's very possible that your husband could be calling himself by the name Judge Branson now. Branson could be a phony identity he's assumed. Something is rotten in Denmark. Ah, listen, my dear, this is too important... I seldom suggest this, but in this case I definitely do recommend getting a second opinion, just to verify that we're on the right track."

"You yourself can't be sure?"

"I am very, very sure, that's just it. I trust what they tell me implicitly. But I want you to be convinced."

"You mean I should call another psychic and see what they say?"

"Yes, I believe you should. And then we can talk again, if you wish."

"Can you recommend someone, Magda?"

"If you like, I can."

After taking down the name and number of the psychic Magda recommended, I felt better, now surer that my own hunches about Allen had been correct. I immediately picked up the phone again to dial Magda's recommendation, Francesca.

A husky feminine voice answered, "Francesca speaking."

I'd decided not to tell the second psychic very much, so as to let her come up with the things I needed to know with as little prodding from me as possible. So I asked, "Francesca, What can you tell me about an individual named Allen Topping, born November 19, 1921?"

Francesca said, "I see many women. This man has married a number of times   not just ordinary multiple marriages. No, this goes beyond that. He's had an almost preposterous number of wives, perhaps two dozen or more. And my dear, I would have to say you yourself were one of the two dozen. I have to say this man is not in good health. He drinks too much. However, if he takes good care of himself, he can live a few years longer."

"He's still alive, then?"

"Oh, very much so!"

I then explained to Francesca about Allen being officially dead and she howled. "He's not dead," she declared. "That's one thing I can tell you absolutely."

"Francesca, does the name Judge Branson mean anything to you?"

"Yes, I feel a very strong current coursing through my heart chakra, hitting me almost like a hammer. The name is integral to this situation. I'm not sure how the good judge figures in, but he is definitely involved in some capacity, and I would have to say it's decidedly not kosher."

"This is very interesting," I said. "Magda said you might be able to verify the answers she gave me, and you have."

We chatted for several more minutes. Francesca told me an uncanny number of totally accurate things pertaining to myself not involving Allen. Then she returned to Allen, and said, "Your husband is not only alive, but I see him involved in something illegal with a woman, or perhaps I should call her a black witch."

"What is it they're involved in?" I asked. "And what does this black witch have to do with it?"

Francesca said, "It concerns an insurance company. And the witch flies. I can't elaborate on that. It just came clairaudiently, and it hasn't been explained yet. This is all I get on it now."

Francesca had confirmed Magda's information and my own hunches. I hoped she wouldn't be offended if I asked whom I might consult for a third opinion. If three psychics could provide input of this accurate a caliber, it would help me to continue on the right track. Francesca was pleased to recommend someone else, saying an excellent medium named Garrett might be able to help me with further answers.

CHAPTER TWENTY-THREE

Garrett's number wasn't answering. On the sixth ring, just when I assumed no one was home, a male voice chirped, "Garrett speaking. Who's calling, please?" Garrett sounded sweet, obviously gay and quite simpatico. I liked him at once. He was presently busy, he said, with some important music he was doing with the Miami Choral Society, but could I phone back later?

I rang Ellen in California to fill her in on the psychics. Ellen had just seen a great psychic on TV who lived in the Miami area, and recommended I call her. The psychic's name was Megan Duffy. I told Ellen I'd phone Megan the following morning.

Later that evening, I rang Garrett's number once more for our reading. He told me the name of the woman involved with Allen was Grace. "Is this correct?" Garrett asked.

"You bet it's correct," I said excitedly. "Right on, Garrett."

"Good. Now I must tell you as well that this woman is a witch, and that she flies."

"What do you mean? On a broomstick?"

"Not exactly "

"Wait! Do you mean she could be a flight attendant? Could that be it?"

"It could be, and as a matter of fact most likely is."

"What about the insurance company?"

"There definitely was an insurance scam involving your husband, involving his phony death. I do feel a Canadian carrier is involved. It's quite possible there could even have been more than one insurance company."

"Can you tell me anything more about my husband?"

"I don't see him in the Miami area at present. He hasn't lived here since around the time of the faked death. Was this man into photography?"

"He sure was. He just about always had a camera in his hand."

"I have the impression of many, many photographs. You yourself were in a lot of these photos, and he was the photographer. The pictures I'm speaking of have been destroyed, they no longer exist, not even the negatives. At one period of time did you have a number of photographs of yourself and of this man that you yourself destroyed?"

"Yes, yes I did! I ripped them all up but one!"

"Well, I have to tell you that it wouldn't do you much good to have these photos today, because this man has not only aged but has changed his face just enough through plastic surgery that he no longer resembles the person you knew. He could not be identified through a photo even if you had one. However, if you saw him in person you would know him!"

"For sure I'd know Allen Topping anywhere!"

Garrett declared that the building Allen had lived in was owned by a plastic surgeon who'd lost his license, that he'd been the one who'd performed facial surgery on Allen. Checking, I later found that Allen's apartment building indeed was owned a physician disbarred from medical practice. Furthermore, Judge Branson, Garrett said, was integral to the fraud Allen had perpetrated.

I was satisfied after talking to Garrett. I was right about the scam and the fact that Allen wasn't dead.

I paced back and forth until the clock told me it was a reasonable hour to phone Megan Duffy. On the dot of ten I dialed the number. Megan answered after seven rings with a sleepy sounding voice. I hoped I hadn't called Megan too early.

"Hallo, Megan here. Who's speaking?" The voice had a decided Irish brogue.

I told Megan who I was, adding, "I'm a friend of Ellen Kingsley Larson, who was formerly in the police department in Miami. I understand you've worked with the police before."

"Many times, many places." I was relieved to hear Megan sounding more awake now.

Megan suggested we meet in person, that it might be better for the first reading. "After that," she said, "I can do you on the phone."

We settled on a one o'clock lunch at Monty's in the Grove. I dressed casually in beige pants, white blouse and navy blazer, called for a driver and took off for Monty's. I hated to go there, as it was so close to Dinner Key Yacht Club, but maybe Megan could pick up more vibes that way.

It was a long drive, but I had a feeling it was going to be worth it. I was deep in intriguing thought when we pulled up at Monty's entrance. I slid out of the car, long legs first, and told the driver to phone in about two hours for an exact pickup time. Entering the restaurant alone, I was uneasy being in the neighborhood. Both Allen and Grace, I knew, used to hang out here. However, I spied Megan right off.

Megan was slim and comely with smiling blue eyes and soft,

shining chestnut hair. She approached me as though we already knew one another, and uttered, "Well, if my intuition is as in tune as I think it is today, you're Victoria Topping, a lady of substance."

I smiled. "You're Megan."

We shook hands and proceeded to a reserved table, escorted by the maître d'. We ordered drinks and lunch. I could hardly contain myself until the waiter left so we could get down to brass tacks. Megan looked at me with a piercing gaze, but also with a warm smile. She said, "You are a lioness, if ever I saw one. A Leo!"

"Who told on me?" I laughed.

"Nobody. I'm psychic, remember?"

"It's that apparent?"

"Leos usually are very apparent, my dear, front and center. Well, now, we have some territory to cover. We're meeting to see if we can find information that could bring your problem to a head."

I nodded approval, eager to hear what Megan might pick up.

Megan said, "Your husband Allen, we already know, is an infernal scamp. But this blackguard did not act alone. No, he was aided and abetted by his lady friend Grace in this insurance scam we've spoken about. Has anyone told you Grace is a witch?"

"I've heard that, yes," I admitted. "I don't know to what degree."

"This woman is evil. On the one hand, she has very little control of her emotions. She'll rage into infantile tantrums with an anger that knows no bounds. One would deduce from this that she lacks control in any area. However, when it comes to witchcraft, she's good at what she does. In the craft, so to speak, the woman has discipline."

I was amazed about what Megan was saying, as she seemed to hit Grace on the head. Although I had not previously thought of Grace in connection with hard core witchcraft, hearing Megan tell it, it had the ring of truth.

"No, absolutely, your husband isn't dead," Megan said. "The feeling I have right in the solar plexis leaves me with complete certainty of that conclusion. This witch, by the way, keeps him well supplied with rum to control him. However, don't forget he's as guilty as she is. They worked this scam together."

"In what way did Grace's witchcraft figure into it? I mean, what application did it have?"

"Let me tell you something interesting about that," Megan said. "Grace works both on her own and with other people. These people are right here in Miami. Cubans, some of them, Haitians also."

"You mean --" I was aghast, almost unable to pronounce the words that stuck on my tongue.

"I mean," Megan said solemnly, "Voodoo and Santeria, Afro Caribbean tradition. All I can tell you is be careful."

It was nearly too much to digest at once. I listened carefully as Megan told more about Grace's methods. Grace, when working on her own, carried out simple "jobs," as Megan referred to them. But for the more involved, complicated things, she required expert help and was willing to pay for it. She frequented Little Havana and the Haitian sections of Miami, where she had a padrino expert in the arts of Santeria, a man named Alejandro, who killed chickens and goats for her, then scattered the body parts into iron pots and lit candles to Yemaya, goddess of the sea, who kept Grace looking "young and beautiful."

I laughed out loud. "Megan, I'd believe everything you say, as far out as it sounds, except in this case I have to tell you you're off base. Grace is not young and beautiful, she's --"

Megan interrupted. "I know! She's old and ugly. But you've heard that beauty is in the eyes of the beholder? All right, Allen perceives Grace as young and beautiful!"

I conceded that it was possible, especially in a haze of alcohol.

"I'll tell you something else that will shake you to your bootstraps," Megan said. "Allen has been a very sick man. He should be dead, but he's not. The reason he's not is due to the work of Grace's Haitian godfather, a very powerful man in the 9th degree, which is the highest you can go in that -- ah -- path."

"Why should Allen be dead?" I asked.

"Cirrhosis of the liver, diabetes, heart disease, ulcers, alcoholism -- these things add up, ducky, they take their toll," Megan said. I was impressed she'd gotten the list of ailments exactly right.

"He couldn't have lasted much longer, but Grace doesn't have the expertise to do what needed to be done to prolong his life, so she called on her godfather, the Haitian. He performed -- I don't know how they say it French or in Creole, I only know the Spanish for it -- it's what they call in Santeria a *cambio de cabeza*, that is, `changing the head.'"

I didn't know what this meant, but I was getting a very spooky feeling as Megan spoke, and my arms were covered with goose bumps.

Megan explained, "Frankly, I don't know how they do it and I don't want to know. All I can tell you is the process is very expensive and highly dangerous. What they do is they `claim' a person. That person then dies, and they literally `change the head,' or take on that person's life."

"But how?"

"They enter the person's head or that person's soul enters their body or ... " Megan's own head and body shook, as if she were trying to free herself from a bad dream. "We shouldn't even be talking about this, it's so horrible," she finished.

"I'm sorry," I apologized, although I wasn't sure what I was apologizing for. Yet I had to know more. I pressed Megan further. "Just tell me, please, what happens after this? Does the person seem the same as before? Can they live a long time? What does it feel like?"

"They can live up to at least a year or two, depending, and then quite possibly they'll have to repeat the process in order to go on living longer. I've heard they could continue this way for ten or twenty years, but I really don't know," Megan said. "And as for how they feel, they don't really live," she concluded, "they merely exist."

I couldn't believe what I was hearing. "How do they look?" I persisted, trying not to let the eerie feelings get the better of me.

"They look the same, except they have a glazed over appearance in the eyes. It's primarily inside that they're really different...they've assumed the soul or the essence, the life force of that other person."

"Judge Branson?" We had touched on the probability that Branson was Allen's new identity.

"Yes, if he was the head `claimed.'"

"And you say it's expensive?"

"At least $50,000, maybe up to $250,000 is what they charge for this. It's not easy to do, it's dangerous, they have to go to the cemetery ... it's risky business."

"God, maybe that's one reason they needed a lot of money and pulled the insurance scam. It sounds grotesque, like something out of Carlos Castaneda or Stephen King, or worse."

Then Megan said, "This makes me tired. These two are so totally rotten. Let me rest a bit, have lunch and we'll come back to it, all right?"

Shaken, I said, "Of course, Megan."

The waiter brought bread and rolls, we sipped our cocktails, made small talk. After lunch, Megan suggested, "Let's amble on over to the beach. I have a feeling about it."

I paid the bill against Megan's protestations and we walked down toward the bay.

Thinking aloud, I said, "Destiny is both strange and cruel."

The sun sparkled on the waves, making them look like liquid

diamonds. I thought of the diamond rings Allen had given me, and it brought tears to my eyes. I no longer wore the rings, but kept them in my safety deposit box in California.

For the next half hour, Megan told me many details about my life, things no one could possibly know about me, about my Nana, Star, my horse and dogs, my life in California, details about Allen. I was particularly amazed when she zeroed in on Mr. Topping, Allen's father.

"I'm seeing the name Joan Crawford in connection with the father. The father was in some way involved with her. They definitely had an affair, a very torrid affair. The sex they had together was of an exotic nature, and I'm seeing that there was an exchange of money, quite a substantial amount."

"Megan, that's amazing. Mr. Topping financed Joan Crawford's career!"

"Yes, and a lot more. You know, father and son were in many ways alike. But the son could never live up to his father's expectations, and this was a great deal of the problem. The father was a drinker too. He had a penchant for stewardesses, chorines, dancers, show girls..."

"Why, yes, that's definitely so. He married a couple of them, too." I recalled Allen once telling me, with regard to the stewardesses, that his father liked them two at a time. Allen said his father used to order strawberry ice cream by the gallon and eat it off the two stewardesses' naked crotches simultaneously.

"I see that both father and son had a war injury," Megan continued. "Now about the son, I'm seeing that due to his war injury he had a plate in his head, and I believe that if you could investigate the cremation, you'd find the ashes contained no residue of metal. If you could obtain this information that would be further proof that the man incinerated at the funeral home in Coral Gables was someone other than your husband. Of course, I doubt you could get this. The mortician was in on the scam as well, his palm was greased. And he's not a well man. He doesn't have that long to live himself."

Megan surprised me no end when she told me my friends Keith and Frank were silent partners with Chicago/Las Vegas organized crime interests. So that was how they came from seemingly nowhere inside of a short span of time to become so established in the motion picture industry.

Finally Megan suggested we go for a drive, saying perhaps this could bring additional information to light about the subject that most fascinated me -- Allen Topping.

CHAPTER TWENTY-FOUR

Megan started the engine and we took off in her green BMW. I felt lightheaded as we drove up in front of Dinner Key Yacht Club.

Megan asked, "Are you all right? You look so pale."

"No, I'm fine."

"Did something shock you about this club?"

"Oh, no, nothing much," I said with a note of sarcasm. "It was just my husband's hangout!"

Megan said, "I feel your husband met the black witch here. He was very drunk and she just about raped him in public. He really didn't know what was going on for a few days after they met. By then it was too late."

"Too late?"

"She had mesmerized him, you see. He was drunk and easy to influence."

"Oh, so that's how it was."

"And I'll tell you something else. She performed another one of her witchcraft rituals on him right away. She got his sperm, and she used it to bind him to her."

"His sperm? How did she do this?"

"Another Caribbean method. There are several approaches. I think the manner Grace used was to put the sperm on a dab of cotton, then place it in a hollowed out lily bulb together with some Spanish fly and quicksilver and a few other ingredients. I can't give you the entire recipe, but that's the basics -- then you ignite it and recite some incantations over it or whatever. It's said to be infallible. The man doesn't have a prayer."

I heard the sound of Megan's voice dimming and felt myself getting strangely weaker.

"There's something else," Megan said, hesitating. "Have you heard of parabiosis?"

"No. Should I have? What is it?"

"In the 1920's, a Russian physician named Alexander Bogdanov conducted research in anti-aging. He discovered this method of rejuvenation called parabiosis in which a patient's blood is replaced periodically with entirely fresh blood that's a mixture of the blood of aborted babies and children under ten."

I was shocked. "And this is something that Allen has done?"
"That's right."
"Oh wow, Megan ... you've blown my mind."

Megan had leaned over and was looking at me with a concerned expression. She said, "Victoria, I'm going to take you home so you can get some rest. And don't worry, we'll find the answers you need. Trust me."

"Thanks, Megan. We'll be in touch soon?"
"Of course. I'll ring you or you ring me."

I got out of the car, walked to the desk at the lobby to get my key and messages. In my suite, I went directly to the bath, dropped my clothes and slipped into the tub. I started to think about all Megan had said, but everything was almost too much -- and some of it too frightening to assimilate at once, so I allowed my mind to wander in other directions.

I thought about my teenage years and remembered the day my grandmother died. Then came the barristers, who told me Nana owed a lot of money, that her home would have to be sold to pay all the debts before the estate could be settled. I cried a lot about Nana. Why did she have to die now and leave me all alone? I felt so frightened and lost. It was a feeling I never got over. Perhaps if I hadn't been so vulnerable, things would have been different with Allen.

That horrible story Megan had told me about "changing heads" was too gruesome for words, so much so that I couldn't even face thinking about it. To put it out of mind, I looked over the documents I had on Allen for possible new inspiration.

Included among the papers attorney Mr. Dunleavy had given me was Allen's marriage license to Gertrude Secomb Monson, tacked onto which was Trudy's current phone number.

Allen had married the then pregnant Trudy in January, 1952, while still wed to Mariana Townsend Look, who did not divorce him until October of that same year ten months after his marrying Trudy. However, at the time of both of these aforesaid unions, Allen was actually still legally wed to Minnie May Walker, with whom he had first tied the knot in 1942, divorced that same year, re-wed in 1944, and not bothered to split from again after that, even though he managed to sandwich in a few more illegal spouses in between.

Allen and Trudy had cohabited only a couple of months, but Trudy hadn't divorced him until 1968, nine years after our first marriage in

Mexico, six years after our second one in Las Vegas. Allen had fraudulently declared his divorce from Trudy came in '59, and said her name was Gertrude Jenkins, not Gertrude Seacomb Monson ... (unless perhaps he might have also wed a Gertrude Jenkins and gotten the two Gertrudes mixed up?).

Wondering if Trudy Topping, the former Gertrude Seacomb Monson, might have anything to say that could shed light on my search, I dialed her number in Newport News, Virginia.

"Hello, is this Gertrude Secomb Monson Topping, who was once married to Allen Topping?" I asked.

An audible gasp came from the other end of the line. A woman's voice, sounding wan and feeble, said, "Who is speaking, please?"

"You don't know me," I began, "I -- "

"I am unable to communicate with you unless I first know to whom I'm speaking," Trudy said, in a not unpleasant though wary voice.

"My name is Victoria Topping. I   "

"Topping, Topping you say? You're a relative of Allen's then?"

"I was his wife."

Another gasp from Trudy. She wanted to know just what this was in regard to, why I was calling.

I asked her if she'd heard Allen was dead.

"No, I hadn't heard," Trudy said, "but I'm not surprised."

"You were expecting it, then?"

"Oh, heavens, no. I hadn't seen or spoken to Allen Topping in years. He upped and disappeared, but he was quite a drinker, you know, and those people don't last."

"I imagine you and I must have had many experiences in common," I proffered, hoping to dig a bit deeper into the warp and woof of Trudy's life with Allen before I'd known him.

"I do hope not. My experiences with Allen Topping were most unpleasant, to say the least."

"You had a child by him, didn't you, Trudy?"

"Yes, indeed, my daughter, Georgianna, who's now a grown woman and looks just like her father, and if you knew Allen you know how good looking he is -- or was."

"I'd heard there was a great resemblance."

"Allen Jr. missed having a very lovely family," Trudy said. "Georgianna is happily married and the mother of two young sons. It's certainly too bad Allen couldn't have had the pleasure of meeting any of his own flesh and blood."

"He never met your daughter?"

"Never. Allen got up one morning while I was pregnant and said, 'I'll see you when you get back in shape.' He cleared out, and I never did set eyes on him again, although I waited a long time, hoping."

Trudy sounded like such a nice, heartbroken old lady. She made me think of Anne Topping. The voices were similar -- well bred, slow, low and just plain sad. I surmised Trudy must probably be over seventy years of age now. She told me she'd been having dizzy spells for a number of years. She sounded tired.

She also told me about her trip to New York to see Allen Sr. She said, "I walked into his office at 159 Varick St. and he seated me, saying, 'Oh, yes, you are Captain Secomb's daughter.' I answered, saying, 'Yes, and I am also Allen Jr.'s wife.' Mr. Topping gasped as he dropped into his chair. He was quite concerned at my being in the family way; his son's lack of responsibility bothered him very much. I begged him not to give Allen Jr. any more money; it was ruining his life to know he could always fall back on his father. I do believe everything could have been different for Allen had he held down a job.

"Mr. Topping tried his best. You know, he was a dear friend of Juan Trippe, the founder of Pan Am. Allen Topping is the only person in the history of Pan Am to be fired three times from the same job, and he can thank his father and Juan Trippe for the fact that he had any job at all at Pan Am."

Trudy said that when I had Allen arrested on bigamy charges, the Miami Prosecutor had wanted her to come to testify against him, but she'd been unable to make the trip from Georgia to Florida because of her health. From all she said, it sounded like Allen had been really mean to her. So mine was not a unique experience. What was it that made Allen behave that way?

Trudy and I ended our conversation warmly, both feeling as though we'd been taken.

Trudy, Grace, Rosamond Stone, Ginny the Guinea's voice ... I'd had contact of sorts with a few of Allen's spouses. Oh, yes, there was another one I'd almost forgotten about.

Allen and I were walking across East 72nd St. in New York. A couple was coming toward us. I noticed Allen grinning that evil grin of his. When the couple reached us everyone stopped. I can't remember if this was Mariana or Marnie, but it was one of the ex's beginning with "M", not Minnie May, Millie or Melissa. She was with her new husband. Brunette and pretty as I remember, but she turned the color of ashes when she saw him.

He introduced us and we all went on our way. Didn't seem to faze him at all. Apparently this must have been one of the same wives Anne once referred to in Woodstock.

The story I got from Barbara was that this girl's father was quite wealthy and owned a breeding farm. Allen of course was a horseman, so possibly that was how they met. Anyway, he married her and when she was pregnant he pushed her down a flight of stairs and she lost the baby. Barbara said the father demanded that he leave and they were divorced. I think Barbara said it was Marnie but it may have been Mariana, I don't recall.

Back in New York, Allen used to hang out at Jilly Rizzo's, Gatsby's, and Gleason's Irish Bar. He was always standing up at the bar alone, staring into space, immersed in his own secret world, talking to no one, communicating only with John Barleycorn. It was the same at Foxy's in Las Vegas too. Allen lived in his own private world, a world of his own invention, and it was a world in which laws, rules, regulations, codes of honor and decency were made for others, never for him.

Would I ever manage to really penetrate that world and discover all the things Allen had hidden from me, and why?

CHAPTER TWENTY-FIVE

It was dinnertime but I wasn't hungry. I took an iced tea to the balcony, where I sat watching the lights twinkling on the water like stars. I fell asleep on the chaise longue and didn't wake till nearly dawn. A great time to swim, I decided, so I went to the pool and did laps for about a half hour. When the sun was rising, I took off for the welcome shade of my suite. Megan phoned and we made a date for the end of the day.

We met in the lobby at five.

"Let's go upstairs and talk," I invited.

Before Megan gave me any new information, I wanted to show her the documents in my possession some of which contained puzzling and conflicting data: the many marriage licenses, the separate wills, a "declaration of marriages" he'd made to the Veteran's Administration in 1972, a power of attorney he'd made out to Grace at a time when they were "divorced," and numerous other things.

"What do you make of all this?" I asked.

Megan shook her head, incredulous at reading the information. She pointed out that the dates Allen had given to the Veteran's Administration for six of his marital unions did not coincide with the dates on the corresponding marriage licenses.

"I noticed that too."

"It's also obvious that this V.A. `declaration of marriage' isn't in Allen's handwriting."

"I figured Grace probably wrote it up. Did you see she has me `divorced' from Allen two years before I first married him? And in fact, Allen and I were never divorced."

"Hmmm ... this is odd, too. The `home address' Allen gives here is actually the address of the Federal Courthouse in Miami -- 400 North Miami Avenue, Miami," Megan said, peering at the papers through tinted lenses. "Most of these documents are suspect. Grace's will is a joke, an obvious forgery. I'm surprised the courts didn't pick up on it."

"From experience, I'd say these courts don't look for facts, they just want to move 'em on out."

"Comparing marriage licenses, one sees Allen repeatedly lied about his marital status. His first marriage to Grace in 1962, when he was still married to you, Trudy, Minnie May, Ginny the Guinea and Rosamond

Stone, he refers to himself as a bachelor. On their second marriage in 1972 he's a tad more honest, says he's been married four times previously."

"What made him do it?"

"Psychologically, the bigamies explain themselves. Allen's upbringing, the dysfunctional family, his disrespect for women including his own mother, the compulsive womanizing, his running away, the sociopathic tendencies. But he trips himself up repeatedly, like so many criminals do. It's as if he's crying out for help. He wants to get caught ... but no one ever catches him."

"I hope it's not too late for that. I'd like to see Allen get caught," I said.

Megan was silent a moment. Then she said, "Victoria, have you asked yourself what creates this tremendous attachment and obsession for Allen Topping? Why you put up with his abuse? Why you couldn't walk away?"

"I tried, but Allen always talked me into going back to him. He was very persuasive and hard to resist when he was on his good behavior. Besides, I felt I had nothing else to go to; I was afraid of being alone. When his father died, I thought we could have a new lease on life, that money would make a difference, he could start a business, he could mellow out. And I didn't take my vows lightly. I believed in 'till death do us part.' All marriages have trouble spots; you have to see it through. There were other reasons, deeper, subconscious reasons." I told Megan about Anne Topping's influence in my life and about Cook's prophesy. "There was a whole dynamic going on," I explained. "A concept ... Prince Charming, soul mate, twin flame, one half of my own being ordained since the beginning of time. I believed it with all my heart and soul and mind. I couldn't let go of it. "

"There were other men in your life who could have treated you well, weren't there?"

"True, but most of the time I didn't give them a chance, I was so tied to Allen. In a way, it was like an emotional prison. But a voluntary one."

"You lived with Allen for a number of years; he was in and out of your life for more than three decades, and yet, there are huge gaps in your knowledge of who this man was, his background, his family and friends."

"Allen had no friends. His only friend, to my knowledge, was the son of Jesse Livermore, the famous Wall Street tycoon who jumped out of a window in the crash of '29. I think they went to Yale together."

Megan said. "And yet, when he took you to Las Vegas, he knew his way around. Right off the bat he got a job only a trusted associate gets, dealing 21 at the Frontier, a notorious mobbed up casino."

"You're saying Allen had some connection to the mob. I always thought that myself."

"Yes, Allen had other `friends.' In Vegas, he introduced you to a couple, a man and wife. One of them had a name beginning with `J.'"

"A married couple? Joyce and Howard Russell. Howard was General Manager of one of the big casinos in town. When we first arrived they took us for a ride in Howard's plane to show me Vegas from the air."

"There was something very mysterious with Howard Russell, a disappearance."

"I never heard the full story. I phoned Joyce and she told me Howard had died suddenly. She claimed not to know how, and furthermore they never found the body."

"He wasn't a sick man and he wasn't much more than forty. Did that strike you as strange?"

"It did, but Joyce was not forthcoming."

"As well she should not have been, since her husband was murdered by the long arm of the Chicago mob."

"Now I remember there were rumors about Chicago and the Tony Accardo crew, how they hung Howard on a meat hook and stuck cattle prods in his penis and up his ass, but it was all so gruesome I tuned it out. However, did Allen get connected with the mob?" I mused.

"The connection actually goes way back to his father, to Prohibition, when gangsters and bootleggers mixed freely with society figures like Mr. Topping. They frequented the same speakeasies and even the same parties."

Other pieces of the puzzle seemed now to fit. Allen once told me his father knew Meyer Lansky, Frank Costello and Lucky Luciano. And once again, the Joan Crawford connection popped up: when an unmarried Crawford was seeking to adopt an infant, she ran into problems finding an agency willing to give her a baby. The man who finally fixed everything and found Joan her child Christina was Meyer Lansky! No doubt through their mutual friend, her lover Mr. Topping Sr.

Megan said, "Allen was actually being groomed to front a casino, only he screwed himself out of it. His drinking loused him up. You knew a lot of these mob people yourself, but you had no idea who or what they were."

I said, "All I knew was that they were a bunch of short, old, funny looking men, that they were very nice, very solicitous to me, and always treated me like a lady."

After Megan left, I relaxed in a lounge chair, remembering those days in Las Vegas again, trying to bring back something that would connect it all. It was too late to talk to all the "nice little men" I'd worked for at the Desert Inn. Moe Dalitz had been murdered right on the Strip in broad daylight in a gang war.

There were so many things going on in Vegas that I never understood at the time. I was so young and unsophisticated, none of it registered with me. In retrospect it now seemed that people all over the place were trying to give me messages I never picked up on.

When my neighbor Kathy Long's boyfriend Hank Whalen, the skim courier, allegedly was clipped by the Chicago boys in a phone booth in L.A., I was supposed to understand why. Everyone else did, but it all went way over my head. Kathy herself used to corral Vegas hookers into the ladies room, where she'd lecture them to quit hooking and let her teach them how to make more money via another method. Apparently Kathy's technique involved hustling high rollers, but I was too naive to understand.

Then there was the doctor at Sunrise Hospital who told me I should have killed Allen instead of trying to kill myself, that nobody would have prosecuted me after what he'd done to me. The doctor knew I worked at the Desert Inn for Moe Dalitz. Here again somebody was trying to tell me something I didn't understand. Moe Dalitz was a man of incredible influence in political circles. He would have pulled strings, that was what the doctor was trying to tell me.

And Moe himself had said if I ever had a problem with Allen, just let him know and he'd take care of it. But I hadn't caught his drift.

The night I was to go to work after slitting my wrists, one of the nice bosses, Solly Enders, who was very close to Moe Dalitz, told me, "You can't work like that, with those bandages. Let's go to the Trop and have dinner."

Afterwards, as we strolled back to the casino, Solly handed me five one hundred dollar bills with the words, "Either go gamble or go home." I went home. It was only later that Kathy Long explained I was supposed to understand the money came from Moe, that he offered it as a gesture. I was supposed to understand all this but I didn't.

Only now did I begin to realize what a fool I'd been. So many people would have helped me because they knew all about Allen.

Once when I asked Allen how he knew these people if he'd never been to Vegas before, Allen's reply was "Don't ask silly questions."

I thought about the question Megan had asked me about Allen, why I'd stuck with him. I guess Cook said it best: "Caant live one widout da otha... no matta how fah, always cam bak togetha ... You and him be one. Two peas, one pod, batty and bench, one spirit." I believed in the veracity of Cook's words, "He bring you good times, bad times ... but you give him you heart and it will work out fie you, you mark my word, it's in your stars."

Most of our reconciliations were hard won on Allen's part, with me fighting and resisting, sometimes as much as eight months. Gradually, Allen always wore me down. All I had to do was open that door the merest crack, and that was it. Could Allen ever be charming when he wanted to be. He was an incredible lover and when he wasn't drinking or in one of his Jekyll and Hyde periods, God knows he was fun, sweet, kind, generous, thoughtful, considerate, loving, caring.

I've often thought back to the champagne bath Allen gave me in New York, my first deep vaginal orgasms, the first time we practiced Imsak, the words Allen instilled in my subconscious. He told me no other man would ever get to me like he could, that we were one mind, one soul, one body, one being, that I would always belong to him. I do believe, in retrospect, that Allen exercised some strange hypnotic power over me, and that he was able to enforce this power in the sexual embrace by practicing a form of sex magick.

What was the alternative to being with Allen? Unlike most people, I had no support system -- no family, no home. Having been abandoned as an infant by the death of my parents and again when my grandmother died, I was alone and rudderless. Allen became the only roots I knew. It was hard to turn my back and confront a void. Added to that, the chemistry was there, the magic, the incredible sex. That alone was hard to give up.

Faced by Allen's destructive patterns, I often went into denial, I repressed my feelings, refusing to admit what was happening. Then the minute Allen held out his arms to comfort me, I was lost, back in the old trap. I felt loved again. I was addicted to Allen, always expecting things to change. After all, Cook had said, "It gwang get bettah."

And sometimes it did.

CHAPTER TWENTY-SIX

Megan and I touched bases again a few days later. She suggested lunch at the Breakers in Palm Beach. We made it for 2 pm.

I dressed in a taupe leather skirt and silk blouse to match, pulling it together with matching pumps and purse.

I was curious about the ways in which Palm Beach had changed, who might still be around, what new people hung out there now. The Topping estate had been sold; I'd heard a lot of the old guard had auctioned their furniture and were occupying empty houses just in order to keep living in Palm Beach.

Appearing at the Breakers for the luncheon appointment with Megan, I felt a warm glow of recognition. I'd forgotten how breathtaking the Breakers was. Megan couldn't wait to tell me the latest piece of information she'd discovered via psychic means.

"Something came to me about your grandmother's death," Megan began. "I know it would be difficult to prove, especially after all this time, but your grandmother did not die in debt. She left a sizable fortune that by all rights should have come to you."

It sounded more than plausible. When I heard Nana died penniless, owing huge amounts, I couldn't believe it. My Nana had always told me some day I would be a very wealthy woman, and I'm sure she was not mistaken. But I was so young, naïve and inexperienced, I was at the mercy of the barristers whom I had no choice but to trust implicitly.

"Ducky," Megan said, "you were screwed. Do you have any idea how much money your grandmother left? You should be worth about 25 million at this juncture."

What a difference even a fraction of that money would have made. As Megan had said, proving her assertions would, especially after such a length of time, be nigh onto impossible; nevertheless, I was sure it was all true. I was engulfed by a sense of loss coupled with injustice. Nana would be heartbroken to know I'd been cheated out of what was rightfully mine. I felt sadness for my grandmother to have trusted and believed I'd be provided for, then going to heaven and discovering the truth, that we'd both been duped.

"Well," I sighed, realizing there was absolutely nothing to be done at this late stage, "at least Allen didn't get the money."

"He couldn't have handled it."

"I guess if I'd had all that money Allen would have hung around until it was gone. What a life that would have been! It was bad enough as it was. Maybe he might have even tried to kill me if he thought I was that rich."

"He practically did, as it was."

"Speaking of killing people, do you have any psychic impressions on why my old boss in Las Vegas, Moe Dalitz, was rubbed out?" I asked.

Megan said, "Dalitz crossed the Chicago mob, the Outfit, by forming an alliance with their arch enemy, Joe Bonnano. So Dalitz' death was a mob hit. Four bullets hit him, but he survived. He was taken to Sunrise Hospital. The Chicago boss, Tony Accardo, (aka `Joe Batters,' also known as `Big Tuna') called for his man in Florida, Gussie Alex, to finish the job.

"Gussie flew into Vegas. He'd touched bases with Sidney Korshak in Palm Springs before he left Fort Lauderdale. Sid knows everybody in Vegas; he's been connected there since the days of Bugsy Siegel."

"Why, I've met Sidney Korshak," I said. "Korshak's an attorney, right? Charming guy! We met in L.A. in connection with Governor Pat Brown's office. I liked Sid. I heard he's been sweet on Stella Stevens and Jill St. John for years. I think he has a wife named Bea. I was even invited to their house for a New Year's party, but I couldn't go."

"Sidney Korshak leads a double life. He's a successful labor lawyer, business adviser to Fortune 500 corporations, friend to Hollywood stars and executives, but at the same time he's described by high level Justice Department officials as `one of the four or five most powerful men in organized crime in America.' He also maintains a close relationship with politicians like Pat and Jerry Brown.

"Sid got his start repping members of the Capone mob. Later he became key adviser to Tony Accardo, Accardo was Capone's bodyguard and took over the reins of the Chicago outfit.

"Gussie and Sid talked over the plot to finish off Dalitz. Gussie told Sid he needed to get to someone at Sunrise Hospital, and Sid set him up with a shady doctor there, who in turn connected him with one of the hospital's orderlies.

"The orderly's name," Megan continued, "was Ben Jackson. He was paid $100,000 in cash by Gussie Alex, who left on a flight for Phoenix the next day.

"The news came shortly thereafter. Moe Dalitz, Mr. Las Vegas, mob boss who started out with the Purple Gang in Detroit, moved on to gangsterdom with the Mayfield Road branch of the Cleveland

Combination and became a legend on the West Coast, had been poisoned in the intensive care unit at Sunrise Hospital. The `godfather of Las Vegas' was dead."

Megan finished the story and said, "Do you understand now?"

I looked long and hard at Megan and asked, "Who are you?"

"I'm a psychic, dear, that's all. Not to worry, I'm not a mob associate, not at the present time, anyway."

"Wow, Megan, that was some story! And you got all that psychically?"

"Not all. Some of it's general knowledge, available at your local bookstore. I filled in the blanks, which is what a good psychic often does."

Somehow, I felt there was more than met the eye here. Until the present I'd not questioned Megan much on her background, feeling she'd tell me what she wanted when she wanted. But now I was curious. I had to know more about her. So I asked.

As I'd come to suspect, Megan had known mob figures in the past. When she'd first arrived in the United States from her native Ireland at the age of eighteen, she'd met and fallen in love with one of the top members of the Chicago outfit, a very rich older, married Jewish guy who owned trucking companies in Chicago and had investments in Las Vegas. She'd become this guy Jake's mistress and he'd given her homes both on Chicago's Lake Shore Drive as well as in Vegas.

After his death, she'd hooked up with another rich married guy with Chicago/ Vegas mob connections, Lou, with whom she had a child out of wedlock. Megan married after that into a totally different milieu; her late second husband, Ed, was Chairman of the Board of one of the biggest banks in Chicago and had thus given her respectability. She became active on the Chicago social scene, planning charity balls and the like. The whole town knew her background and not only accepted it but was proud of it. The psychic stuff made it even more so. After Ed died, Megan moved to Florida.

I was glad Megan told me her story. I felt I knew her better now.

The very next day, something totally unforeseen occurred. Hoping to discover clues about Joan Crawford's relationship with Mr. Topping, I took out a biography of the star from the library.

After reading the chapters on the first part of Crawford's life, I tried to pin down the likely years for the Crawford/Topping affair to have been carried on. I decided this would have been when Crawford was eighteen to nineteen and Mr. Topping twenty-six to twenty-seven.

In 1924 Joan Crawford was beginning her career and had been spotted out of town by J.J. Shubert who signed her for Broadway, where she appeared in "Innocent Eyes," a review starring the French singer Mistinguett.

I already knew that Mr. Topping belonged to the tradition of rich playboys who hung out at stage doors seeking the company of chorines, bestowing expensive gifts for their favors. He had also frequented the Harlem club scene so popular with society figures where Joan Crawford moonlighted. Allen's father and Joan also spent time in the same famous speakeasy on West 56th Street.

Late in 1925, Joan was offered a Hollywood contract and went out to California. For that reason, I zeroed in on 1924-25 to have been the likeliest time for their affair to have been at its peak, when the honey incident(s) occurred. (The relationship could well have continued after that as well).

Mr. Topping must have married Anne around 1919, since Allen was born in 1920 (he sometimes gave the date as 1921). By 1924, Anne, retired from the stage, was the mother of two young pre-schoolers. Knowing Anne, it's easy to assume she eschewed golden showers or anything kinky. No doubt she was too straight laced for Mr. Topping's exotic tastes, whereas the effervescent, ambitious Joan Crawford was eager to go along with just about anything. This one gathers from her reputation, at least.

That made sense. But there was something more that I was unprepared for -- Joan Crawford's brother, Hal Le Sueur. As I went flipping through the book's photo section, I couldn't believe my eyes when I came upon Le Sueur, pictured with his sister.

I could have been looking at Allen Topping! The exact same features -- the teeth, the brows, lips, jaw, the smile, and those eyes. Cover the lower half of the smiling face and you see that Hal's eyes are angry, just like Allen's eyes. The hands were the same as well. Hal's hand was raised to his chin, showing long fingers, absolutely square in shape, with beautiful nails -- everything identical to Allen.

It was then I remembered the incident so many years ago in East Los Angeles in front of the seedy hotel on Alvarado Street. That time warp was playing tricks. I looked at the photograph again and remembered "Hal." He was Hal Le Sueur, Joan Crawford's brother!

I read on, seeking any information on Hal Le Sueur I could find.

He was a failed actor and alcoholic who went to work as a night clerk in a dumpy hotel on Alvarado Street, the book said.

Interesting that Allen and Hal seemed to lead parallel lives of sorts, both alcoholics, both night clerks in derelict hotels.

Then I read that Joan Crawford, née Lucille Le Sueur, and her brother Hal Le Sueur's mother's maiden name was Anna Bell Johnson. Bell? Could Anna Bell Johnson be related to Grace Bell Topping? Were Mr. Topping and Joan Crawford cousins? Did that spell incest?

Allen Topping and Hal Le Sueur had to be related! What else would I yet discover about Allen that I didn't already know?

CHAPTER TWENTY-SEVEN

In my attempt to understand Allen Topping, I wondered if there might be something in his family history that could explain his strange pathology. Anne had said there was nothing genetically wrong with her son, but I wasn't so sure. So I researched the Topping family tree back through the centuries. I learned many Toppings had an alcohol problem. That defect definitely seemed to run in the genes.

Rich WASP playboys, mostly Yale men, the Toppings led charmed lives surrounded by yachts, planes, and beautiful women. Many Toppings besides Allen were multi married: cousins Dan and Bob Topping between them had some twelve wives, six apiece, including one they shared, actress Arline Judge, who herself had six or seven husbands and at one time was the most married actress in Hollywood. Other Topping wives included glamorous stars like Lana Turner, Kay Sutton, and Norwegian Olympic skating champion turned Hollywood movie star Sonia Henie.

Toppings were also associated with sports: their ranks included renowned world class polo players; Dan and Bob were into baseball as owners of both the Brooklyn Dodgers and the New York Yankees. Allen's aunt, Dorothy Topping Bomeisler, married Yale all-American football star, Douglas Bomeisler.

Toppings died young. Dan was 54, Bob 61, Mr. Topping not much older. Topping spouses also often went to early graves, including Douglas Bomleiser at 61. Allen seemed to have outlived them all.

Ever since my first reading with Megan Duffy, something had been gnawing at me that I had relegated to the back of my mind. This concerned what Megan had told me about "changing heads," the Afro Caribbean magical process performed at cemeteries that had saved Allen's life. Although it terrified me, I knew I must not delay. If I were to come closer to discovering what happened to Allen, I would have to investigate the closed, hidden society of those people -- Haitians and Cubans who performed these peculiar rites.

I had entertained notions of doing so in Miami, but then during a visit to New York, a friend mentioned she knew local people, deep initiates in this practice, who could help answer my questions. My friend reassured me that these people would not pull any scare tactics such as animal sacrifice and the like.

Nevertheless, it was with trepidation that I accompanied my friend on that first visit to Spanish Harlem to meet "the Old Man," as he was called, the palero or padrino, the godfather. My friend said he was the "head of the White Table" in New York City and a very important man in his religion.

The Old Man greeted us at the door of the ground floor four room walk through apartment he shared with his wife and ten children. He was slender and youthful looking, with a head of closely cropped grey hair, no baldness, the perfect picture of health. Bare chested, barelegged, he wore only a pair of tan cotton shorts. His legs were sturdy and strong. At least a dozen or more necklaces of colored beads and silver chains hung around his neck. I admired how firm his arm and chest muscles were and the fact that he had a beautiful set of teeth, although I didn't realize at the time they were false. Actually, The Old Man really wasn't particularly old, appearing to be in his robust early 60's, but he had been called "the Old Man" ever since coming to the States from his native Cuba a couple of decades ago.

In Cuba, the Old Man had been Fidel Castro's padrino, and as an expert in Molotov cocktails, a key figure in the revolution. Born into a rich family, at 12 he had run away to live with "the people of the wood," to study their ways. Later on, after he became a palero, he performed many rituals for his *ahiyado* Castro, including immersing the leader in a bathtub full of blood to give him the magical power to survive all attempts on his life.

The Old Man ushered us into an area of the railroad flat that had been partitioned off to function as a consultation room. This room was unlike anything I had ever seen before. It contained many rocks and a number of iron pots with dirt and various objects inside them. There were flowers everywhere, white and yellow chrysanthemums and red roses, and fragrant sandalwood incense was burning. Two white doves on perches cooed softly. The lighting was dim, but not so dark that I didn't notice a few cockroaches crawling about the walls and even some tiny mice scampering through holes. When I recoiled, the Old Man laughed and gestured with a not to worry attitude. He spoke no English at all and at that point we had to rely on my friend's mediocre command of Spanish.

"Don't worry, Victoria," my friend soothed, "all creatures are friendly here." I wasn't so sure but took one of the folding chairs offered me.

Just then, I noticed a tiny mouse on top of one of the rocks, drinking from a silver cup. I learned this mouse was special, that he belonged to one of the orishas, or gods. No attempt was made to get rid of mice because they served a purpose as helpers in the religion. Roaches were another matter; the Old Man and his wife had been after the landlord to get the exterminator in to take care of them.

The Old Man first threw a set of four coconut rinds a number of times. Based on whether the white or the dark sides came up, and in what pattern, the Old Man could provide answers to my questions.

At that point, Kitty, the padrino's wife, arrived home with six young children in tow. The members of this brood ranged in age from 12 on down. Four older children were yet to come. Telling the bigger kids to mind their siblings and help them with their homework, Kitty joined us in the consultation room. She was a short, chubby Puerto Rican woman with a wonderful warm smile, Afro style dyed red hair, and an air of wisdom about her. She was also obviously very pregnant with a set of twins, I was to learn. Kitty was about 40, much younger than her husband. Not all the kids belonged to the padrino, but were Kitty's by former marriages. She'd started in at sixteen and wasn't ready to quit yet.

Fortunately Kitty was completely bilingual, thus I got all the answers and explanations I needed. The coconuts revealed that Allen definitely was alive, that he had indeed perpetrated the insurance scam with Grace, for which they had collected "*mucho dinero.*" Just to be completely certain, the Old Man checked and rechecked, and over and over the confirmation was definitely yes on all my questions. The Old Man kept talking to the coconuts and asking, "*Mi confirma,*" then he'd toss the rinds again and exclaim, "*Si, señor!*"

After checking the coconuts to satisfaction, the Old Man threw a set of seashells which were identical to the ones Cook had used back in Jamaica, and just as the coconuts had given positive answers to my queries, now the shells were also *si, señor* on all counts. Kitty and the Old Man explained the patterns to me.

Nor was this by any means an exercise in mechanical hocus pocus. I was aware that the atmosphere in the little consultation room was highly charged with an electric energy, that the longer we continued, the deeper we went into it, the more power the room seemed to contain.

Kitty and the Old Man conversed in Spanish for a few minutes before Kitty turned to me. I was very moved by the tenderness of her gaze. She now told me I must try to think way back in time, thirty years ago, to be exact, when I had had contact with Allen's father, when he had given me a thorough analysis of my husband's problems that I had failed to heed.

I met Allen's father only once. It was shortly after he had proposed the sum of one million dollars in exchange for my signing papers to commit Allen to an institution. When next we spoke, I suggested a face to face meeting and Mr. Topping offered to send a car for me the following day.

At 10 a.m. a chauffeured black Cadillac arrived. Ominous, I thought. I tapped on the glass partition of the vehicle's black interior to ask the driver, "Where are we going?"

"To Long Island," the driver replied. "Mr. Topping thought you might be more comfortable at his house rather than in the office. "He told me it was not a business meeting, Mrs. Topping."

I closed the window, enjoying the scenery. I was finally going to meet this "gargoyle," as Allen called his father. I was uneasy.

Two and a half hours later, we arrived at Beach Lane in Old Quogue. The Toppings' large white brick home stood facing the water, a circular driveway leading to its front entrance. As the chauffeur extended a gloved hand to help me out of the car, the Atlantic breeze brought to me the fragrance I always smelled on Allen's chest of salt sea, air and sun.

Almost automatically, the front door opened and a butler ushered me in. As I stood on the threshold in anticipation, I took in the surroundings. The house interior was decorated in 17th century New England style. The butler showed me into the library and said, "Mr. Topping will be with you shortly." Through glass doors, I caught sight of the 150 foot Topping yacht, "Careless Babe," moored at the end of the dock. Rich or poor, I thought to myself, it's nice to have money.

Next to the door, framed in gold leaf, was a family crest with a large dark arm in a fist at the top, and at the bottom, an eagle with wings spread.

Just then, a tall, tan, fine looking gentleman with white hair entered the room. I thought I was looking at Allen Jr. a quarter of a century hence. Mr. Topping was dressed casually in white cotton twill trousers, matching Brooks shirt and navy blazer, on the pocket of which was repeated the design of the family crest.

Out of respect for Mr. Topping's age, I immediately stood up. He was smiling cordially as he extended his hand to greet me. Shaking it, I was surprised to feel how cold it was.

"Well, well," he said, in the same privileged, blue stocking Anglo Saxon patrician tones his son used, "it's certainly a pleasure to be meeting my elusive daughter-in-law at last!"

"Elusive?" I repeated. "I haven't been hiding anywhere, Sir."

"Then let's hold Allen Jr. responsible for the breech in good manners," Mr. Topping said. "Please be seated, Victoria. Don't be nervous. I don't bite. Your eyes look as large as tea cups. You needn't be uncomfortable."

I noticed he shivered slightly, and at that, he went to the thermostat to turn up the heat. It wasn't cold out. This was summer, yet Mr. Topping was cold? Strange. We sat down facing each other. His eyes were the same vivid blue as his son's.

He said, "Victoria, you are a lovely girl, but far too young to begin to understand Allen Jr.'s problems. And believe me, he has many."

"Mr. Topping," I said, "I should like to know what these problems are and how you expect to deal with them by institutionalizing Allen."

Mr. Topping looked stern when he replied, "An institution is the only place qualified to deal with Allen's situation."

My heart had started jumping. Mr. Topping prefaced his remarks by saying he really did not want to tell me the whole story, that he was afraid I wouldn't be up to hearing the truth, but I insisted. "Allen is my husband, Mr. Topping. I have a right to know; you must tell me everything."

"All right," Mr. Topping agreed reluctantly. He began by describing two spoiled children whose mother could not discipline them but always had to phone her husband in the city to come home to Tarrytown to spank them. Allen, according to his father, was a bright, precocious student at Irving Prep and was admitted to Yale, but never seemed motivated and lacked ambition. Mr. Topping was convinced that Allen's enlistment in the Army prior to the outbreak of the war was a deliberate act to spite his father.

Along the way, there were innumerable problems with alcohol, with handling money, finding the right vocation in life, and in assuming responsibility, just to mention a few areas. There was also the matter of his war injuries, which had worsened things considerably. Furthermore, Allen's relationships with the opposite sex had convinced my father-in-law that his son hated and wanted to punish women, that he had a Don Juan complex and was a latent homosexual. In Mr. Topping's opinion, Allen was a charming sociopath and worse, a psychopath. Ordinary rules did not apply to Allen; he considered himself above the law.

"I apologize if this sounds harsh, my dear," Mr. Topping said, adding that he had tried to soft soap everything, that there was even more he hesitated to tell me.

But I had heard quite enough. This could hardly be a true picture of my beloved Prince Charming. Somewhere along the line there must have been a terrible misunderstanding for a father to judge his own son in such an unfavorable light. Obviously, Mr. Topping had an axe to grind. He was prejudiced against Allen. I was more determined than ever I would never do as my father-in-law wished, never sign the papers to commit my husband.

Mr. Topping must have perceived my distress, for he asked, "Do you want a glass of water? You've turned so pale."

"No, thank you," I replied. "I don't want your million dollars, sir. I love Allen with all my heart and soul. I couldn't sign his life away. Allen would die having to live locked up. And in my opinion, he doesn't need institutionalizing."

Mr. Topping saw it was no use. He said, "Would you like some lunch before you go? It's rather late. You must be hungry."

"No, thank you, sir. I really should be getting back to the city."

"I'm certainly delighted to have met you, Victoria," he said, rising. "We must see one another again. After all, you're family now. And who knows, perhaps given more thought, you may change your mind about what we've discussed." He rang for the butler and ordered, "Call the car. My daughter-in-law Mrs. Topping is leaving now."

When we shook hands I noticed his palm was still ice cold. For a brief instant, I had the impression of him as a young man, licking honey off of Joan Crawford's crotch. However, I erased this thought, smiled and said, "I'm glad to have met you, too, Mr. Topping."

"Don't be a stranger, now," he returned warmly. "Let's be in touch soon."

He phoned the next morning to tell me he had purchased and would be paying the premiums on a life insurance policy on Allen's life. "Just in case," he said. Mr. Topping added that should he die himself, the premiums would be fully covered through a trust. I didn't ask who the beneficiary was but assumed it must be me.

Aside from all the true things Mr. Topping was trying to tell me about my husband, my strongest impression of Allen's father was his shivering in the middle of summer and the coldness of his hands. Later on, I was to learn these were signs of slow arsenic poisoning.

A few short years after that, my father-in-law died, according to Allen and Barbara, by slow arsenic poisoning administered by Glad Ass.

"Your father-in-law gave you the facts. He wasn't making anything up. If you'd listened you might have had second thoughts," Kitty said, "to say nothing of a million dollars. But of course, love is blind."

Why did Allen always have me so chained to him? The Old Man said even though Allen and I hadn't been together in years, I still was still chained and asked did I want to get free? I looked startled. I assured the Old Man, through Kitty, that yes, I did want to be free. Kitty asked what I was doing Sunday morning. Could I come up to the Bronx? The old man kept his many *prendas* and his "foundation" there and we would be able to work more extensively in this location than at the apartment in the barrio. The old man would perform a ritual and would be able to check deeper on the matter of "changing heads."

I paid the Old Man twenty dollars for the consultation and agreed to come to the address in the Bronx Sunday.

Alone early Sunday morning, I was feeling faint hearted as I followed Kitty's directions and boarded the uptown Lexington Avenue number 6 subway. The train was empty but for a few somnulent passengers, which increased my uneasiness. I tried to look hostile, unobtrusive and poor, praying I wouldn't be attacked by the type of criminals New York is full of. I got off the subway right by a huge old armory and as Kitty had instructed, walked six blocks full of mom and pop Spanish language stores, turning a corner before I came to the address. I walked through a ground floor garbage can/plastic bag laden courtyard and knocked on the rear door. A rotund Hispanic man of about thirty admitted me. He introduced himself as Mike, superintendent of the building, and led me to a huge basement, part of which had been sectioned off with particle board.

A door had been built inside this room leading to yet another room, which housed the old man's foundation and his "*prendas*." I wasn't sure about the significance of the *prendas*, but they, like the objects back in the barrio apartment's consultation room, were all of iron and rock, however far more extensive. Here the iron and rocks were piled up one on top of the other, resembling a cave and reaching some 20 feet in all directions, right, left and upwards. There were a number of huge cauldrons as well. Votive candles burned in several nooks and crannies. It was very awesome and impressive.

The Old Man greeted me with a big hug and a kiss. He was still wearing shorts and a pile of necklaces but this time had put on a tee shirt saying "New York Mets." Kitty embraced me with a warm smile.

I accepted the invitation to sit down on one of the folding bridge chairs. The Old Man passed out cigars to all. Everyone lit up, so I followed suit. The old man puffed away, blowing his smoke ceremoniously at different angles and into different pots and rocks. He intoned prayers in an African language, sang songs, drank several mouthfuls of liquor from a Gordon's gin bottle, gulped more gin and spat it out in the direction of his *prendas*. Then he went into a sort of trance, in which his whole personality seemed to change into someone else's.

Everyone continued puffing on the cigars, so I did likewise, although I was puzzled. The Old Man seemed to be babbling and I had no idea what he was saying. Then he started to gag and kept pointing his finger at me. I wondered what in blazes was going on.

Kitty said, "Do you remember when you gagged like that? You were a little girl. You didn't like oatmeal."

This was uncanny. How could anyone know that? "Yes, I hated oatmeal as a child, I gagged on it and couldn't eat it. Once I was forced to remain at the table for five hours without being able to keep it down. After that I never had to eat oatmeal again."

The old man was still gagging, clutching his stomach and pointing at me.

"You see," Kitty explained, "you were very stubborn. You decided you weren't going to like oatmeal, and nobody could persuade you otherwise once your mind was made up. It was the same with your husband, stubborn devotion to an idea. That was part of the problem, but one side only. What else do you remember about your childhood?"

Very little, I was afraid. I strained to recall...

... I am a long, skinny, red baby with huge blue eyes and very long legs who cries all the time. I walk around in my crib wearing pajamas with feet. I have whooping cough and I'm screaming ... Nana is talking to the nurse, saying I'm a sick child because I have no mother.

... Now I'm three. I'm always running and falling down. Nana always scolds me because "little ladies don't run."

... One day Nana dresses me up in a pink organza dress, a bonnet, gloves and a pink and blue parasol. She tells me not to run. As soon as I think I'm out of Nana's sight, I begin running, pushing the parasol up and down in the air. I trip and fall. Nana scolds me. I have skinned my knees again and ripped my first pair of silk stockings. I must be three or four years old.

... I'm seven or eight now. I've been taught to set the table for a dinner party already, and I know how to manicure my fingers and toenails. "Well-bred young girls are always well groomed, well dressed, and never leave soiled panties for the servants to wash, because it's too personal," I've been told.

... I don't go to any school and Nana says I never will until I'm eighteen. Private tutors teach me. I love Nana. She has never punished me except once because I played tennis with a colored boy. Nana whacked me with a tennis racket then. The reason I have no friends is because I don't know anybody my age... I'm always in the kennels or the stables when I'm supposed to be in the house... I like horses and dogs much better than people."

The room seemed to reel and I felt like I was losing my equilibrium. Kitty, speaking in a low and reverent voice, told me that the orishas, the gods of the religion, were present. I could certainly feel it, for the whole atmosphere had become charged with magnetic current. A loud yell escaped from the Old Man and his body almost snapped in two. Kitty said the spirit had possessed him, and he was going to speak as that spirit.

Kitty translated the Old Man's Spanish: "You were devoted to the ideal of your twin soul, whom you called Prince Charming. First of all, it's true, he is your other half. When God created the world, he created man and woman, one being. Later God split us all up and now we are always looking for that other half.

"Most people can live their lives with a mate who may not be the twin soul, just someone they're friendly and compatible with. Not you. You had the idea in your mind that you must find your true other half, you found him and you couldn't let go, even if he couldn't live up to your expectations. The reason he couldn't do better by you, the spirit says, is that he was injured; this man was not a whole, healthy person.

"You had very firmly planted the Prince Charming concept in your subconscious. Most young girls dream from early childhood about their Prince Charming just as you did, but they lose this idea once they have their first boyfriend at about age 15. You never lost it. You fell in love with the idea you had created in your soul and couldn't let it go.

"First there was your conditioning. Do you remember a black woman in the Caribbean who prepared you that it was definite? She said you should stick with him no matter what. You took her advice to heart.

"Other than that, did you ever feel that your husband hypnotized you? Do you recall a special kind of sexual practice in which he hypnotized you?"

I certainly did remember. Imsak. I had suspected as much.

"He bewitched you, enslaved you, brainwashed you from the time when you were a teenager. You had to obey. He subjugated your will, locked you in, tied you up in knots. You were unable to move even when you wanted to. Whenever you had the feeling you must get away, there was always an interference or obstacle, a reason why you couldn't.

"You even had to contend with his mother begging you not to leave him. She was a very seductive, manipulative woman, wasn't she? You had a deep desire to please this woman, your mother figure, just as you wanted to please your grandmother. You never had a real mother, so you transferred these feelings to these other women. You thought you had to please them or they wouldn't love you. You did as your mother-in-law asked, just as you did as your grandmother asked.

"Allen used every angle possible. He had a powerful mind. With one glance he could break all your resolution. Your need for security was so strong, you longed for the sense of family, of roots. Growing up, you lived in a vacuum with no friends, nobody to interact with, you had no experience to help deal with life's realities.

"You never had a father. You had a mother substitute but no father figure at all. This husband of yours, an older man, assumed this role in your subconscious. You were always attracted to older men because of that unresolved father problem. Perhaps the lack of a father convinced you that you deserved to be abused by a father substitute? Your subconscious was conditioned not to accept any other man in your life. It was a transference you made, it was all consuming and it was absolute.

"Your Nana wanted to protect you from the world, but she couldn't protect you from yourself. You cultivated this hope, this dream, the idea of Prince Charming. And on one level, it is real. Your husband is that other half of yourself. The black woman was right. The tragedy was he was impaired, unable to function in a healthy manner.

"You kept expecting if you could be the good girl you were brought up to be, Prince Charming would recognize it. Why didn't you wake up to reality? Stubbornness, a stunted consciousness, and self punishment, a guilt over something you feel you deserve to be punished for.

"The black Caribbean woman said you owed him a debt and that was true. The debt has been paid. It was paid with your love, your devotion and your suffering, all your pain and sorrow. You tried to be kind, but in this lifetime he can't be helped. Only God can help him."

I wept, as much for Allen as for myself.

By now, the Old Man was coming out of his trance. He took several deep breaths and sat down. Kitty offered him a cup of water which he drank quickly. Everyone was silent. Mike had put out his cigar. The Old Man looked tired. Kitty was concentrating her full energies on him, as if waiting for a signal. Gradually, he seemed to return to normal. Then she turned to me.

"Do you have any questions?" she asked.

I wanted to know if the Old Man had been able to check out the "changing heads" business. I asked, "Did Allen have the *cambio de cabeza*?"

Kitty and the Old Man talked for a few minutes, the Old Man nodded in my direction, and then Kitty told me yes, absolutely Allen did have the "head change."

"Was it successful?" I asked.

"Oh, yes, the person whose head was claimed is now dead and buried, so it is successful for your husband. Not for the other person, of course."

"Could you tell me something about it?"

They told me the process was arduous, that very few paleros knew how to do it, that it was a very "big job" commanding a lot of money. The Old Man had performed this ritual many times in his native country, but things were different in the U.S.; people were scared of it, it was hard to find the right graveyards, and you had to bribe the cemetery owners, which was one reason it cost so much. The climate of receptivity might improve over the long haul, however, given the large influx of Latino and Caribbean peoples now settling here. Changing heads was in their culture, and some of them were going into the cemetery business, thus it might become easier to perform the rite in the future. Allen had had his head change done in a graveyard outside Tampa, Florida, I was told.

"I've heard this method sometimes may not last indefinitely," I said.

"True, it's a temporary fix," Kitty answered. "In most cases it can give the same number of years which the victim, that is, the person whose head was 'claimed' might have had left to live out, but not always. For instance, if one of your husband's vital organs were severely damaged, he couldn't continue living beyond a certain point no matter what."

I asked just how long they thought Allen had left on earth. The answer was probably no more than two years. Due to drinking, his liver was in bad shape. The changing heads might have to be repeated again in an attempt to give him a bit more time, but there was a limit after the body broke down.

All the psychics said Allen was still alive; all along, I felt he was, now the Old Man had confirmed it. How was I to prove Allen and Grace had perpetrated the insurance scam? The insurance carrier, at my behest, was carrying out a full investigation.

What could I accurately deduce? I had already speculated that it was someone else, a patient near death, who had been admitted to the V.A. Hospital under the name of Allen Topping, that after this person's demise and cremation, Allen had assumed the identity of Judge Branson, married Grace under that name, and taken off with her for parts unknown (which several psychics believed to be Canada).

How was I going to locate Allen and Grace? Private detectives assured me this could be done, but to initiate the search demanded a minimum $10,000 retainer with no guarantee that more wouldn't be required. At that point, I could not afford it and decided to take California psychic Joan Brooks' advice and write this book, which Joan declared would lead to the capture and arrest of Allen and Grace. The Old Man now repeated what Joan had said; once the book was out, the amount of publicity generated would assure Allen and Grace being found.

I accompanied Kitty and the Old Man from the Bronx basement to the subway station. Kitty was so great with child she was having difficulty walking. I had paid the Old Man $30 for the ritual, and when we got to a corner flower stand, he insisted on using $6.00 of that money to buy Kitty and me each a bouquet of yellow and white chrysanthemums, which he offered with a great flourish.

I was touched by his gesture. Both Kitty and he were such sweet, good hearted people. As bizarre as my two experiences with them had been, I felt comforted in their presence. From what I'd already known about Allen's "head change," I had to find people who understood what was entailed to explain it all to me, even though I'd been frightened. Trepidations notwithstanding, I'd forced myself to be open to the Old Man's unorthodoxy, and my reaching out into left field had brought a serendipity: these people, in the short span of time I'd known them, had offered me more compassion than I'd received most of my life. Isn't it amazing, I thought, that people of such diametrically opposite lifestyles and cultures can meet, focus their energies in a one pointed manner, and break common ground. If only Allen and I had had more of that.

During the subway ride Kitty and I chatted like two old friends. I told her, "From the day I met Allen Topping, my life became a tragedy. I never knew Prince Charming was a false prophet until it was too late."

Kitty said, "You were so young, a teenager with no roots, too young to be turned out in the world alone. You had no money, no contacts, no support system. Where could you go? I know women who are afraid of making the trip between the Bronx and Manhattan, that's how scared of being on their own they are. With nowhere to turn, they find a man and they stick with him even without the illusion of Prince Charming. Some of them, believe it or not, experience a whole lot worse than you did. It isn't easy being poor. This is life, this is reality. It is like that for some women."

I embraced both the Old Man and Kitty and we said our farewells. A lot of my questions had been answered and I had a greater understanding of the long voyage I'd taken over the past three decades. Allen would always be a part of me, but now there was a shift in perception of the tragedy he'd brought to my life.

I was overcome with "ifs": if I'd been older and wiser; if I hadn't believed in Prince Charming; if Cook hadn't told me Allen was it; if I'd tried to make a go of things with Andrew; if I'd had a family; if I hadn't been swayed by my mother-in-law; if I'd accepted Mr. Topping's offer of the million dollars; if I'd listened to Amanda, kept on modeling; if I'd said yes to Don; if Allen hadn't taken me out of New York; if I hadn't let him make decisions and handle the money; if I'd accepted Moe Dalitz or given Howard Koch the green light; if Denny Slater had lived; if I'd kept my resolutions to shut Allen out instead of caving in to him; if Allen had gotten the help he needed; if I could have relinquished my dreams ... and so on. But none of this happened. Instead, my love fueled the fire; I allowed Allen Topping to be my all in all.

For some readers my story will seem unresolved. But how often am

I reminded of the thousands of people living unresolved lives -- couples nationwide whose children are missing, some even for years on end. How hope must surge in their hearts that someone, recognizing their child's photo on a brown paper bag, would phone the hotline and deliver to these parents' the resolution of their most fervent desire: assurance their child was still alive.

I also think of the families of veterans missing in action for decades who haven't relinquished hope, people who will continue praying for answers until their final breath. They too are leading unresolved lives. I feel for all who, like me, have lived in the precarious state of limbo. Not knowing is a trying and challenging state to be. Is there is no answer? What is one to do if there is nothing to be done? How to get on with one's life? In my case, I go on believing Allen Topping lives and will be found. Perhaps someone reading my book will unlock the tangled mysteries I am seeking to solve.

If Allen himself should see this book, what would I want him to know? I have written these pages with more pain than I thought I could endure, yet much remains to be said. Allen, please do pick up a phone, reach out to the wife who truly loved you, who will love you always no matter what. And please remember: it's supposed to get better.

I believe that with all my heart.

######

FIN

ABOUT THE AUTHOR

Jeanne Rejaunier graduated from Vassar College, and did postgraduate studies in Paris, Florence, Rome, and at UCLA. While a student at Vassar, she began a career as a professional model, and subsequently became an actress in Manhattan, Hollywood and Europe, appearing on and off Broadway, in films and television, on magazine covers internationally and as the principal in dozens of network television commercials.

Rejaunier achieved international success with the publication of her first novel, *The Beauty Trap*, which sold over one million copies and became Simon and Schuster's fourth best seller of the year, the film rights to which were purchased outright by Avco-Embassy. Rejaunier has publicized her books in national and international tours on three continents in five languages. Her writing has been extolled in feature stories in *Life, Playboy, Mademoiselle, Seventeen, BusinessWeek, Fashion Weekly, Women's Wear, W, McCalls, American Homemaker, Parade, Let's Live, Marie-Claire, Epoca, Tempo, Sogno, Cine-Tipo, Stern, Hola, The New York Times, The Los Angeles Times, The Washington Post*, and countless other publications.

Branching out as a filmmaker, Rejaunier produced, directed, filmed, and edited the four hour documentary, *The Spirit of '56: Meetings with Remarkable Women*.

#####

BOOKS BY JEANNE REJAUNIER

The Beauty Trap
The Motion and the Act
Affair in Rome
Mob Sisters
Odalisque at the Spa
Everybody's Husband
Hollywood Sauna Confidential
My Sundays with Henry Miller
Titans of the Muses (with Noreen Nash)
Planes of the Heavenworld
Everything You Always Wanted to Know About Heaven But Didn't Know Where to Ask
The Kingdom of Heaven and 4th Dimensional Consciousness
The Afterlife in the Here and Now
Living in Eternity Now
The Eightfold Path and the 8th Plane of Heaven
Modeling From the Ground Up
The 50 Best Careers in Modeling
Runway to Success
Astrology For Lovers (with Lu Ann Horstman)
Astrology and Your Sex Life (with Maria Graciette)
The Paris Diet (with Noreen Nash and Monique de Warren)
The Complete Idiot's Guide to Food Allergy (with Lee Freund, M.D.)
The Complete Idiot's Guide to Migraines and Other Headaches (with Dennis Fox, M.D.)
Japan's Hidden Face (with Toshio Abe)
The Video Jungle (written under nom de plume)

#####

CRITICS' COMMENTS ABOUT
THE BEAUTY TRAP, by JEANNE REJAUNIER

"Here is a novel that can't miss, crammed with all the ingredients that make a blockbuster." - **Publishers Weekly**

"A startling closeup of the world's most glamorous business, an intensely human story." - **The New York Times**

"Jeanne Rejaunier has concocted a sexpourri of life among the mannequins that's spiked with all the ingredients of a blockbuster bestseller."- **Playboy**

"A fascinating inside story of the most glamorous girls in the business, absorbing to read." - **California Stylist**

"A powerful novel that takes off like 47 howitzers." - **San Fernando Valley (CA) Magazine**

"New York's most sought after women find themselves having to make desperate decisions that will affect their very lives." - **Wilmington (DE) News Journal**.

"The novel is rich in esoteric commercial lore about modeling...." **Saturday Review**

"Possibly the most honest novel to appear by a female writer in the past decade."- **Literary Times**

"Crammed with all the ingredients of a blockbuster. ...Beasts in the Beauty Jungle... authentic, searing exposé." **London Evening News**

"Miss Rejaunier is most interesting when she goes behind the scenes in the modeling world." - **Detroit Free Press**

"If a male author had written *The Beauty Trap*, he'd be hanged by the thumbs." - **UPI**

#####

Manufactured by Amazon.ca
Bolton, ON